Hollywood Heir

ALSO BY RUTH CARDELLO

WESTERLY BILLIONAIRE SERIES

Up for Heir
In the Heir
Royal Heir

LONE STAR BURN

Taken, Not Spurred
Tycoon Takedown
Taken Home
Taking Charge

THE LEGACY COLLECTION

Maid for the Billionaire
For Love or Legacy
Bedding the Billionaire
Saving the Sheikh
Rise of the Billionaire
Breaching the Billionaire: Alethea's Redemption
Recipe for Love (Holiday Novella)
A Corisi Christmas (Holiday Novella)

THE ANDRADES

Come Away With Me

Home to Me

Maximum Risk

Somewhere Along the Way

Loving Gigi

THE BARRINGTONS

Always Mine

Stolen Kisses

Trade It All

A Billionaire for Lexi

Let It Burn

More Than Love

TRILLIONAIRES

Taken by a Trillionaire

Virgin for a Trillionaire

TEMPTATION SERIES

Twelve Days of Temptation

Be My Temptation

BACHELOR TOWER SERIES

Insatiable Bachelor

Impossible Bachelor

Hollywood Heir

RUTH CARDELLO

This is a work of fiction. Names, characters, organizations, places, events, and incidents are either products of the author's imagination or are used fictitiously.

Published by Montlake Romance, Seattle

www.apub.com

ISBN-13: 9781503903845
ISBN-10: 1503903842

Cover design by Eileen Carey

Printed in the United States of America

This book is dedicated to my niece Valerie and her little girl, Viv. No matter how far we wander, family always finds a way to bring us home. Thank you, Val, for bringing me home.

Don't Miss a Thing!

www.ruthcardello.com

Sign up for Ruth's Newsletter:
https://forms.aweber.com/form/00/819443400.htm

Join Ruth's Private Fan Group:
www.facebook.com/groups/ruthiesroadies

Follow Ruth on GoodReads:
www.goodreads.com/author/show/4820876.
Ruth_Cardello

Westerly
Family Tree

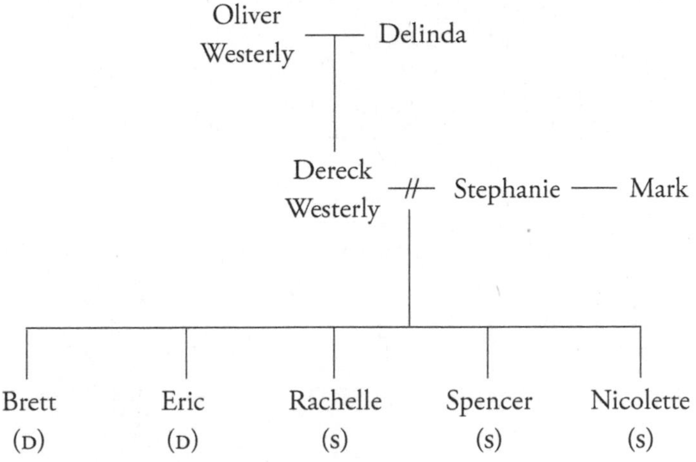

(D): stays with Dereck after the divorce

(S): stays with Stephanie after the divorce

A note to my readers:

What is a water bear?

Water bear bugs (a.k.a. tardigrades) are eight-legged creatures that live in water and are said to be able to survive even an extinction-level event. They would not only survive without water for thirty years but also in the vacuum of space. They are popular enough in some circles that people sell plush-toy replicas of them.

I may have to give one to my children, just to see their expressions when I do. Water bears—so ugly they're cute.

Chapter One

"Sorry it took me so long to get here—traffic was a pain. What's the emergency?"

Sage Revere motioned for her best friend, Bella, to sit across from her at a small table in a busy London coffee shop. She pushed a cup of black coffee across to her. "He's not here yet, but he will be. He comes every day just about this time."

Bella took a seat and lifted the paper cup to her lips, blowing on the hot liquid. "I should have known this wasn't urgent. We need some kind of code in case you actually need me one day."

"It *is* urgent. I need you to look at him and tell me why I can't get him out of my head. Today. Before this goes further."

"Is he a potential client?"

"I don't think so. He haunts me, though. Does that make sense?"

"No, but I'm used to this side of you," Bella suggested with a knowing smile. "You're cursed with a gift. Instead of seeing dead people, you see unhappy rich ones. What's his issue? Did he just win the lottery and lose all his friends? Is he retiring from a lucrative, cutthroat career and discovering he's alone? Don't worry, whatever it is, you'll find a way to bring him around. You always do." Her voice was thick with *but I love you anyway* sarcasm.

"I don't think he has money."

Bella sipped her coffee. "He must. Your radar doesn't work for unhappy poor people."

Ouch. Sitting back in her chair, Sage crossed her arms over her chest. "You're in a mood today."

"Sorry." Bella leaned forward and placed a hand on Sage's arm. "I have a lot going on at the office. And I know I sound like a jerk sometimes, but someone has to keep you grounded. You're not psychic."

"I never said I was."

"The people you help usually deserve to be alone."

"That's a horrible thing to say. To love and be loved—isn't that what life is all about? What could be more important? And you know as well as I do that money doesn't make anyone as happy as they think it will. You were miserable before you met me."

Bella sighed. "I was ten."

"I helped guide you. Admit it, you're a thousand times happier working in law than you would have been running your mother's cosmetics company."

"Why are you making a case for yourself? Are you about to do something that I'll have to defend you for in court? You're not stalking this guy, are you?"

"Of course not. Well, not technically. Does coming every day when I know he'll be here constitute stalking?"

"It could—depends on whether he becomes one of your clients or takes out a restraining order against you."

Sage's attention was drawn to the door. "That's him."

By the time Bella turned in his direction, he was faced away, ordering a coffee. "Nice ass. Nice back. I'm going to go out on a limb on this one and say that your fascination has less to do with how he feels and more with what you'd like *to* feel—those quads. At twenty-six, it could even be your biological clock. Either way, damn, that man sure knows how to fill out a pair of jeans."

"Wait," Sage said.

He turned, as if he could sense them looking at him. His temple and cheek were darkened with a thick layer of cover-up that didn't fully conceal a scar that ran down both. Whatever had happened to him had disfigured one side of his face, leaving it rounder and painful looking. A somber gaze met Sage's briefly before he turned away again.

Bella said, "What happened to him?"

"I wish I knew. He looks so lost, doesn't he? He sits alone, finishes his coffee, then leaves without talking to anyone."

Bella waved a warning finger. "Be careful—you don't know how he got that scar. For all you know, he earned it."

"Or maybe not. I want to go over there and hug him."

The man looked up from the table he'd chosen and met their attention with a glare.

"I wouldn't advise that. That's a man who prefers to be alone."

"No one does. Not really."

Bella touched her arm again, pulling Sage's gaze back to her. "I know you have a good track record for leaving people better than you found them, but you were right to ask me about this one. Don't get involved. My gut tells me his scar isn't his biggest problem. On the other hand, I have a neighbor who recently bought a fourth Maltese. Why don't you visit her and see if you can find out what emotional hole she's trying to fill with canines? That's more your style, not this guy."

Sage shook her head, sending her ponytail flying back and forth. "Everyone comes into our lives for a reason. Maybe this is a sign that my radar is evolving. Lonely is lonely, no matter how much or how little a person has. He needs me."

"You realize if you start taking on financially challenged clients, they won't be able to pay you. When you chose independence from your parents, you chose all the bills that came along with that."

"I can take on other clients while I work with him. This will be pro bono. If I do it right, he'll just think of me as one of his friends."

"You brought me here for my opinion. It's no. Emphatically—*no*."

"I can't accept that—"

Bella took out her phone and snapped a photo.

"What are you doing?" Sage asked.

Bella replaced her phone in her purse. "If this guy hurts you, at least now I have a photo to show the police."

The man rose, crushed his coffee cup in his hand, and threw it in the trash. Sage stood. "He saw you take the picture of him."

"Good."

"No, not good. What if he doesn't come back because of it?" Sage looked from her friend to the retreating man. *Great, now we embarrassed him.* "I'll call you later. I have to speak to him."

"Sage," Bella said.

Sage paused a few feet away. This wasn't the first nor would it probably be the last time she went against Bella's advice, but she was still glad she'd included her. Sage was used to following her instincts when it came to people. Those instincts were what led her to reach out to complete strangers on a regular basis. She was beyond caring what others thought of her self-designed career choice. Bella's comment about seeing sadness only in the wealthy stung a little, but Sage had been born into money. That didn't mean she didn't care when others were in pain. She worked substantial philanthropy into every happiness plan she designed. When it came to helping people on an individual level, however, she was drawn to the ones she knew how to heal.

My gift? Bella had once accused her of compulsively helping people find happiness because she hadn't yet found it herself. *Which might explain why, despite how many people I've helped, Bella is my only friend. She thinks I'm so afraid of being left again that I put an expiration date on how long I let people get close to me. She may be right. I care about people deeply, but then I always walk away.*

None of that changed the fact that she felt compelled to help one angry-looking man find his smile again.

"Be careful," Bella warned.

"Always."

"Call me later, and don't you dare go anywhere alone with him."

"I won't," Sage promised as she rushed out of the coffee shop and onto the busy sidewalk. The man's long stride had taken him a good distance. She darted between people to catch up with him. When she finally did, she said, "Excuse me."

He kept walking, not sparing her a glance.

Sage wasn't easily deterred. She doubled her pace to keep up with him. "I'm sorry about my friend."

He stopped then, and she came to a skidding halt beside him. His eyes burned with anger. "Who are you?"

She held out her hand, then lowered it when he didn't shake it. "Sage Revere."

He leaned closer and growled, "Whatever you want, I'm not interested."

Rather than intimidate her, his warning had her cheeks flushing and her heart racing. All pity for him melted away beneath a slam of attraction. "Do you have plants?" she blurted out.

He scanned her face. "What?"

"Plants." Of all her introductions, this ranked as one of her least polished. She took out one of her business cards and handed it to him. "I'm a plant psychologist. Botanist extraordinaire."

He took the card and inspected it before asking, "Is this some kind of joke?"

"No joke. I can give you references if you'd like."

"Thanks, but no thanks. I don't have any plants. The shrub over there is looking a little sad, though—perhaps you should counsel it." He tried to hand the card back to her, but she refused to accept it.

He wasn't the first to start off thinking she was crazy. Admittedly, it was an odd career choice, but it was also a nonthreatening cover that allowed her into the homes and lives of people who needed her. She reminded herself the delivery method didn't matter as much as the message. "It's a scientific fact that plants are good for people. If you're not happy for some reason, buy one. And then, if you have any questions about how to care for it, call me."

He pocketed her card and leaned closer, so close she thought he might kiss her. His breath caressed her lips. "Stay the hell away from me."

He turned on his heel and walked away.

Sage watched him go, knowing it wouldn't be the last time she saw him. That wasn't the way this worked.

Bella appeared at her side. "Let him go, Sage. I'll give your card to my neighbor. She has bearberry bushes that I'm sure you can convince her are depressed."

Eric Westerly entered his studio apartment and slammed the door behind him. He strode to the bathroom to inspect himself in the mirror. It pleased him that his features still reflected how he felt: hideous, damaged.

He traced his fingers along his prominent scar and the altered shape of that side of his face. His rehab counselor had warned him that recovery would be a process. They'd assured him, though, that a normal life was possible.

What's normal?

Am I capable of recognizing it?

Or even deserving it? He slammed his fist down on the bathroom counter. *I need to be more careful. If those women recognized me—.* A knock on the door interrupted his thoughts.

"You in there?" a familiar voice demanded.

Eric crossed the room to let him in. "I told you not to come here."

Reggie, his employee and friend, breezed past him as if he'd been invited. "I can't do it anymore. I can't handle your grandmother's beady little eyes. You have to come back. She's staring into my soul."

"No," Eric said as he closed the door. "Not until I'm ready." There was a time when Reggie, his wife, and his two children were not as openly a part of his life. Reggie had moved them into an infrequently used wing of Eric's home. Once Eric had fully acknowledged the agreement, it had brought him the closest thing he had to a family. Alice, Reggie's wife, could always be found chasing her children: Axton, a precocious twelve-year-old; and Liana, his pint-size six-year-old sister. Their antics had given Eric's empty home new life—but that wasn't enough to get him to return.

Reggie looked him over and shuddered. "I'll never get used to your face like that." He walked around the room, kicking the legs of the threadbare furniture. "Honestly, I don't see the appeal of this place, either."

"You don't need to. I don't expect anyone to."

After wiping crumbs off the cushion of a chair, Reggie sat. "You are one fucked-up dude. What's it going to take for me to convince you to give this up?"

Eric shrugged and pocketed his hands in his jeans. "I am not going back yet, Reggie. I can walk down the street here without being followed. No one wants anything from me. Most people don't even look at me."

"You taking anything?"

"No."

"Not even to sleep?"

"Nothing."

"Prescription?"

"I'm clean."

"Your phone rings constantly."

"Turn it off."

"You sure you don't want it?"

"There's no one I want to talk to."

"Not even your sister? I thought you were getting close."

"Rachelle is married with a baby on the way. She doesn't need my stuff on top of all that."

"I told the studio you were in Vandorra for a few weeks doing some Vandorran stuff. I don't know; I made some shit up. They seemed to accept it."

"I'm not concerned about them."

Reggie sighed. "Don't kill yourself. I really like my job, and my kids enjoy living in your house. They might even love the pool more than they love me."

Eric smiled with wry amusement. "I'm glad they're happy there. They're good kids. Don't worry about me, Reggie. I'm just taking a break."

"I'm working on a surprise for you."

"I don't want anything."

"You need this even if you don't know it yet. It's expensive, though. Keep that in mind when you check your bank balance."

"You know I don't care about that."

"You should." Reggie shook his head as if disgusted and looked around the small apartment again. "Is this the life you really want?"

"I don't know yet, but that's what I'm here to find out. Not everything I heard at the clinic rang true to me, but one thing did. It wasn't even from one of my counselors. It was an older man who was there to break an addiction to pain medication. He asked me why I was there, and I told him the truth—I didn't know why. Maybe I needed to say it out loud. Anyway, he said every life was a gift, and if I couldn't see that anymore, it was time to make a change—a drastic one. I asked myself what I wanted, and here I am."

"You can't hide forever."

"I don't intend to. I was in a bad place before I went to the clinic. I wasn't even angry anymore, just numb. When I visited those sick kids at the children's hospital, I felt—ashamed. There has to be more to this existence than I've seen."

"You chose a strange neighborhood to look for the meaning of life. I was almost mugged right outside your door."

Eric looked Reggie over. "Is that my watch?"

Reggie pushed his sleeve back, revealing a Louis Moinet Magistralis watch—an $800,000-plus gift from his father. Eric had never worn it, anyway. "Yeah. I use it to keep the time while driving your McLaren."

The admission didn't bother Eric. "Keep both, but it's probably safer if you don't bring either here."

Reggie stood. "Good point, but no thanks. It would take all the fun out of borrowing them. I might even give my title back. I admit it was cool to be knighted by the king of Vandorra, but it's too much responsibility. They invite me and my wife to events now. I can't sit around in one of your tuxes and talk to old, rich people all day. I have too much shit to do."

"Like that surprise you're making for me."

"You're going to fucking love it."

Eric laughed. Reggie was one of a kind—tall and pale with dark hair and the stare of a creepy extra in a movie. His official title was house electrician for the sprawling estate Eric owned in London, but Reggie stepped in and helped whenever he saw the need. He made sure everyone was paid and that Eric's estate ran smoothly. He was also one of the few people Eric trusted.

Eric shook Reggie's hand. "Thanks for covering for me."

Reggie nodded, then wagged a finger at Eric's marred face. "Hey, can you get laid like that?"

"I don't know. I hadn't put much thought into it." An image of the plant lady from the coffee shop came back to him with disconcerting clarity. She'd been curved in all the right lush places. Absolutely batshit crazy, but fuckable at the same time. Not that it mattered, since he had no intention of seeing her again. He was reasonably certain neither she nor her friend had recognized him, but they'd already taken a photo of him, and he wasn't about to give them a reason to share it.

"That's the first thing I would have asked myself. I guess you could get creative, though. Lights off. No hands. I'll experiment with Alice and get back to you with some tips."

"Not necessary."

"No trouble. We've been together long enough we need to shake things up now and then. She might even get a kick out of putting makeup on me."

"'Bye, Reggie."

"I'll be back next week to check on you."

"I'm fine."

"Can I use your jet?"

"No."

Reggie walked to the door and shrugged. "How about the yacht?"

"No."

"Great. I'll only tell you if I dent something." With that, Reggie slipped out the door and closed it behind him.

Alone again, Eric returned to the mirror. Slowly, using a special cream and expertise that came from years of experience in theater, he peeled off the scar.

I really am a fucking mess.

Who am I to judge a woman for thinking she can talk to vegetation?

Her words came back to him: *"It's a scientific fact that plants are good for people."* He took her card out of his pocket and placed it on the carpet of his bedroom, focusing on it as he did push-ups.

Without fame, money, or the face my fans call perfect, could I get laid?

God, I want to fuck someone who doesn't know me—who wants nothing from me.

For that kind of sex, I could tolerate a little crazy.

Chapter Two

He'll be here. No one comes to the same coffee shop every day, then stops just because someone takes a photo of them.

I did also chase him down and tell him I talk to plants, but most people find that intriguing rather than off-putting.

Sage sipped her coffee and tried to occupy herself by reading the news on her phone. It was never good, but she wanted to stay informed even if it always left her wishing she could do more. It also made her miss her grandmother.

Sixteen years ago, her death had shaken Sage and contributed to the ugliness of her parents' divorce. Her father, English by birth, had relocated to the United States and started his own import business. He'd done well and married an American model. As a child, Sage had traveled extensively—and considered home wherever her nannies were. She had fond memories of her grandmother, although so many of them had faded over time.

The death of her grandmother had brought her family to a whole new level of wealth, and Sage's mother had decided to leave with her fair share of it. Still reeling from the loss of her grandmother, Sage had spiraled out of control while her parents used her as a bargaining chip.

They both decided she wasn't worth it, compromised, and sent her off to boarding school.

At first, Sage had been convinced one of her parents would wake up and come for her. Family had to be about more than social status and luxuries. People didn't just give up and walk away from the ones they loved. Her parents didn't come, though, and Sage withdrew from her classmates and teachers. She'd felt lost and adrift, alone and scared. What could possibly matter when she knew *she* didn't?

She might have turned to drugs or alcohol, as many there did, if not for a garden renovation project her dorm mother convinced her to participate in. It was there that she'd discovered how connected every living organism was and how good contributing felt.

Bella's British parents were still married at the time, but both were so busy they had no time for her. Like Sage, she had lived everywhere and nowhere.

Unlike Sage, Bella had been dragged into the garden project as community service for repeatedly skipping classes. She and Sage hit it off from the first day they met and had been each other's family since.

Bella pushed Sage to speak up for herself. Sage showed Bella all the reasons she still had to be happy. Sage's secondary career had taken root during those early school days. A new student, Kim Bradley, had arrived at the school and quickly landed in disciplinary probation for acting out in class. Sage and Bella were asked to befriend the girl. Her parents had died in a boating accident, and her uncle thought the school would be the best place for her. Helping Kim heal and fit in inspired Sage to reach out to another troubled student, then another. And her gift—*or curse*, as Bella jokingly called it at times—blossomed.

Sage's cell phone ringing brought her back to the present. "Hi, Dad."

"Miranda will be in London tomorrow. She wants to take you shopping."

"I don't need anything, but I could do lunch—"

"Don't talk to her about your mother."

"I would never."

"Or Sylvia."

"Why would I—"

"Or Caroline."

"Dad. I get it. I'll pretend she's your first wife instead of your fourth."

"I don't appreciate your tone, Sage."

Breathe. "Will you be in London as well? I'd love to see you."

"You know I can't get away right now. Just give me your assurance that you won't do anything to upset Miranda."

"What is it you're afraid I'll do?"

"Caroline and I were fine before she went out to visit you."

"Oh my God, Dad, she was fucking her makeup guy and bragged about it in front of me. Should I not have mentioned that? Because I thought that was something you'd want to know."

"It was none of your business, Sage. Marriage is complicated. You're not a child anymore. You need to learn to keep your mouth shut."

Sage threw one hand up in the air. "Fine. I won't tell you even if I find out Miranda's hosting an orgy on your dollar."

Her father sighed. "I can't deal with you right now. I'll tell Miranda you're traveling."

"You don't have to lie to her, Dad. I can—"

"It's probably for the best. She already thinks you should be involuntarily committed for your own protection. I thought shopping together might help the two of you bond."

"Hold on. I'm trying to wrap my head around this conversation. Why the hell would she think I need to be committed?"

"Let's not have this conversation again. You know how I feel about your lifestyle."

"My *lifestyle*? You mean the one where I work a job, pay my own bills, and never ask you for anything?"

"You've always been odd, Sage. I'm getting tired of trying to explain you. Is this the year you spend the holidays with your mother?"

Since it was still summer, it would be difficult for her father to claim he already knew he'd be too busy to see her. *I'm an adult. These are no longer visitations. It's just—just that I want to see him.* "No, that was last year."

"We'll figure something out. I'm late for a meeting."

"If you don't want me to come, Dad—" Sage would have said more, but her father had hung up. She took several deep breaths. *Don't let him do this. It only hurts if you let it.*

Feeling calmer, she looked around and met the brooding eyes of the man she'd been waiting for. He was watching her from several tables away. Had he been there all along? How much had he heard?

Her face flushed as she remembered how he'd warned her off the day before. Would acknowledging him send him scurrying away? She decided to risk it and waved at him once.

He didn't wave back.

Instead, he stood up and threw his coffee in the trash. Sage forced herself to look away. Her grandmother used to say every action a person made needed to come from love, because it made the world either a better or worse place. Her parents had thought *she* was crazy, too.

"Why did your friend take a picture of me?"

Startled, Sage nearly knocked over her coffee. The man was standing beside her table, blocking her view of everything beyond him. Her body came alive. From his perfectly shaped lips to his T-shirt stretching over his biceps and broad chest, Sage doubted there was a woman alive who wouldn't find it difficult to remain composed around him. He oozed virility. She wondered if he was self-conscious about his scar. There was no need to be. He would have been too perfect without it, the kind of unflawed Hollywood idol few women would dare approach. The scar gave him a realness, a depth Sage couldn't resist. "She thought you might be dangerous. Are you?"

One corner of his mouth curled. "I suppose that depends on your definition. I'm pretty fucked-up."

Maintaining eye contact, Sage asked, "Do you hurt people?"

"I've been known to disappoint my share."

"Me too," Sage said. "Some to the point where they think I require professional help."

"You may."

Ouch. "Thanks for the vote of confidence."

"Come for a walk with me."

"Now?"

"You have somewhere you need to be?"

"No. It's a slow week." She stood. "I'd love to." She disposed of her cup, picked up her purse, then stepped outside the shop with him. They walked side by side on the busy sidewalk without speaking. Finally, Sage asked, "Your accent is American. Have you lived in London long?"

He stopped and looked down at her with that somber expression of his. "I don't want to talk."

"Oooo-kay." She ran a hand through her long hair as she tried to discern his mood. "Not even your name?"

Another long, measured look as if he didn't want to disclose that, either. Finally, he said, "Wayne Easton."

"It's nice to meet you, Wayne." Sage started down the sidewalk again, and he fell into step beside her. There were a thousand things she wanted to ask him, but helping people meant valuing each person and their experience. He was telling her what he needed. Someone or something had hurt this man, and he wasn't ready to share his story yet. One day he would be. If there was anything plants could teach people, it was patience. No flower bloomed before it was ready, no matter how much a person wanted it to.

Their walk took them to Leicester Square, where they both paused to watch a young girl laugh and play in the spouts of water at the base of a fountain. She looked to be about four or five and was running barefoot back and forth with such joy on her face Sage couldn't help but smile along. She glanced at Wayne. Sadness filled his expression as he watched the young girl.

"The theater district is one of my favorite areas," Sage said. "It has an invigorating energy. So much talent. So many possibilities. If I could, I would talk to everyone here."

"Why?"

Sage waved at the people rushing past as well as the ones grouped in circles. "Aren't you curious about their stories? Are they students? Actors? Is this their first visit, or are they locals? What do they see when they look around?"

"I doubt anything past their cell phones."

"That's true for some—more concerned about the selfie they'll share than the history of the square. There are others, though, who are savoring this." She pointed to a couple on a nearby bench who were watching the little girl dance in the water. "I bet they saved up to come here and they don't want to miss a single moment of it."

"How do you know they don't live around the corner?"

Had Bella asked her that question, Sage might have joked that it was her gift to know, but the reality was that people were not really that difficult to figure out. "She is clutching her purse like a tourist, and he has his wallet in his front pocket. People don't tend to do that in their hometown. There's something wrong, though. They're too serious. This isn't a simple vacation for them."

Wayne looked at her with a good amount of skepticism.

"Look closer," she urged. "He's comforting her."

Wayne turned his attention back to the couple. His eyebrows rose and fell as if he were mildly impressed. "You're very observant."

Sage shrugged. "I like people. I hate to see them upset. Let's make them smile." Not waiting for him to answer, she grabbed his forearm to take him with her. Touching him felt right. She couldn't explain it;

there were a great many things in life she didn't understand, but she refused to let that stop her. She dragged him out of the small park that surrounded the fountain and across the busy street.

"Are you buying them a plant?" he asked as they approached a florist shop.

Sage pulled him past it. "Who gets a plant on vacation? It's unlikely they could take it home with them. No, this calls for something a little different." She let his arm go when they arrived at the party store that was a few doors down. Minutes—and a hundred pounds—later, Sage exited the store with a still-grave Wayne. She led him back to the middle of the square, this time off to the side, where they could watch without being part of the scene.

As requested, a clerk from the party store appeared with a large bunch of balloons. She announced it was a promotional giveaway, one balloon per child. A group of children instantly surrounded the woman. She asked them to line up from shortest to tallest. The little girl who had been dancing in the fountain rushed to ask her parents if she could have one. They walked her over to join the line. Sage's joy spilled over for the little girl and her mother, who was still clutching her purse like a tourist. Her reward was how happy the couple and child looked as they walked away.

"It won't fix whatever they're dealing with, but I'd like to think they'll leave London with at least one good memory now," Sage said, happy with herself until she looked at Wayne.

He was scowling at the departing couple, then the line of children that remained.

Sage couldn't help herself. She asked, "What's wrong?"

"Nothing."

"You don't like kids."

He shook his head, but she wasn't sure if that was confirmation that she was correct in her assessment or completely misreading his response.

Some might have given up and walked away from the sour-looking man, but seeing him like this only made her more determined to discover the root of his problem. "I have an idea. Let's see a show."

"No."

She threw his earlier question back at him. "You have somewhere you need to be?"

He glared at her rather than answering.

She remembered being that angry with the world once. More than one teacher had given up on her, but thankfully, her dorm mother hadn't. Giving up on people was an easy, but lonely, choice. "I'll take that as a no. So, let's catch a matinee. We can buy last-minute tickets right across the street."

"I can't do this." Looking as unhappy as he had earlier, he started to walk away.

"Because you don't like live theater?" she asked as she trotted after him. "I don't believe that. You wouldn't come to this district every day if that were true."

He stopped and bit out his answer without turning toward her. "I don't need to explain how I feel about anything."

Sage raised her hands in concession. "You're right."

"It is none of your business where I go or what I do."

"I completely agree."

His head snapped in her direction. "Are you capable of silence?"

Sage put a hand on one hip and cocked an eyebrow at him. "Now you're getting rude. I'm not the one who suggested this walk, so you can stop scowling at me. I didn't do whatever it is that has you so angry, and I refuse to let you ruin my good mood." He stood there, holding her gaze for long enough that her confidence wavered. Was there a chance he couldn't afford the ticket and was too embarrassed to admit it? She hated the idea that she might have put him in that position. "The tickets would be my treat."

"Why would you offer me anything? I'm so *rude*."

Since you asked. "You know all those people you think you've disappointed? I'm not one of them. Not yet. Consider me a clean-slate friend."

He shook his head, turned on his heel, and strode away. She watched him go until he disappeared into a crowd of people. Only then did she release the breath she'd been holding. She was tempted to call Bella, but she wasn't ready to hear what she knew her friend would say.

He's angry.

His problems aren't your business.

You can only help people who want help.

She scanned the area for the couple with the child again. They were gone. There were endless possibilities as to why the woman might have been upset. Giving their child a balloon hadn't actually made anything better for them.

But I couldn't pretend I didn't see their pain.

Does that make this about me or them?

Does Wayne Easton actually need my help, or is my present lack of male companionship messing with my radar?

He really does have an amazing ass.

Eric walked without a destination in mind. He needed to put distance between himself and the woman who was reopening old wounds. He'd gone to see her out of curiosity and after a sleepless night that had provided him with far too much time to fantasize about her.

He didn't want a relationship, just sex. The last thing he needed now, while he was figuring himself out, was for some woman to mess with his head. Been there. Done that.

He'd expected Sage to be outrageously eccentric, fundamentally unlikable. She was a self-professed plant psychologist, for God's sake.

The question he'd pondered as he'd headed off to meet her that morning had been if he'd be able to tolerate listening to that crap long enough to screw her.

She wasn't supposed to have a smile that made his stomach do flips or eyes he couldn't look away from. He'd been there for her sweet little body, not the way she pursed her lips when he said something obnoxious. She wasn't the first woman to tolerate his bad behavior, but those women were normally using him to advance their careers. Many prettied up the exchange of sex for photo ops and introductions by pretending it was part of a relationship. Others didn't even bother. They chased him, hunted him, offered him everything and anything he wanted, all in exchange for something else.

He was no saint. In his early twenties, fresh from a broken engagement that had jaded his view of women, he'd accepted a fair share of what he was offered. As the years went on, though, he turned down more and more. The last date he'd gone on had been more than a year ago.

Like a bout of food poisoning after a certain dish, his last date had left a bad taste in his mouth. He'd come home after leaving her at a club to find she'd beaten him there, sneaked past his people, and ambushed him, naked, when he'd gone to bed. She wanted a role in his next movie.

The whole exchange sickened Eric. Everyone wanted something. Some were simply better at hiding it than others. He walked past the small theaters, trying to remember when he'd still enjoyed acting. A small stage, energy from an audience he could see, story lines that mattered.

Was all that lost, along with his faith in humanity?

He thought about the little girl from the fountain. His daughter, had she been allowed to live, would have been about her age. Passing years had numbed the pain, but sometimes when Eric saw a young girl, he still wondered about her. No matter how it had ended with Jasmine, he would have loved his child. He knew what it was like not to be wanted and would have made sure his little girl never felt that way.

He hadn't been given that chance.

A phone call from Jasmine's doctor to check on her after a procedure had unraveled an otherwise well-executed deception. Jasmine had never loved him. She and one of his college classmates, Sven, had duped him into funding their superhero movie, *Water Bear Man.* They'd needed his support, and it hadn't been as if he didn't have the money. A favor for a friend and the woman he loved . . .

The contract had been designed to screw him and the scriptwriter out of millions. Sven and Jasmine would then split and enjoy the cash together. They might have gotten away with it, had Jasmine not gotten pregnant, then angry with the situation—angry enough to spill her role in the deception. In a fit of anger, she'd incriminated Sven, the man she claimed as her true love. She'd said it had been Sven's idea for her to distract Eric enough to sign without reading the full contract. Their last conversation had been ugly. She'd mocked everything Eric had disclosed to her about his dysfunctional family just to hurt him; then she'd torn into their engagement. She claimed to have been disgusted by Eric's touch and relieved when she'd learned about her pregnancy early enough to terminate it. She'd said the baby had been a little girl. Had it? Or had she thrown in the detail to hurt him more deeply? He'd never know.

Only Reggie knew the full extent of what she'd said. He'd been doing electrical work in Eric's then-modest London apartment and overheard Jasmine's vile ranting. After she'd left, Eric had stood in the living room, devastated, asking himself how he could have thought what they had was love.

Because life has taught me to have low, low, low expectations of people.

Reggie had walked out of the kitchen and said, "That bitch played the wrong man. Aren't you filthy rich?"

At the time, revenge had been the last thing on Eric's mind. He'd never been the vengeful type. "I am," he'd said to the then-near stranger.

"You must have an army of lawyers. Don't let those fuckers get a dime from your movie."

They hadn't. Eric had made sure of that, but it hadn't made him feel better. Jasmine's view of him as someone who was unloved because he was unlovable had rung true to him. Wanting nothing more to do with *Water Bear Man* or the money that came from it, he'd donated his earnings from it to charities. Rather than close that chapter of his life, it had only brought a surge of interest for a sequel. Eric had had no intention of producing or starring in another film that involved him prancing around in a gray spandex superhero costume, but his publicist had begged him to meet with the writer and cast from the original movie before deciding.

One of the cast, a man Eric had forgotten had even been in the movie, said he'd been living in his car before *Water Bear Man*. Eric had offered him money, but the man had refused, claiming he didn't want a handout, he wanted a career. One day, the man professed, he would become like Eric, rich and powerful and dedicated to giving back to the community.

A real hero.

Eric had tried to explain to the man that there was nothing heroic about his life. He was a disappointment as a son, a distant sibling to those who claimed to love him, and even what appeared to have been done out of kindness hadn't been.

Eric offered the man the role as Water Bear Man in the sequel, but the public wanted Eric. They loved Eric Westerly, not onstage performing classic theater or for who he was in person, but as his on-screen, over-the-top character. More spandex. More swagger.

"You're a role model, Water Bear Man."

I shouldn't be. I've never done a damn thing for anyone but myself.

Eric sometimes told himself the *Water Bear Man* franchise was his good deed, but in his heart he knew the truth. He employed more people than he could keep track of. Many successful actors had used his movies as starting points for their careers. In the industry, Eric had a reputation for generous support of his fellow actors. They didn't know how little of it had been by design.

He didn't tell anyone the reality of how he felt about them or the industry. It wasn't their fault that no matter what he did, how insane he shaped the plot to be, or even that he moved his base to the UK—nothing slowed the brand down. No matter where he went or what he did, he was Water Bear Man. Every time he thought he might break free, the brand grew and sucked him in deeper until he couldn't even look himself in the mirror without seeing the character he'd come to hate.

He touched the fake scar on his cheek and temple. Yes, it was a lie, but a necessary one. It was a passport to a second chance to be himself—just a man.

His thoughts drifted back to Sage. Part of him wanted to track her down and apologize for his behavior. None of what he hated about his life was her fault. She couldn't have known that watching that little girl had been tearing him apart on the inside or that going to a play would only remind him of a world that was closed to him.

Her concern in response to ingratitude reminded him of his sister Rachelle. As he walked on, he thought about what a mess he'd been when Rachelle had come to London—determined to connect with him. She and her royal husband were the reason he'd agreed to the rehab clinic. They were good people—better people than he deserved.

Like Reggie.

Eric didn't remember asking him to come to London, but he was grateful he had. Reggie and Alice made sure his household ran smoothly. Eric had a feeling that if he gave his fortune away, they would still show up to give him shit on a regular basis.

Eric smiled as he imagined Reggie taking his kids out for the weekend on the yacht Eric had told him not to use. He didn't expect anyone to understand their bond. Eric had two biological brothers, one older and one younger. His older brother, Brett, was a brainwashed, condescending heir to the weight of the Westerly dynasty. In other words, he'd taken over the family company and stepped into their father's shoes. His wedding had been the first of his siblings'. Oh yeah, and there was the little wrinkle of his wife having first been engaged to their youngest brother, Spencer. Not to be outdone, Spencer was a self-made tech tycoon and just as much of a workaholic as Brett. Or he had been until a few months back, when he'd married some woman who was raising her niece. Both of them adopted the little girl and claimed they'd never been happier. Although Eric had attended all the weddings, he'd felt like an outsider. He had more in common with any of the strangers walking past him than with any of them.

In addition to Rachelle, Eric had another sister—Nicolette. He knew next to nothing about her other than that she was traveling for her photography and spending as little time with the family as possible. She sounded like she had a good head on her shoulders. Survival was best achieved via distance.

That fundamental belief clashed with Eric's gratitude toward Rachelle. She advocated for family and for everyone being stronger together. Even if Eric wanted one, though, he couldn't imagine a healthy version of his family—nothing as uncomplicated as he had with Reggie, Alice, and the kids.

Thank God Reggie was keeping his grandmother occupied. Delinda would never understand what Eric was doing in the theater district any more than she understood him lately. To her, he was a success. Money and power were how she measured a person's worth.

I've earned more on my own than I would have inherited from her—how could I possibly not be happy?

Fuck.

As Eric walked by a group of young women, one of them looked up at him, then stepped away from the others. She was tall, blonde, and looked college age. Eric looked away, hoping she'd get the message.

"Excuse me," she said.

He didn't respond.

She continued, "Are you—"

No, don't recognize me.

"—from around here? We're looking for Heathbright. Our GPS said it was right here, but I don't see it."

Relief flooded him. He pointed to a side street, where the entrance to a small but highly acclaimed theater was located.

"Thank you," she called out as she sprinted back to her group.

He nodded. He'd considered coloring his hair or donning a weight suit to change his physique, but sometimes simple was more effective. Superman could become Clark Kent with only a pair of glasses because people believed what they saw, regardless of how glaringly obvious the truth was.

I can do this. I can be Wayne Easton.

A short time later, Eric approached his building. A single mother from the first-floor apartment began yelling out her window in a foreign language to her teenage son, who was standing with his friends on the corner. Eric doubted it would do much to deter the young men from whatever mischief they were plotting. As he watched, the group turned their attention to the elderly woman from the third floor who was walking down the sidewalk pulling a metal cart of groceries. Eric tensed. Surely they wouldn't—

The boys walked toward her, and Eric began to as well. He stopped, though, when he saw the elderly woman smile at the boys. The boys walked with her to the steps of the building, then one removed her grocery bags from her cart and handed them out to the other boys before folding the cart and offering to help the woman up the stairs. She spoke in a different language and tried to pay them each with coins, but they refused to take her money. The woman from the first-floor window said something to the boys that sounded like praise.

Eric made his own way into the building, but he couldn't stop thinking about what he'd witnessed. He would gladly have pulled up a chair and watched that scene a hundred times over.

He once considered people watching essential to advancing his craft. He studied the nuances of their expressions, savored the uniqueness of each. Somewhere along the way, his views had become jaded and he'd stopped looking, stopped caring. That moment revived something in him.

He wondered what Sage would have noticed about his neighbors. Would she have formulated a theory on the circumstances that had brought his neighbors to that building? The whereabouts of their families? Their sons? Their husbands? Would she have marveled, as he had, that a difference in language had not stopped them from caring about each other?

They didn't have fancy houses.

They walked where they needed to go.

He'd wanted to believe there was good in people. So many people he knew cared more about what they owned than those who worked for them. They saw differences when they should see commonalities. He'd begun to believe everyone was like that—but his fellow tenants weren't.

The building had more wrong than right with it, but the people in it took care of each other. They were what he'd been looking for—proof that there was more to life than what he'd experienced. For the first time in a long time, he didn't feel trapped. He didn't dread the hours that stretched between him and sleep. He exercised in his apartment, went for another long walk, then did what he'd found impossible to do in his past life—he slept until morning.

Chapter Three

Even though she wanted to, Sage didn't return to the coffee shop the next morning or the morning after that. She wanted to give herself time to sort through her obsession with a man who clearly did not feel the same way toward her. She investigated a potential new client to distract herself, but that prospect didn't hold her attention for long. After stepping out of the Tube station near her apartment, she decided to update Bella. "Good news about Mrs. Hartman. She just likes dogs."

Bella laughed. "My neighbor? I didn't have a chance to give her your card yet, and I never even told you her name. Maybe you are psychic."

"Or maybe I stood in your yard and listened for barking."

"You're a nut, but I love you. So, you knocked on my neighbor's door, gave her an informal evaluation, and deemed her sane?"

"Oh, she's batshit crazy, but not unhappy. She had chairs made specifically so each of the dogs could sit at the table. Clothing for every occasion. They're adorable. She said she was lonely after her husband died and needed something to smile about. Her grandchildren come around more now. There are photos of her family all laughing and playing with the dogs. If she's broken, I don't want to fix her."

"Have you seen coffee man again?"

"Not since our walk."

"That's probably for the best."

"I wish I agreed. He's so unhappy. It's heartbreaking."

"What's his name?"

Sage hesitated. "If I tell you—you'll do a background check, won't you?"

"Abso-fucking-lutely."

"He's not a criminal."

"You don't know that."

"How about we wait until he gives me a reason to believe he's dangerous before we violate his privacy?"

"How about we find out everything we can so we don't have to worry about him violating yours?"

"I don't see everyone as a potential threat, you know."

"And I don't believe tossing fairy dust makes the world a safer place. Come into my office tomorrow and I'll introduce you to an older couple who wish they'd had a background check done on the painter they hired . . . the one who came back with his friends to beat and rob them. I'm not paranoid. I'm aware."

I hate it when she corners me with a good point. "Wayne Easton. That's his name. That's all I know."

"Don't be upset, Sage. I worry about you. You're a pleaser—that's not always a good thing. Don't cut anyone excuses just because you think they're dealing with something. Everyone has problems, but not all of us let it affect how we treat other people. People need boundaries."

"Speaking of which, did I mention that my father thinks I need professional help?" Sage updated Bella on the conversation she hadn't until then been ready to repeat.

"He's the one who needs help. I know he's your father, but he's also an asshole."

Another point I can't argue. "What do they say is one sign of insanity? Doing the same thing over and over and expecting a different result? What is wrong with me that I always think if I'm just a little nicer, try a little harder, he'll see something good in me?"

"Oh, Sage. There is more good in you than in most people I know put together. I wish I could wave a wand and give you the parents you deserve, but life doesn't work that way. They never came back for you at boarding school, Sage. They're not coming now. I'm sorry. You need to start accepting your relationship with them and stand up for yourself."

As if on cue, Sage's phone beeped with an incoming call. "It's my mother. Can I call you back later?"

"Sure. Especially if you need me. I'll be working on a case tonight, but just reading for it. I can take a break."

"Thanks, Bella."

"Sage. Practice this word—*no.* Whatever she wants, it's probably the right response."

"I'll try."

"Are you fifty years old?"

"No."

"Are you blonde?"

"No."

"Can I have five thousand dollars?"

"I don't have that much, but—" Sage stopped herself with a laugh. *I do have a problem.* "No."

"Exactly. Okay, you sound ready. Good luck."

"Love you, Bella."

"Love you, too."

Sage pressed a button on her car panel to switch the call. "Mom?"

"Sage, how are you, sweetie?"

"Good." *Sweetie?*

"How's Bella?"

"Great. I was actually on the phone with her. She has a new apartment in—"

"Yes, well, I was wondering if you could do me a tiny favor."

"Okay." *Shit. Should I have said no? How could I when I don't even know what she wants?*

"I received a call from a very prominent woman from Boston. She's in London for a short time. I still can't believe she called me. I mean, I know who she is, but I had no idea she knew who I am. This woman is old money. Better connected than God. She's dating royalty—that kind of connected. Anyway, she bought a small estate, only ten bedrooms, and is looking for someone to help her expand the rose garden. Finally, there's hope your education wasn't a complete waste. If you swear to me that you will keep your craziness in check, it would mean a lot to me if you met with her and talked me up."

Wow. "I have all the clients I can handle right now, Mom." *Not true, but my mother never could understand my faith that more work would come.* "If this woman is as connected as you say, she'll already have found someone."

"This is important, Sage—make the time."

"I can't. And what you said was hurtful."

"Stop. Don't make this all about you. If you don't want to do it, just say no."

"I don't want to do it."

"You would say that to me after everything I've given you? When do I ask you for anything? Anything? This is what happens when you give your children too much—they become little brats who won't do a single thing that doesn't immediately benefit them."

Here goes nothing. "No."

Her mother sighed. "I'm asking you to do one thing for me. One thing. Meet this woman and tell her your mother is a wonderful person. Is that so hard to imagine yourself doing?"

Sage made a pained face. "Mom."

"I told her you'd meet her for dinner tonight and texted you her contact information. If you can't make it, if you're so damn wrapped up in your own life, then cancel with her—but don't think I'll be very happy with you."

"You never are." *That actually felt good to say.*

"Don't try to twist this into an argument." Her mother made a frustrated guttural sound, then in a forced pleasant tone said, "I heard that your father is coming to London."

"He's not. Just his wife."

"Have you met her? It's so sad what the plastic surgeon did to her nose."

"I don't want to talk about her, Mom." *Not with you.*

"Fine. Sage, wear something nice when you meet Mrs. Westerly, and try not to speak too much. I hear she's a real stickler for formalities."

"I already said I can't g—Why do you care what she thinks of either of us?"

"One day I'll get news that you were switched at the hospital. There's no other explanation for the way you are." With that, her mother hung up.

Sage let herself into her apartment and stood in the middle of the room, hugging herself. *What would accepting that my relationship with my parents will never get better look like? Would I stop seeing them?*

They're all the family I have.

Them and Bella—that's it.

Until I have my own. If I ever do.

She sat on her couch, kicked off her shoes, and opened the text message from her mother. Delinda Westerly. *I have to at least tell her I'm not coming.* She touched the number to make the call.

"Hello," a woman answered.

"Mrs. Westerly?"

"Yes."

"My name is Sage. I'm Victoria Revere's daughter. About tonight—" Sage paused, trying to decide on a polite way to cancel.

"Six o'clock," she said in a sharp tone. "Don't be late. I abhor being kept waiting."

She sounds delightful. "I'm actually calling because I won't able to make it this evening."

"Pardon me?"

"Although I appreciate that my mother recommended me for your garden project, my schedule is packed at the moment. I can, however, send over a list of other highly qualified candidates."

"Nonsense. I've already cleared my schedule for you and made arrangements with my cook. Surely whatever else you had planned for this evening can wait one more day."

Growing up as she had, Sage was no stranger to Mrs. Westerly's attitude. Rich. Demanding. Entitled. The problem with the wealthy was that they were often surrounded by people who wanted something from them, and therefore they weren't often told when they were out of line. An unchecked ego could grow to ugly proportions. "Unfortunately, that's not the case—"

"Miss Revere, I would think very carefully before turning me down."

"Mrs. Westerly, how old are you?"

"What a question!"

"Seventy? Eighty? I'm guessing by your voice."

"What does my age have to do with anything?"

"More than you think, but either way, I don't have time for another client."

"With your lack of professionalism, I can't imagine you have any at all."

Sage leaned back and closed her eyes. *If I were a better daughter, maybe I'd apologize and say something amazing about my mother, but both of them are more privileged than either deserve.* "Listen, my mother is a horrid, social-climbing, English-accent-faking American. My gut tells me you're a hypercontrolling socialite battling chronic loneliness with a tangible amount of regret. I've never been able to reach my mother, and you are likely beyond my skills as well. So, although I must pass on your dinner invitation, please consider inviting my mother instead. The two of you have quite a lot in common."

Sage hung up without giving the other woman a chance to respond and dropped the phone beside her on the couch. It didn't take long for Sage to feel bad about what she'd said. Even though Mrs. Westerly had been condescending, she hadn't deserved what Sage had volleyed back.

I took out my frustration with my mother on a little old woman, who will now likely eat dinner alone because of me.

She glanced over at the Polyscias in the corner of her living room that a client had given her after she'd brought it back from the brink. It had done well in her apartment for years, but suddenly it was drooping.

Great. Just great.

It had been several days since Eric had gone on the walk with Sage, and he'd spent most of his time telling himself he didn't care if he saw her again. Yet he swore as he entered the coffee shop, looked around, and once again did not see her. He gave his order, then took it to the table that was no longer his haven.

Where was she? Had she already come and gone? Perhaps his poor attempt at being charming had driven her to choose another shop. He knew next to nothing about her, but the uncomfortable truth was that he wanted to see her again.

It wasn't just her rounded little ass or her lush curves that stood out against the reed-thin women in his circle. By entertainment-industry standards, Sage's hair was too wild, and the color in her cheeks looked as if it might be . . . *gasp* . . . from actual sunlight. He knew many in his circle would have considered her beauty natural but unpolished.

There was an earthiness to her. She hadn't flirted with him or name-dropped to impress him. She'd been as open as a springtime window and just as refreshing. Despite the way they'd parted, thinking about her made him feel—hopeful.

He couldn't stop thinking about how she'd bought those balloons for the children near the fountain. When was the last time he'd looked at the people around him and asked himself what they needed? Somewhere along the way, his focus had shifted inward. Even as he'd watched Sage bring happiness to the young girl, his thoughts had been on himself and the darkness in his own life. It was a realization that had haunted him since.

While in rehab, he'd come to terms that there were parts of his life he resented. After his parents divorced, his childhood had become lonely. As one of five children, three boys and two girls, he should have scars from wild adventures, memories of laughing until his stomach hurt, and embarrassing stories about each of his siblings.

He didn't.

His mother had taken the three youngest with her and built a new life with another man. Money was the evil she'd blamed for the failure of her first marriage. She'd turned her back on everyone and everything associated with it—including her two eldest children, Brett and Eric.

Brett aligned himself with their father and grandmother and became as cold and judgmental as they were. Eric withdrew from his two families, not comfortable in either. He found solace in books—and later in theater.

Wealth came at a heavy cost. His father's obsession with the family business had made him absent from not only Eric's life, but Brett's as well. For a long time, Delinda had been Eric's only family.

There'd even been a time when he'd believed she understood him, but as he'd grown up, he'd realized she viewed even him only in terms of achievements. She didn't ask, nor did she care, how he felt as long as he was the best at whatever he did. Only scoring the lead role was celebrated, and then only if his performance had been flawless.

The entire Water Bear Man series had appalled her. She'd warned him not to take the role, then lamented the loss of his ability to be taken seriously by anyone once he had. Her complete rejection of the project had already driven a wedge between them before he realized how right she'd been. He shouldn't have taken the role. Jasmine had seen him as nothing more than an ATM.

Delinda had predicted that as well when he'd announced their engagement. When it came to having a brutally clear vision of how things worked, Delinda was often painfully right. He'd won her approval back when Water Bear Man exceeded everyone's box-office expectations again and again, but it had been an empty victory. He felt like the joke Delinda had warned him he might become.

So he'd done what he did best—withdrawn.

One counselor had outright asked him if he'd taken the anesthetic drugs because he wanted to kill himself. The question had shaken Eric. He hadn't seen how far he'd sunk until then.

He didn't want to die.

He wanted a reason to get up in the morning, a friend who didn't care about his fame or fortune. He had more money than he could spend in his lifetime, with profits rolling in daily. It was a burden his counselor hadn't been able to understand—similar to survivor's guilt.

Why me? Why not someone more deserving?

And what is wrong with me? How could anyone have as much as I do and not be happy?

The door of the coffee shop opened, and Eric's breath caught in his throat. Sage. Their eyes met across the room. She nodded once at him before looking away. Eric stood and knocked his coffee over, spilling it. One of the workers, a young man, rushed over to mop the mess off the table. Eric absently tried to help, but his attention remained focused on the woman who hadn't seemed the least bit excited to see him.

He thanked the worker, slapped a generous tip down on the table, and stepped around him. She turned from the counter with a coffee and scone in her hands and made her way to the table where she'd sat with her friend. His hand instinctively went to his scar as he strode to her. Without asking permission, he took the seat across from her.

She didn't smile at him, but she met his gaze and held it without blinking for a long moment. He was accustomed to female attention, but this was different.

He drummed his fingers on the table before him, then said, "I'm sorry about the other day. I shouldn't have left the way I did."

Her expression softened. "Was it something I said?"

"No." He realized he was drumming his fingers again and stopped. Women didn't normally make him nervous. It was a novel feeling. Yes, she was attractive, but had she offered to fuck him right then and there, he would have been disappointed. Somehow, although he couldn't explain how he knew it, she was meant to be more. "It's complicated."

"*You're* complicated," she said, maintaining that steady gaze of hers.

"Not really. Just an ass." Her eyebrows shot up, and he had to admit that even *he* was surprised by his comment. He wanted her to like him, so why was he still pushing her away?

She sipped her coffee. "There's a cure for that. Our behavior is really the only thing we can control."

He wondered if anyone in his family would agree. Money allowed them to shape their environment. Even his younger siblings, the ones who thought they'd been raised outside the influence of their wealth, had never known real adversity. Brett had covertly paved the way for them. There was no loan they hadn't gotten, no grant they were passed over for. For Brett and Eric, their financial status had shaped their lives, defined how people saw them, even dictated whom they interacted with. It was both the wings that had allowed them to fly and the tool that had reined them in. "Because a handful of powerful people make the decisions the rest of us have to live with?"

She cocked her head to the side. "Or think they do. I prefer to make my own path."

He nodded. Yes, that was part of what drew him to her. She lived by her own terms.

All the reasons why he shouldn't start a relationship with a woman while his life was still off-kilter didn't matter now that she was in front of him again. He savored the way she looked him directly in the eye when she spoke. She wanted nothing from him. She was simply a confident woman having a conversation with a man. He pushed aside his attraction to her because he craved this part of her as well. "I missed you."

His words hung in the silence that followed. He hadn't expected to say it, but he didn't regret that he had. Another woman might have volleyed back that he didn't know her well enough for that to be true. Many would have taken it as an invitation for much more than he was offering. In his experience, everyone had an agenda.

What was Sage's?

She broke her scone in half. "Would you like a piece?"

He shook his head. "Do you live in this area?"

"No. I have a place in Acton."

"What brings you here every day?"

She broke eye contact to look down at the napkin she began to fold into smaller and smaller triangles. "Nothing in particular."

She's lying.

He was fascinated. "Do you work?"

"I told you what I do." She tore off a piece of the napkin and rolled it between her fingers before repeating the action. "Go ahead, say it's ridiculous. I'm used to being mocked for it."

He leaned forward and cupped her chin with one hand, raising her eyes back to his. The feel of her sent desire shooting through him. Her eyes widened as if she felt a similar jolt. He dropped his hand. Holy shit, he wanted her, but not the way he had the first time he met her. He didn't want to wake up and slip out while she slept. When she looked at him that way, he wished he really were Wayne Easton. Wayne hadn't left more women than he could remember the names of. He wasn't a pathetic sap who would fund a movie for a woman simply because she said she loved him. "People aren't kind to what they don't understand."

She shrugged, but there was sadness in her eyes. "Like I said, I'm used to it."

He would have accepted her answer from most people, but he felt a sudden protectiveness. He himself had joked about her choice of career, and he regretted not being kinder. "How did you become a plant psychologist?"

She took a bite of her scone, chewed, then sipped her coffee before answering. "I have a master of science in ethnobotany. It's essentially the study of human-environment interaction and the sociocultural importance of plants around the world."

"Impressive." And not at all the response he'd imagined.

"The subject is. Plants are complex creatures humanity has underestimated. Science is proving that, although their movements occur at a rate too slow for our eye to register, they make choices, and some believe they even feel pain. People are driven to explore space, but there's so much here on our own planet that we don't understand."

"Feel pain? Don't tell vegans that. If science gives lettuce a voice, they're screwed." She didn't smile, and he regretted making the joke. He hadn't been making fun of what she did. Hell, he still wasn't sure what that was yet. "That was stupid, sorry."

"No, it was funny," she said while looking down at her napkin and demolishing it again.

He'd disappointed her, but she wasn't going to say it. Although he'd spent his life dreading the constant criticism he received from his family, he didn't like that she accepted his bad behavior as her due. "You didn't think so."

"What I think isn't going to change your mind."

God, how many times had he thought exactly that? "So, tell me to fuck off."

She choked on nothing, then said, "I would never do that."

"Try it. It might feel better than you think."

She swirled her coffee in her cup. "It wouldn't. I'm still feeling crappy about the last time I lost my temper."

Now this he had to hear. "What did you do?"

Sage raised her eyes to his. "I said hurtful things to a person who didn't deserve it simply because I've never been brave enough to say it to the person who does."

"And that bothers you." He'd done much worse and felt less remorse about it. Like someone witnessing a miracle, he wanted this to be real—wanted her to be real. He leaned forward in his seat.

"Of course it does. I want to make people happy, not hurt them."

He studied her expression again, seeing the strain in her eyes this time. "No one is perfect."

She shook her head in disgust. "I'm well aware of that."

Silence hung heavy between them again.

She spoke first. "Sorry. It's been a tough week."

"Tell me about it." He couldn't remember the last time he'd said those words—to anyone.

This time he saw an uncertainty and yearning in her that mirrored the state of his own soul. "Ever look at yourself in the mirror and not like what you see?"

"Every damn day," he said in a low tone.

She looked at his scar, and a flush spread across her cheeks. "Oh my God, I'm sorry. That was completely insensitive of me—"

He reached across the table and put his hand over one of hers. "No, it wasn't—"

"Yes, it was. That's what I'm talking about. I pride myself on being able to sense what people need, but this week I feel like I'm stumbling blind. What I said was thoughtless, and I apologize."

He gave her hand a squeeze. Now that it was in his, he didn't want to let it go. "I don't accept."

Her eyes darkened. "You don't?"

"No." Okay, so it probably wasn't fair to take advantage of what she'd admitted, but he wanted to see her again. "The only way I'll feel better is if you agree to go to dinner with me."

Her gaze skirted away. "Like a date?"

A smile tugged at his lips. "Exactly like that."

"Oh, I don't know."

Disappointment welled within him. His hand went to his cheek. He'd deliberately sought to make himself unattractive. Still, a part of him had hoped she could see past the superficial. He was tempted to rip the scar off and confess the truth, but that would change everything. Instead, he sat back and told himself to calm the fuck down. "I understand."

She leaned forward and touched his arm gently. "I don't think you do. Before I say yes or no, could you answer a question for me?"

"Yes," he said in a tight voice. Did she know?

"Why wouldn't you see a play with me?"

Now there was something he could be honest about. "Acting was my passion when I was younger, then . . ." Her lips pursed in that adorable fashion that made him forget what he was saying. She raised her hand as if she might touch his scar, and he yanked his face back.

"Is it painful?" she asked, a husky tone inflecting her words.

"Not physically. I'm more messed up on the inside."

"I'm sorry."

"Don't be. You didn't do it." He squared his shoulders. "Instead of dinner, do you have plans for this morning?"

"Yes. I need to find a new client if I have any intention of paying my rent."

"How much are you short?" He didn't want to bring money into their relationship, but he didn't like the idea of her struggling, either.

She waved hand. "Only a hundred dollars. I'm not worried."

"That's about how much you paid for the balloons the other day."

She smiled, and it transformed her face. "It was worth it."

"If you need—"

"I don't, but thank you." This time when she touched his arm briefly, his heart did a somersault. She stood and began to gather the clutter from the table. "It was nice seeing you."

Shit, she was leaving. He was on his feet in an instant, blocking her retreat. "Let me help you."

"I'm fine," she said, misunderstanding his offer, while she gathered the last of her trash.

"I know a lot of people. Some have plants." Reggie could arrange something without anyone ever knowing.

"Oh. Thanks, but I don't think so."

"Why?"

The corner of her mouth twisted in a half smile. "It's complicated."

Not really. Not for me anymore. I don't want our time together to end yet. "Are you married?"

"No," she said, sounding shocked.

"Engaged?"

"Not even close."

"Then it's not complicated at all. Say yes."

She looked uncertain. "I usually work alone."

"I'll be as quiet as a mouse."

"What I do is important to me."

"Understood." He was well versed in negotiations. This wasn't a refusal—she was clarifying her terms. "I'm genuinely interested."

Her chest rose and fell as she took a few deep breaths. "I couldn't handle another person doubting me right now."

"I wouldn't do that to you." *Again.* He hated that he'd made fun of her profession the first time they'd met. He'd never been anyone's hero, but she brought out a protective side of him. In a way she reminded him of who he might have been, had no one opened his eyes to the reality of human nature.

She seemed to sense his inner battle. "I'd love to say yes."

Never had he wanted to kiss a woman more than he did in that moment, but she looked upset again. "Then say it."

"I don't know. I'm not usually indecisive. Everything is normally clear to me, but this week—with you—"

He cupped her cheek with one hand. "What would you say if I told you it's the exact opposite for me? When I'm around you, I feel like a shipwrecked man who has just spotted a boat on the horizon."

"That sounds good." She let out a shaky breath that warmed his lips.

"It is."

Her gaze searched his. "Only one person in the whole world knows what I do. If I let you in, you have to swear to keep my secret."

"You have my word." Lost in her eyes, he would have promised her anything.

She stepped back and picked up her purse. "Okay, then, let's go find my next client."

Chapter Four

Delinda Westerly accepted the hand King Tadeas offered her as she stepped out of a Rolls-Royce in front of her grandson's estate. Michael, her driver and butler, closed the door behind them. Delinda sighed. "Do you think Eric is here? If not, I'm not looking forward to this visit. I have never in my entire life met anyone so frustrating to converse with as Reggie."

"I like him," Michael said.

Delinda narrowed her eyes at him, then steadied herself on the arm the king held out to her. "What about you?"

"I'll admit he's an acquired taste, but he did save your granddaughter's life," Tadeas said in a tone as neutral as Michael's.

"Yes, he did." She shuddered, not wanting to remember the day she'd almost lost Rachelle to a madman and his son. "Eric lets him run his establishment as if it's his. How do we know he's not stealing from Eric?"

"We don't," Tadeas parried, stepping forward and guiding her along with him. "He did, however, refuse the substantial bribe you offered him. He also fell asleep at the last gala we took him to. He's certainly not a social climber."

Delinda shook her head in frustration. "With the prime minister in attendance. It was mortifying."

Michael trotted up beside her. "Or refreshing. He's not intimidated by anyone."

"I doubt he's intelligent enough to realize he should be," Delinda snapped.

"Now, now, Del, your anger is misplaced," Tadeas said.

His words cut through Delinda's defenses, and her shoulders shook beneath her jacket. "It breaks my heart that Eric won't see me."

Tadeas placed his hand over hers on his arm. "I know."

"We used to be close. Why didn't he turn to me when he needed help?" She raised her head and blinked back tears. "I don't care what I have to do to keep him safe. I won't lose him the way I lost Oliver."

Tadeas leaned across and kissed Delinda's temple. "No one should go through what you did. I cannot imagine the pain that must still be in your heart, but Eric is not Oliver. Don't let your fears cloud that."

"My fears are justified," Delinda answered tersely, even though she wanted nothing more than to lean on the man who had taken up residence in London simply because she was there. "If Rachelle hadn't come to find him . . . if Eric had continued to take that drug—"

"But she did find him, and he went to rehab, Del. He's going to be okay," Tadeas said.

"Is he? Then why is he hiding in some awful neighborhood pretending to be someone else? Doesn't that sound like someone who requires *another* intervention?" Delinda turned and faced Tadeas. "I'll stop if you look me in the eye and tell me you're certain Eric doesn't need my help."

The king's confidence wavered. "I cannot."

Delinda squared her shoulders and walked away from her two companions. Tadeas fell into step on one side, Michael on the other.

Michael cleared his throat. "Are we here because Miss Revere wouldn't meet you?"

"Miss Revere?" Tadeas repeated her name slowly. "Who is she?"

Delinda didn't explain herself as a rule, but Tadeas didn't ask questions merely out of curiosity. He cared. "Sage Revere. She comes from a horrible family and has attached herself to Eric. My sources tell me—"

"Sources? Are you having Eric watched?" King Tadeas took hold of one of Delinda's arms and pulled her to a halt. "Did you not learn your lesson with Rachelle? You'll drive him away if you hold on too tightly."

Delinda looked down at his hand on her, then met his gaze with fire in her eyes. "The same could be said to you. Kindly remove your hand."

"I'll meet you both back at the car," Michael said as he beat a hasty retreat.

Tadeas rose to his full height but did not release her. "I know you are acting out of love, but that doesn't mean you can disregard how others feel. Stop. Let Eric find his own way."

"You speak as if you haven't shaped your son's entire life. You dare to tell me how to behave with my own family?"

"I do," the king said in a low growl that sent a flush to Delinda's cheeks. Tadeas was still a handsome devil, far too accustomed to getting his own way. "But only because it would please me to see all of your grandchildren at our wedding."

Delinda flushed. "I've told you—I'm too old and too busy to marry again."

"Then we shall have a long, torrid affair. Either way, Delinda, your place is at my side"—he lowered his voice—"and in my bed."

Flustered, Delinda flipped her head. "You're shameless," she said.

"And you're gorgeous." Tadeas pulled her into his embrace with the skill and strength of a much younger suitor. His lips brushed over hers, sending warmth flooding through her.

Delinda raised a hand to caress his cheek as he continued to kiss her. She still wore the wedding band Oliver had given her, and wanting another man felt like a betrayal, but she'd been alone for decades.

Only recently had she realized how much of herself she'd buried with her deceased husband.

Tadeas raised his head. "You're not alone, Del. Not anymore." He raised a hand and wiped a tear from her cheek she hadn't realized she'd shed. "And I'll take you in my life on your terms, but I won't stand quiet when we disagree. I care for you too much to do that."

She sniffed delicately and smiled ruefully. She would have been disappointed if he did, but she wasn't about to tell him so. "I suppose a certain attitude must be expected when dating a royal."

Tadeas laughed heartily. "Oh, my dear. You may not be a queen by blood, but you could go toe to toe with any royal I've ever met."

"A compliment, I'm sure," Delinda said while arching one eyebrow at him.

He laughed again. "Of course. You've brought joy back to my life. I want nothing less for you."

After decades alone, her heart was well fortressed, but Tadeas had laid siege to it. She already found herself looking forward to their time together each day. He was a friend who wanted more. Until him, she had thought that part of her life was over. The idea of it starting again was both terrifying and exciting. So instead of facing it, she focused on her other concerns. "I'm worried about Eric, Tadeas. Really worried. I don't like this woman. He needs someone stable, someone strong. I've looked into her, and there isn't anything about her lifestyle I approve of. She's rebellious and flighty. She's a charlatan. She targets people with money and fleeces them. That's how she supports herself. Does she sound like someone Eric needs?"

"No, but perhaps she is more than she appears."

"I was willing to give her a chance. I asked her to meet with me, but she refused the invitation."

Tadeas looked as if he were holding back a smile. "Did she? Well, then, we should string her up."

"Sarcasm is rarely helpful."

"Is this better?" Tadeas claimed her lips once more, and she was twenty again, feeling desire for the first time. She clung to him, knowing from experience that such moments were to be savored.

From just beside them, Reggie said, "King Tadeas, normally I wouldn't interrupt lovebirds, but my kids are home today, and it's hard enough to explain the shit they see on YouTube."

Delinda jumped back from Tadeas. "There most certainly is nothing to explain."

Maintaining one arm around Delinda's waist, Tadeas shook Reggie's hand. "Good to see you again."

"Is it?" Although Reggie towered over both of them, he made a pained face. "She scares me a little bit."

"I should," Delinda said, straightening her back despite Tadeas's hand.

Tadeas clucked in reprimand. "We're here because we're worried about Eric. Have you seen him recently?"

Reggie gave them both a blank stare that would have frustrated any cross-examiner. Delinda wanted to reach out and shake him, but she settled for glaring at him instead. He refused to answer any questions regarding her grandson—as if she were the one Eric required protection from. Was he so dim-witted that he didn't realize she already knew everything?

"He's spending time with a woman of dubious character, and I'm concerned." Delinda decided to lay her cards on the table and see if that would shake any information out of him.

"Is he? Good for him," Reggie replied.

Losing patience, Delinda leaned forward and growled, "Could you at least pretend you care what happens to my grandson?"

"Del—" Tadeas started to say.

"I don't know anything about a woman," Reggie said, cutting the king off. "But I don't have to pretend anything. I don't work for you. I don't even like you." He shrugged like a child would. "Sorry."

Delinda tensed and turned to Tadeas. "Do you see how he speaks to me?"

Tadeas looked from her to Reggie. "Careful, Reggie. I respect your loyalty to Eric, but she's his family."

Reggie rocked back onto his heels as if doing so helped him absorb that reminder. He directed his answer to Delinda. "You're not the only one who cares about him. I've tried being nice to you, but maybe you need to hear this—he doesn't want to see you. He doesn't want you involved in his life right now. When he changes his mind, I'll be the first one to open the door, but for now he wants to figure things out on his own—without you."

Delinda snapped, "Who do you think you are?"

Reggie folded his arms across his chest. "I'm the one he's *not* hiding from."

She gasped.

Tadeas pulled her closer to his side. "This isn't helping anyone."

Undeterred, Delinda snarled at Reggie, "I only want the best for him."

"Then give him time," Reggie said quietly before turning and walking away.

"That man—" Delinda started.

"Is a good friend to Eric. Come on, Del, let's go home."

Shaking with emotion, Delinda said, "I can't stand by and do nothing."

Tadeas began to guide her back to the car. "Sometimes you have to. We're here if Eric needs us."

When they arrived back at the car, Michael ushered them inside. Before getting in, Delinda searched Tadeas's face. "We? Don't you have a country to run?"

"Magnus can handle my duties," he answered.

Doubt bubbled within Delinda, then burst out. "I don't know if I can wait for Eric to come to me."

"You will do what's right. You're the strongest woman I've ever known." He kissed her again, briefly, then said, "I believe I understand some of Eric's struggle. I've spent much of my life surrounded by people who bowed to me. I was more king than man to them. My role had become my identity. I see Eric as someone who is searching for his purpose. What is a man without one? When I realized Magnus was old enough to take over my royal duties, I began to wonder who I was. My journey felt over—then you demanded I meet you for tea. Demanded. You opened my eyes to how much more I could do. It was the proverbial kick in the pants I required. I don't know how long I have left on this earth, but I know how I want to spend the remainder of my time—with you."

"You, sir, are quite the charmer." Delinda chuckled and gave his hand a pat.

He laced his fingers with hers. "Only with you." He brought her hand to his lips and kissed her knuckles.

Delinda's cheeks warmed. She felt younger and almost giddy. In an effort to keep herself grounded, she reminded herself that she was too old to fall in love. It was a battle she was slowly losing, though. "I can't let this woman derail Eric."

Tadeas sighed. "Delinda, has anyone ever told you that you are an incredibly stubborn woman?"

Chin held high, she turned to look out the window of the car. "Once or twice."

Chapter Five

"Which way are we going?" Eric asked. He didn't care, but they had been standing on the corner for several minutes.

She hugged her purse to her side. "If you have somewhere you need to be—"

"I don't. I'm just curious about your strategy for finding your next client." He didn't honestly mind if they stood there all day. Everything about her was interesting, and he delighted in having no idea where the day led.

"My clients come to me." She looked down one street, then the other, but didn't take a step in either direction.

"How do they know what you do?" He half expected her to pull a sign out of her purse and wave it at passing cars.

"They don't."

"I see," he said, even though he didn't. She probably left her cards in jars or on bulletin boards at business establishments. Her eyes darted up and down the streets around them, as if she were anticipating the arrival of someone. Perhaps he'd misunderstood when she'd said she needed to find a new client and she worked with referrals. "Is one meeting you here?"

"Not exactly." She chewed her bottom lip and gave Eric a once-over. "You're messing with my radar."

"Is it my piercing blue eyes or the broad shoulders that you find most distracting?" he joked, hoping to bring a smile back to her face.

"No, it's your humility I can't resist," she snarked, but her eyes slid over him, and she blushed.

She does find me attractive. I knew it.

His chest puffed with pride. Over the years, major online magazines had bestowed titles on him based on his appearance. World's Sexiest Man. Hottest Superhero. None of it had ever mattered to him. However, when Sage glanced at him from beneath those long lashes of hers, he felt like a schoolboy discovering his first crush liked him back. They looked into each other's eyes long enough that Eric began to lean in.

"Let's walk," she said, and sidestepped away from him.

He followed, releasing his breath slowly as he lengthened his stride to keep pace with her. There'd be plenty of time later for what he'd just vividly imagined doing with her. This day was about getting to know her on a different level. "I should have said it at the time, but what you did for that little girl at the fountain was—intense."

Sage slowed her pace. "Thank you. I hope it helped their family in some way."

He nodded. "I'm sure it did."

She pocketed her hands in the front of her jeans. "You didn't seem happy with me at the time."

"It wasn't anything about you."

"Do you want to talk about it?"

"Not really."

She hunched her shoulders forward. "Well, if you change your mind—I'm a good listener."

He already knew that about her. They walked in comfortable silence for a couple of blocks. Unlike many people he knew, she didn't take every pause in conversation as an opportunity to talk about herself. It piqued his curiosity even more. "You obviously didn't grow up in London. What brought you here?"

"A friend."

"Male?"

She shot him an odd look. "No."

"What's her name?"

"Bella."

"She's your . . . ?"

"Best friend."

"Ah." He wouldn't have cared if their relationship had been more intimate, but it was nice to know he wouldn't face that kind of competition. "Longtime friends? Let me guess, she lived across the street when you were little." He liked the idea of Sage having that Norman Rockwell kind of childhood.

Sage shook her head. "Boarding-school buddy."

"Which school?"

"Wordsloe Academy."

His gaze snapped to her profile. She didn't give off the vibe of someone who'd had an expensive education, but he didn't doubt it. What he didn't yet understand was how she'd gotten to a place where she was struggling to pay her rent. "Impressive."

"To my parents, perhaps. I can't complain. It provided me with a solid foundation in my chosen path of study." She smiled. "And I met Bella."

"Are your parents in the London area?"

"Not often." There was a sad wistfulness in her tone.

"Are you close with them?"

She stopped walking and turned to Eric. "Do you want the truth or the public version?"

He ran his hand lightly down her arm in a move that initially had been meant to reassure her but that felt instantly intimate. "Whichever you're comfortable sharing with me."

She held his gaze for a long moment before saying softly, "I play six instruments. I speak four languages fluently and can understand at least nine others. Yet for as long as I can remember, I have been an utter disappointment and embarrassment to my parents. I'm their only child. You'd think that would make me special, but it doesn't. They don't come see me because they don't want to. Their lives are easier when I'm not part of them. That's the real relationship I have with my parents."

"Come here." He pulled her to his chest for a hug. He could have said he understood, but this wasn't about him. Someone else might have told her to ignore her parents' opinions, claiming it didn't matter. Eric knew it did. He'd never known how to connect with either of his own parents. His mother hadn't known how to fit him in with the new family unit she'd created for herself after leaving his father. His father had remained aloof yet judgmental. Yes, he knew exactly how much family could cut one to the core. So despite the people passing them on either side, he simply held her.

She stood awkwardly in his embrace at first, then laid her forehead on his chest and seemed to give herself over to the moment. It wasn't a dramatic, tear-filled scene—but it was packed with more emotion than Eric had allowed himself to feel in a very long time.

Eventually she raised her face. "Sorry. I don't usually vomit my private life on people like that."

He traced her chin with his thumb. "You can vomit on me anytime—" He stopped and shared a smile with her. "Figuratively, I mean."

"Thanks." She stepped out of his embrace, looking bemused. "I appreciate both your offer and your clarification."

To lessen the tension, and because he wanted to maintain their connection, he offered her his elbow. "Shall we continue on?"

"We shall." She placed her hand on the crook of his arm and fell into step beside him.

They came across a small, tree-shaded park. It reminded him of another day and place. "I almost had a daughter once. At least, that's what Jasmine said. She would have been the age of the girl at the fountain."

"Almost?" Sage's hand tightened on his arm, but she didn't break pace.

"I was engaged to a woman who didn't love me. She aborted the child when she discovered it."

Sage gasped. "I'm so sorry."

He shrugged, downplaying how he felt out of habit. "It was probably for the best."

She stopped then and looked up at him. "You don't believe that."

She saw past his act, and it knocked him off-balance. "No, I don't," he said tightly as his throat closed with emotion.

"Did you love the mother?"

"I thought I did," Eric said, and realized the memory of Jasmine no longer had the power to sadden him. "She didn't want me, though, only what I could do for her."

He waited for her to say something trite or inspirational, but she didn't. Instead, she nodded and urged him to walk with her again. He knew in that moment that she understood him in a rare way. He didn't require reassurances. He would have rejected any declaration that he would one day have that daughter—as if children were interchangeable. Even if he and some future woman bore a dozen children, a corner of his heart would always belong to the daughter he'd never met.

Once inside the small park, Sage released his arm and sat on a bench. Eric joined her, close enough that they were almost touching. They sat for a while before either spoke again. Oddly, the quiet was comforting.

Sage finally asked, "Do you remember the person I told you I regretted telling off?"

Eric turned to face Sage more. "Yes."

"She didn't seem like a very nice woman."

"So maybe she did deserve what you said."

"Maybe, but that doesn't change how I feel. I want to apologize to her. I just can't decide if that will make things better or worse." Her small shoulders rose and fell. "Bella says sometimes it's best to leave well enough alone. What do you think?"

Eric grimaced. "I'm no expert. I've never been accused of being a good person."

She scanned his face before saying, "I didn't ask you what you've been accused of—I asked you what you thought."

Nothing he'd ever experienced, no drug he'd ever taken, had ever felt as good as being given a chance to redefine himself. With Sage, Eric didn't carry the weight of every mistake he'd ever made. He could finally, simply, be himself. "You should trust your own instincts."

Sage clutched her purse on her lap. "I don't want to be anyone's doormat, but I need to leave people better than I found them."

Need? Leave? The words stood out to him. She wasn't seeking a relationship with this woman she felt compelled to comfort. So why care about her at all? What drove Sage? When he'd first met her, he'd thought her profession was a flighty fantasy. She hadn't come across as someone he could take seriously. He was beginning to believe she had scars as deep and dark as his own. He was choosing the best way to phrase his next question when she slapped a hand on his thigh.

"I've found my next client," she exclaimed in an excited whisper.

He fought his body's lusty reaction to her touch and looked around. There were several people in the small park. "Who?"

"The man sitting on the bench behind you."

Eric tensed. He didn't like the idea of her looking at, forget about working for, another man. He swung around.

Sage grabbed his arm and said quickly, "Don't be obvious."

I'll be what I need to be, Eric thought, giving in to a novel wave of possessiveness. Relief flooded in when he realized that the object of her attention was an older man of small stature and silver hair. "Him?"

Still holding Eric's arm, Sage whispered, "Yes, him. Now turn around before you scare him off."

Eric obediently turned back toward Sage. Pink rushed to her cheeks, and the fire in her eyes made saying no to her unthinkable. "Do you know him?"

She shook her head, sending her ponytail whipping back and forth. "No, but he has to be the one."

"The one?"

"I told you—my clients find me. He came to this park for a reason."

"And you think *you're* that reason?" He regretted the question as soon as he voiced it. It sounded more sarcastic than he'd meant.

She looked away and then back. Her back straightened with defensive tension that he'd put there. "You don't have to believe in me or in what I do, but please leave if you don't intend to be helpful."

Leave? No chance in hell. "What do you need me to do?"

She studied his expression, seeming to gauge his seriousness, then stood. "Follow my lead."

He stood and squared his shoulders. "Let's do this."

She placed her hand back on his arm, but as if he were a prop rather than a partner in crime. Like him, she didn't give her trust easily. She'd told him that only one other person knew what she did.

He hoped it wasn't because it was criminal.

He couldn't overlook pickpocketing, no matter how adorable she was. He wanted to believe she was about to offer to help the man with a plant issue, but how could she know if he had one? The way she talked, it sounded more like he was a target than a potential client. Eric took a closer look at the man they were approaching. Hunched forward, he stared blankly ahead, holding a collar and leash in his hands. A profound sadness hovered about him.

Somehow, Sage intended to help him. At least, that was what Eric wanted to believe—needed so fucking much to believe. He pulled Sage to an abrupt stop beside him. "About that woman you offended."

"Yes?"

"Apologize to her. Not because it'll make things better, but because it's the right thing to do."

A huge smile spread across Sage's face. "Thank you. You get me."

I hope to God I do.

◆ ◆ ◆

Sage had never shared this part of her process with anyone else—not even Bella. She had described it to her best friend, but it wasn't something Bella would have understood. It required trusting in a way that defied logic. Sage didn't have any special powers or even a gift. What she did have was an open heart and a desire to help people. The formula required no magic—just patience and the belief that people were often much more than they first appeared.

Wayne was the perfect example of the last part. He'd been rude and dismissive, then withdrawn and angry. Yet, a few moments earlier, he had not only comforted her but had also shared something that still hurt him deeply. He was reaching out.

When she'd first met him, she'd thought he would be her next client. He was definitely troubled enough. Being with him was so much more complicated than that.

Sage didn't share personal information with clients. She certainly didn't tell them about what she did. The people she helped hired her to care for their plants. While in their lives, she did what she could to bring joy back into everything. They paid her for her work with their plants. That was simply how it worked.

So if Wayne wasn't a client, what was he?

That thought was put aside as she and Wayne reached the older man. Sage tugged on Wayne's arm. "You're so wrong," she said in a playful voice.

It took him only a heartbeat to fall into step with her. "I don't believe I am," he said just as lightly.

"Here, I'll get us a tiebreaker." Sage stopped just in front of the man who was too lost in his own sadness to notice her. "Excuse me, sir?"

The man looked up as if startled and stashed the leash away as if the act of holding it and the collar was shameful. "Yes?"

"A friend of mine has been quite sad recently. I'm looking for the perfect houseplant to cheer her up. Which do you think she'd prefer? Fuchsia or snapdragons?"

"My vote is for the snapdragons," Wayne said smoothly.

The man blinked a few times, as if the question required returning from somewhere far off. "I—I don't know. I'm sorry."

"Lilacs give off a constant mood-lifting aroma. On the other hand, begonias are hardier and can be transplanted outdoors. My friend has been so down. This is an important decision. Which would cheer you more?"

The man rubbed a hand roughly over his face, stood, and stuffed his hands into his jacket pocket. "I'm sorry. I don't know much about plants. I came to the park to be alone."

"No. No. We're sorry. We didn't mean to intrude." Sage held out a card to the man. "I'm a plant psychologist, so I take vegetation very seriously." She smiled with warmth and waited.

"A plant psychologist?" The man frowned and accepted the card, turning it over as if it did something special.

Sage nodded. "Keep my number in case you ever find yourself with a droopy houseplant." She leaned forward and placed her hand lightly on his forearm. "Or with a home in need of a little uplifting. Plants have health benefits. They increase indoor oxygen levels, raise the humidity, and have even been known to lower anxiety. I suggest one houseplant per hundred square feet, but that's just my preference."

He looked back and forth between Sage and Wayne. "If you're selling anything, I'm not interested."

Sage hugged Wayne's side. "I don't sell plants, just counsel them, right, Wayne?"

Wayne gave her a strange look, as if what she'd just said had made him uncomfortable. Sage tensed, hoping her partner would stay in character. His features transformed into an easy smile, and he wrapped his arm around her waist, holding her closer. "As far as I know, that's all she does."

"Thank you, but I don't have any plants," the older man said as he held the card out for Sage to take back.

Sage didn't. Instead she tugged on Wayne and began to walk away. "Keep my card in case you ever do. They really warm a home up. I also help people introduce new plants into their lives—even ones they've bought at convenience stores. Well, it was nice to meet you."

"I guess," the man said slowly, pocketing the card.

They were several feet away when Wayne said, "Sorry that one didn't work out for you. I have some friends who might be interested—"

Sage stepped away from Wayne. Walking with him as if they were a couple was playing havoc with her senses. "He'll call me."

Wayne looked back over his shoulder at the man, still standing where they'd left him. "I wouldn't bet your rent on it."

"I would. In fact, I am. When you send good out into the universe, good comes back."

Wayne made a sound of disgust. "That's not how things work. I know—I mean, there are plenty of horrible people who are wealthy beyond what they deserve."

"Who are probably the unhappiest people on the planet. Would you really want to trade places with them?" Sage paused and turned to look up at his face.

"No. No, I wouldn't." He lowered his mouth to hers. Sage swayed forward into his unhurried, tender kiss. His hands cupped her face as he explored her lips and delved in to meet her tongue with his.

Warmth spread through Sage, but not just from desire. Being with him felt right and beautiful. As a person who followed her heart, right then she could hear it screaming that he could be the man she was meant to spend the rest of her life with. Bella saw enough divorced couples come through her office that she didn't believe in soul mates, but Sage still did.

Wayne raised his head. His ragged breath matched Sage's.

"Wayne—"

"Don't call me that," he growled, his hands dropping from her face.

Still muddled from the kiss, Sage blinked fast and shook her head. Had she said the wrong name? *I think I said Wayne. God, I hope I said Wayne. What else could I have said?* She reached for him. "Did I—"

He stepped back. "Forget it."

How could she? Whatever she'd called him had just ruined what had possibly been one of the best moments of her life. "If I said something wrong, I didn't mean to."

His expression darkened, and he pocketed his hands. "I said drop it." He started to walk away. She almost let him go, but then chased after him.

When she caught up to him, she grabbed him by the arm and hauled him to a stop. "No. No, you don't get to kiss me like that, then talk to me as if I don't matter to you. You want to be with me? Be *nice* to me. You want to be an asshole—go, but don't come back. Maybe you're angry with the world and maybe it has something to do with whatever left that scar on your face, but I had nothing to do with that."

He looked at her hand on his arm, then met her gaze. The torment in his eyes pulled at Sage's heart. "I shouldn't have kissed you."

"Okay." Sage let out a long, slow breath. She wanted to demand to know why, but in her experience, people shared when they were ready.

"It would be easy to fall into bed with you."

"Not *that* easy," she felt the need to protest. She'd never had sex outside a relationship.

His nostrils flared, and the air sizzled between them. "I'm not in a good place right now. I'm still figuring out a few things. Fucking you would just confuse me more."

Sage released his arm. What did a woman say to that? "Well, I'm glad we've covered how *you* would feel about it."

He shrugged. "You'd be devastated when I moved on. And I would move on. I always do."

"Wow." *That's quite an ego he has there.* "I really dodged a bullet." She didn't attempt to disguise the sarcasm in her voice. *How did I imagine he could be the one for me? Maybe I do need to get my head checked.*

He gave her a funny look. "All I'm trying to say is that I have a lot more shit going on in my life right now than I can talk to you about. Starting anything with you wouldn't be fair to you."

Sage folded her arms across her chest. "That's fine."

"I thought we could be friends, but every time I'm near you, I really want to—"

"Got it," Sage said, while raising one hand up for him to stop. The last thing she wanted was to hear another person make excuses for why they didn't want to be with her. "Well, this is it. Thanks for helping me find my next client."

He frowned but didn't say anything for a few minutes, just glared at her. "What happens if that guy calls you?"

"What do you mean what happens?"

"Don't meet up with him."

"Wait, you don't want to be with me, but you think you can tell me what I can or can't do?"

"I don't want to see you get hurt."

Sage rolled her eyes skyward. "He's a little old man practically crying in the park over a dog. Did he look dangerous to you?"

"You're too trusting."

"Even with you?"

He swore beneath his breath. "Even with me."

Sage hiked her purse farther up on her shoulder and met his angry gaze. "That's a real shame, because I was starting to like you."

With her chin high in the air, she turned and walked away. He didn't follow.

"He has so much shit going on in his life," she muttered as she walked back to her apartment. "Too much shit to share. It wouldn't be fair to me."

A man in a suit at her side gave her an odd look, then said, "He's married." He walked on by.

Sage gasped. "I didn't even think of that. That bastard probably has a wife."

Just then her phone rang. Bella. Coincidence or message from the universe? "Hi, Bella."

"Hey, Sage. Just checking in on you. How are you?"

"I'm fine. Why wouldn't I be fine?"

"Easy, tiger. I'm not suggesting anything. Best friend here. I call all the time, and usually you don't jump down my throat about it, but now that you have, I need to ask—what's wrong? Because you sound upset."

Sage sighed. "Did you do the background check on Wayne Easton?"

"Oh, shit. No. I forgot. This case kind of sucked me in. Why? Have you seen him again? Is there a problem?"

Sage slapped a hand on her forehead. "No. No problem. At least not on his side."

"Oh boy. What happened?"

Sage arrived back at her apartment and let herself in. "If I tell you, you're going to think I'm crazy."

"You are crazy, but I still love you. Spill it."

Sage kicked off her shoes. "I took him with me today to find a client."

"Wait, so you no longer think he needs help?"

"Oh, he needs help. I just don't know if I'm the one meant to do it."

"You're beginning to worry me, Sage. I think you should stay away from this guy."

"That's pretty much a moot point now."

"Good."

"Not good." Sage collapsed onto her couch. "He kissed me, and for just a second I thought I saw—forever."

"Sage—"

"Don't say it, Bella. I know. It's ridiculous. He's obviously troubled. I'm probably transferring my abandonment issues to him. I realize he can't fill that void. I didn't sleep with him. It was just a kiss. It didn't matter. And I'm not going to see him again, and it's probably for the best. Okay?" Sage sucked in a breath only when her rushed speech came to an end.

After a pause, Bella asked, "Which wine would you like me to bring over tonight?"

"You choose. You have good taste." Sage could have said she didn't need the wine or the comfort company, but she missed Bella. It would be good to see her. "Hey, on a happier subject, I met my next client today."

"You did? Who?"

"I don't know his name yet, but I already have a plan for him if he calls me. It came to me the second I saw him holding on to a dog collar so sadly, like he'd just lost his best friend. He looked so lonely. I might need your help."

"My help?"

"Just with the introductions. That's it. We get them in the same room, and if it's meant to be, it's meant to be."

"Sometimes when you start talking, Sage, I feel like I tuned in right in the middle. Am I supposed to know who we're discussing?"

"Think, Bella. Who do you know who loves dogs?"

"My neighbor?"

Even though Bella sounded skeptical, Sage was never bothered by her comments, because at the heart of their friendship there was acceptance for their differences. Sage could never imagine sitting in an office all day poring over paperwork, but she didn't judge Bella for thriving on the challenge of it. Bella worried about Sage, but that didn't stop her from celebrating Sage's successes with each client. Mutual trust. That's what it came down to for Sage. She felt suddenly sorry for Wayne, because he sounded like someone who needed someone like that in his life.

"It won't happen for about a week," Sage said with confidence. "I gave the man my card. First, he has to call. We'll go shopping for plants together. Then I'll figure out if Mrs. Hartman would even be a good fit for him."

"Don't meet him alone," Bella interjected.

"You sound like Wayne now. You know I'll be careful. We'll meet somewhere busy. I've done this a hundred times. Don't worry."

"I'll try. You must have kick-ass guardian angels, because things always seem to work out. Just make sure to tell me when and where you're meeting this stranger who may try to lock you up in his basement."

Sage chuckled. It wasn't the first time Bella had tossed out that dire possibility. "I will, but trust me, he's not dangerous. I have a good sense about these things."

"Let's hope we don't have to test that theory. See you at seven? Your place?"

"I'll make dinner. Come hungry."

"Great. See you then."

Sage pushed herself off the couch and headed to her kitchen to see if she had what she needed for dinner. As she rummaged through her fridge, she remembered the woman she'd canceled having a meal with and the apology she owed her. She almost called her then but decided it could wait one more day. She felt emotionally drained.

Chapter Six

When it came to fucking up a good thing, Eric's record remained solid.

Eric slammed his fist into the cushion beside him. Being with Sage had been amazing. Her view of people and how things were supposed to work was so different from anything he'd ever experienced. Prior to meeting her, he wouldn't have believed people like her actually existed. Sweet. Caring. Dedicated to doing good.

Although I'm still not exactly sure how she's going to help that man.

I'll probably fucking never know now.

The door of his apartment opened. "Hello, sunshine. How was your week?"

"I'm not in the mood, Reggie."

Reggie planted himself in the chair across from Eric. "Yeah, mine wasn't that great, either. It's your grandmother. She plays with my mind like a ninja, and I think she's winning."

Eric stood and walked to the window. "So avoid her."

"I can't. I've started to feel bad for her. You have to go see her."

"I don't have to do anything."

"You're going to feel like shit if she dies and you didn't visit."

"I feel like shit already."

Reggie clocked Eric on the side of the head.

Eric spun on his heel, his hand flying up to where he'd been hit. "What the fuck was that?"

"That's what my dad would have done if I said shit like that. Come back to the house. I'm almost done with my surprise, but what I've finished might be enough for now."

Still angry, Eric leaned in and growled, "Don't ever fucking lay a hand on me again."

Reggie raised both hands in front of himself in mock fear. "Hey, I've tried everything else. It was worth a shot." He smiled.

Eric's anger faded away. "You're such an asshole."

Reggie shrugged. "Come on home. The kids miss you."

Eric brought a fisted hand to his chin. "Maybe I should. What the hell am I doing here?"

"You're asking the wrong person. I wouldn't have chosen this place even if I were broke."

"It's not so bad. I actually like the people."

"You? Like someone? This I have to hear."

Eric described the scene he'd witnessed earlier in the week, then said, "It wasn't an isolated case. They look out for each other. It's nice to see."

Reggie nodded slowly. "Have you spoken to any of them?"

"No. Half of them don't even know English."

"What about the half that do?"

Eric shrugged. "You know I'm not good with chitchat."

"That's because you don't like anyone, but since you seem to actually like these people, you might want to do something crazy like talk to one of them."

"I did meet a woman," Eric confided. It felt good to say it aloud.

Reggie smiled. "See, even with a scar, you've still got it."

"It's not like that."

"No? Then how is it?"

"I feel different when I'm with her. I smile more. Not just because she's pretty. She just has . . . I don't know how to describe it . . . a presence I could get addicted to. I like her."

"That's awesome."

"No, it's bad. I've already fucked it up."

"In one week? That was fast."

"I'm serious. She thinks my name is Wayne Easton and that this scar is real. I outright told her she can't trust me. There's no coming back from that."

"Yeah, that is fucked-up. Well, on to the next woman."

Eric punched the wall with the side of his fist. "I don't want the next woman."

Reggie looked as if he were weighing options. "I bet she'd forgive you anything if she found out you're richer than hell."

"I don't want that, either," Eric growled.

"I know, I know. You want to be loved for you. I was just throwing it out for consideration." Reggie cracked his knuckles in front of him. "So, to recap: you're living in a building with people you like but don't know, and you've met a woman who makes you happy but you've lied to her about—everything."

"Not everything. Just my name . . . and this." He touched his scar.

Reggie made a raspberry with his lips. "I'll make you a deal: come back and see your grandmother once, and I'll help you figure the rest of this shit out."

"What is up with you and Delinda all of a sudden?"

Reggie raised and lowered one shoulder. "She loves you, and you don't make that an easy thing to do."

Eric groaned. "I don't want to hear the laundry list of what she thinks I'm doing wrong."

"Tell her that."

"I've tried. She doesn't listen."

Reggie clapped a hand on Eric's shoulder. "One time. Meet with her one time. Give her a chance to be different. I like to think there's hope for everyone."

Eric turned to meet his friend's gaze. "You really believe that?"

Under pressure, Reggie faltered. "No, but she's camped out in London and has no intention of leaving until she knows you're okay." He looked around the room. "Go back for a few days. Smile, play nice. All this will still be here when you get back." He kicked the frayed chair beside him. "It's not going anywhere."

Eric dreaded the idea of spending time with Delinda when he was already at a low point in his life. Visits with her were best done when he was feeling his most confident, and even then she could reduce a person's confidence with one well-aimed criticism. If it were simply about Delinda, Eric wouldn't go back. However, his friend had been holding her off for weeks now. It was time to go back and save Reggie from the evil queen. "Two days—tops."

"Great. Do you want to meet with your publicist while you're back?"

"Might as well." Eric headed toward the door, with Reggie at his heels.

"Don't you need a few minutes to pack?"

Eric turned and scanned the room. Just like the life he was returning to, there was nothing in it he would miss. He wondered where Sage was that evening and if she would be disappointed when he didn't go to the coffee shop the next morning, then shook his head and walked out the door. Even if she did want to see him again, where could anything between them go? Eventually she'd realize his scar wasn't real. He'd be forced to either lie more or tell her the truth. Neither scenario held much promise.

Reggie tossed him the keys of his Pagani as they approached it. Eric caught them and headed to the driver's side. He ground the gears as he pulled out, just to see if it still made Reggie wince. It did. It was good to see some things didn't change. "So, tell me about this surprise you're working on for me."

"It's something you need to see to appreciate. I'll give you a hint, though. Don't drive up the main road to your house. Take Beasley Street and enter your property from the rear entrance. The wrought iron one."

Reggie looked more excited than Eric could remember seeing him in a long time. Whatever he'd made, Eric would pretend to love it. Obviously, it meant a lot to his friend.

The drive to the estate was spent talking about the recent antics of Reggie's children. Eric drove up to the back gate of his property, just as Reggie had instructed. As he approached it, the gate swung open. "Nice touch," Eric said.

"Hold your applause until you see the rest," Reggie said. "Go to the old barn."

"Okay."

"Now drive into that bush next to it."

"You mean park in front of it?"

"No, I mean drive into it."

The car was in perfect condition, but Eric was curious enough to do as Reggie said. He headed right toward the bush. Just before he connected with it, the foliage parted to reveal a tunnel that went beneath the barn.

A smile spread across Eric's face. "You made me a Batcave?"

Reggie waved for him to drive inside. "Every superhero deserves one."

As they drove, lights came on, illuminating their way deeper beneath the barn. Eric felt almost giddy. He couldn't wait to see what the tunnel led to. "How did you dig this out?"

"I didn't have to. It was here, an old storage area. All I did was modernize it."

The tunnel led to a large, dimly lit space. Eric parked and hopped out to look around. To one side a well-lit, mirrored changing area revealed two wardrobes. He opened one. It was full of designer clothing, expensive shoes, and suits. He crossed to the other and laughed out loud. It held worn jeans, washed-out T-shirts, and a variety of sneakers. "What is this?"

Reggie came to his side. "This is where your two lives meet." He pointed to a wash station and cabinet. "You should lose that stage makeup before anyone sees you."

Eric's hand flew to the scar he'd forgotten was there. It'd been so long. "Oh . . . yeah." He looked around again. In another area of the enormous room was a car—an old, beat-up-looking, brown two-door. "Is that for me?"

Reggie walked with him to inspect it. "Sure is."

"What is it?"

"An old Ford sedan. No one wanted it the first time around. I figure it'll be safe to park in any neighborhood. Vintage plates, so the police won't bother you."

Eric ran his hand over the old paint and pulled open the driver's door. Manual rolling windows. Worn but not torn leather seats. A radio that looked like it belonged in either a museum or a dumpster. "I love it."

"I knew you would."

Eric slid into the driver's seat. He expected the interior to smell bad, but it didn't. "Does it run?"

Reggie's chest puffed out. "Of course. It has to transport you back and forth, doesn't it?"

Eric started it up—it purred. He cut the engine and gripped the steering wheel with both hands, and it felt right. Even though Eric was floundering, Reggie wasn't standing in judgment. The cave was proof of that. More than anyone in his life ever had, Reggie saw the real Eric and didn't feel compelled to change him. Eric stepped out of the car. "Thanks, Reggie."

Reggie shrugged. "It wasn't all me. Axton was asking about you. I can't lie to my kids—you know that. When I explained where you were, he was excited that Water Bear Man had finally chosen a secret identity."

A sad smile tugged at Eric's lips. "Water Bear Man isn't real."

Reggie walked over to a table and picked something up. "Real enough that you hate him."

Eric nodded. That was undeniable.

Reggie tossed a wallet at Eric. "You want to be normal. Most superheroes do."

Eric shook his head. "You're crazy."

Reggie continued. "Really? Superheroes have family issues. Check. They screw everything up in the beginning. Check. Then, often with the help of a sidekick, they get their shit together."

"I'm no one's hero."

"Classic trope."

Eric rubbed a hand over his forehead. "And what is my power?"

Without missing a beat, Reggie said, "You inspire people. Water Bear Man is fucking ridiculous, often the butt of jokes from other comic heroes. No one respects him, but he doesn't let that stop him from doing what's right. He gets knocked down, but he always gets back up. That's why my kids love him. You can hate him for robbing you of whatever the hell life you think would have been better than the one you have, or you can learn to control your gift instead of letting it control you."

Eric scanned the room again. "By doing what? Living a double life?"

Reggie made a face. "Triple. Technically, you still have to be Eric Westerly, or someone will accuse me of killing him off."

The idea sounded insane—and then so, so tempting. He'd felt trapped in his life, but having a documented second identity would allow him to escape when he needed to breathe. He opened the wallet in his hand. There was a license with his face on it, scar and all, with a name beside it. "Tim Toadhill?"

"I didn't know you'd pick your own name. I'll have it all changed to Wayne Easton." He tossed a flip phone to Eric. "I'll put this under Wayne as well."

Eric returned to the changing area and placed the phone down in front of Wayne's wardrobe. He removed his scar and changed into a silk shirt and trousers. Reggie handed him his top-of-the-line smartphone. "So I guess this makes you Alfred, my *butler*?" Eric asked as he pocketed the phone.

"Fuck you," Reggie said, but he smiled. "I'm an independent electrician. Hand me your coat and I'll stuff it down your throat."

Eric laughed, and Reggie joined in. It was a moment of true friendship that reminded Eric of something he'd said to Sage. He'd told her he didn't trust anyone beyond Reggie. That might have been true at one time, but it wasn't anymore. He also had his sister Rachelle. She didn't know about his secret identity, though.

It's better to keep some things a secret.

Eric's smile faded as he imagined trying to explain not two but three separate identities to Sage. He'd once doubted her mental stability, but he was now certain he couldn't defend his own. A thought came to him, and he said, "I'm surprised you didn't make a section for my costume."

Reggie walked over to the wall and flipped a light switch. A panel slid upward, revealing his Water Bear Man costume, hanging just as it did in his movies. Eric laughed again. "This is absolutely nuts, you know that, right?"

"Alice prefers the term *eccentric*."

"You told your wife, too?"

"Of course I did. Enjoy lying and keeping secrets while you're single. Once you're married, there's no hiding anything."

Although it wasn't meant to, that sounded pretty damn good to Eric. Even as he stood in his secret lair, he couldn't stop thinking about the one woman he wished he could show it to.

◆ ◆ ◆

Across town, dressed in a cotton pajama set, Sage poured another glass of wine for her similarly clad friend. Normally she would have gathered the dishes from the coffee table and rinsed them before bed, but it could all wait until morning—at least, that was what her buzz assured her.

Bella had just finished describing her latest case—a sad and brutal cautionary tale that would have been a mood killer if Sage hadn't balanced it with alcohol. Her heart broke for Bella when she spoke of the unimaginable as if it were the norm.

Sage wasn't blind to the ugly side of humanity. No one with a television could be, but she didn't want to live her life looking at every person she encountered through that lens.

She knew to be aware when she walked alone.

She kept her doors locked even during the day.

None of her clients knew where she lived.

In her opinion, there was a gray area between being careful and being paranoid. She liked to think that was where she resided.

"Feel like watching a movie?" Sage asked.

Bella took a sip of wine before answering. "Whose turn is it to choose?"

"Mine," Sage answered with a huge smile. "But I'll be kind."

"Please, no sappy angel movies."

"Hey, I sat through the documentary on bee colonies." Sage tossed a crumpled napkin at her friend.

"And you're a better person for it."

"Definitely, but you could benefit from something with a happy ending tonight."

"You're probably right. Bring it on," Bella said with a wave of her hand.

Sage picked up the remote and began to flip through the available movie categories. She paused over the action/sci-fi section and clicked on one of the titles. Unless she was shitfaced and imagining things, Wayne Easton looked an awful lot like Water Bear Man.

"Oh God, no," Bella said with a groan. "Anything but those movies. Could you pick something at least loosely based in reality?"

Disregarding her friend's request, Sage played the trailer. Water Bear Man, in his tight gray spandex costume, stopped in the middle of fighting an alien creature to pose for a child with a camera. He stood with his feet apart, his hands on his hips, and his powerful chest puffed out. Sage froze the image. "Bella, is it the wine or does he look like Wayne?"

"They say everyone has a doppelgänger." Bella smiled. "But probably the wine."

"I'm serious, Bella. Look at his face."

Bella put down her wine and did for a moment. "Hang on a minute." With a frown, she pulled out her phone and opened her photos, then held up the photo she'd taken of Wayne. "Outside of the scar, yes. They could be twins."

Sage returned to studying the face on the screen. "What's the actor's name?" She read the information below the title. "Eric Westerly. Westerly. Is he related to the Delinda Westerly my mom wanted me to help?"

"He's her grandson. Wait, you didn't tell me Delinda Westerly was the woman you turned down. Hell, I would have gone in your place."

"Really? Why?" Like her, Bella was not usually impressed by money. "I don't watch a lot of television."

"She's not on television, that's how powerful she is. Her family is an American dynasty and the closest they have to royalty—which is probably why one of her grandchildren married a prince and she has a king courting her."

"Since when do you care about titles?"

Bella's face flushed. "It's not like that." She picked up her glass of wine again. "What's your fantasy version of yourself? Wings with a magic wand? Well, for me it would be to be Delinda Westerly for a day. To know the kind of people she does. Just for a second, imagine that no one in the world is off-limits to you. Think of all the interesting people you'd meet, the conversations you'd have, the difference you could make."

"You make a difference already." Sage threw another napkin at Bella. "And I don't dream of having wings." She smiled and conceded, "Although I would love a wand."

Bella volleyed the napkin back with playful force. "No wand for you. You're dangerous enough as you are."

Sage leaned over and hugged her friend, jostling her arm. "And you don't need to meet world leaders to make an impact. You make a difference every single day just by being you. I love you."

"And I love you." Bella patted her shirt where the wine had splashed, then put her now-empty glass down. "Even though I'm now sitting in wine-soaked pajamas."

Sage grinned. "Sorry."

Bella chuckled and stood. "Luckily we're the same size. Mind if I go change?"

"Mi closet es su closet."

Bella took another look at the man on the screen. "He does look an awful lot like your friend at the coffee shop."

"I know, right?"

"Wayne Easton. Eric Westerly. Delinda Westerly. Weird. It feels like a puzzle I should be able to figure out. Hey, I didn't tell you yet, but I had my friend run a quick background check on Wayne after we spoke earlier. He couldn't find anyone by that name who fit his description. Are you sure that's his name?"

"I didn't check an ID, but that's what he said."

"Maybe none of this is related, but my gut tells me I'm missing something obvious."

"Your gut? Is that like my radar? Or are you drunk?"

"I don't get drunk." Bella wagged a finger at Sage and said, "I'll be right back. Save some wine for me. The answers might be in the bottom of that bottle."

Wanting to continue the conversation, Sage wobbled after her friend to her room and spoke to her from the doorway while she changed. "The last time I saw him, Wayne did say something odd. He told me not to trust him."

While buttoning up a clean nightshirt, Bella froze. "Don't see him again, Sage. I know you think I'm paranoid, but people don't say that shit unless there's a reason to. He's hiding something, and that's never good."

Sage crossed her arms in front of her. "You and I look at puzzles differently, Bella. I don't fear what I don't know."

Bella finished getting dressed, then went to join Sage at the door. "And that's exactly why I worry."

Chapter Seven

The next morning Eric woke in his ornate, king-size canopy bed. It, along with the other gilded antiques in the room, had been Reggie's idea of a joke. Eric hadn't cared enough to meet with the decorators, and Reggie had warned him that if he didn't, *he* would.

The room didn't embarrass Eric, but neither was he proud of it. He cared as little about it as he did the massive estate it was part of. They were just things. He'd originally bought the place because it had been in a sad state of disrepair and he'd considered it a shame to let such a building be lost to future generations. Restoring it hadn't brought him the joy he thought it would. He didn't care about *things*.

Eric pulled himself out of bed and trudged to the bathroom that was the size of his apartment. It had been renovated, along with the rest of that wing, in Reggie's tongue-in-cheek, tacky style. Eric suspected that Reggie pushed the envelope at times because he was seeking a reaction. He didn't get one. Eric honestly didn't care.

In reality, his secret lair was the only material possession Eric could remember getting excited about. Creating it had probably cost less than his last car, but it was perfect—simply perfect. The placement of it on his land would allow him to come and go away from the eyes of the house staff. Even though they'd signed NDAs, that didn't mean he could trust them to not let a photo slip out to the press. No, this was best kept to himself.

The more he thought about it, the more his mood improved. He could literally be Eric in the morning, Wayne during the day, and Eric again if there was a need. Reggie had given him something he'd yearned for but hadn't figured out how to achieve—his freedom.

That realization brought a smile to his face while he showered and dressed. The day didn't loom before him as it normally did. Instead, it felt full of potential. He paused by a table in his room. The night before, he had placed his smartphone and flip phone side by side. He picked both up, weighing them in his hands, and decided to keep both with him that day. He didn't have to choose.

He walked out of his suite down to the main part of his home with a bounce in his step. He greeted his staff as he came across them. None seemed sure how to respond. He thought of all the times he'd walked by them, more irritated by their presence than grateful for their help. He'd previously viewed them merely as necessary to maintaining the estate, but now he saw them as people. Did they enjoy working for him? Did they have families? Where did they live?

He felt a wave of shame that he didn't know anything about them.

His smartphone rang. On any other day, he would have let it ring through to his messages, but he felt better than he had in a long, long time. "Hello."

"Eric, oh my God, I can't believe you picked up," his sister Rachelle said in rushed relief. "Where are you?"

"At my house." He continued to the kitchen and popped his head in. There was a clatter of pans being dropped and a sudden silence. "Hang on, Rachelle. Morning, everyone." He spoke to the open-mouthed kitchen staff. "Would you mind whipping me up some eggs and toast? I'll take it on the back patio. And coffee. I'd love a coffee."

"Of course, sir," one woman said.

Eric had begun to close the door but stopped. "What's your name?"

The woman's face reddened, and she suddenly looked nervous. "Mrs. Carn."

"Thank you, Mrs. Carn," Eric said.

"Y-you're welcome," she answered.

Pleased with the exchange, Eric headed toward the patio. "Sorry, Rachelle. That was important. I'm starving."

"You sound happy this morning."

He paused before answering. *Yes.* "I am. I've made some changes in my life, and they're beginning to jell."

"That's fabulous. Anything you can talk about?"

"No," he said out of habit, then realized he didn't have to be that person anymore, either. This was Rachelle, the family member who had found him at his lowest point. Part of his recovery was staying honest with himself and with those who loved him. Hiding from them, withdrawing into himself, had led him to a dark place he never wanted to return to. He'd like to pretend that part of his life had never happened, but he needed it as a reminder not to repeat it. "Yes. I've been living like a man with his back to the wall. I couldn't walk away from my career because it supports too many people. I felt trapped."

"But now?"

"Now I see I have options. It doesn't have to be all or nothing. With a little juggling, there just might be room for what I want as well."

"That is so great, Eric. You have no idea how good it is to hear you like this."

Eric threw the doors to the patio open and took a deep breath. The air was fresher. Every color in the garden was brighter. "And I met someone."

"Really?"

"She's amazing. Bold, sweet, quirky. Just thinking about her makes me smile."

"Eric, I'm so happy for you."

"Things are a little rocky right now, but they're about to get a hell of a lot better. I understand how she and I could work now. It's doesn't have to be full disclosure versus lies. There's always a third option." Standing in the bright morning sunshine, Eric felt young and alive. Invincible. "I'm creating my own third option."

"Eric, what are you talking about?"

"Water Bear Man will do appearances again. So will Eric Westerly." He left off Wayne Easton. Secret identities were best kept—well, secret.

"Should I worry that you're talking about yourself in the third person?"

"Maybe." Eric chuckled. "Does Vandorra have another cause that would benefit from some publicity?"

"Well, the children's hospital would love to have you back. Finn asks about you constantly. His heart transplant went well, and he's home, but it has been a tough road for him."

"What about Tinsley?" Eric asked, remembering the little girl with huge blue eyes and big dreams of visiting Disney. "Did she—did she go?"

"Not yet, but the doctors say soon."

Eric blinked back a tear at the memory of that little girl. He credited that visit to the children's hospital as the catalyst for realizing he needed to make changes in his life. He hadn't realized until then how truly low he'd sunk. Had he not met the kids and done some serious self-reflection afterward, he probably would have refused to go to the clinic. He might already be dead. He owed those children, as well as Rachelle and her husband, more than he could ever repay. "I know you have it covered, but tell me when you know the date she'll be going home. I have friends who can add even more magic to the trip. Also, send me a date that works for another visit and I'll be there—in costume."

"Oh, they would love that, Eric. The children adore you. Magnus will be pleased as well. He was worried because you weren't returning his calls lately."

"I needed time to figure a few things out, but tell him I'll ring him this week."

"He'd like that." Rachelle cleared her throat. "I hate to even ask, but have you seen Grandmother?"

One of his staff hovered near the door with a tray. Eric waved for the woman to set it down on the table beside him. After she did so, Eric said, "Hang on, Rachelle. What's your name?"

In a quiet voice the woman said, "Mia Taylor."

"Thank you, Mia."

"Is there anything else you'd like?" she asked.

Eric looked the tray over then smiled at her. "No, it all looks perfect."

She withdrew.

Eric sat, placed the phone on speaker, and set it down on the table. He poured himself a cup of coffee. "Rachelle, what did you think of my staff? They seem pretty awesome."

She laughed softly. "They were wonderful."

"I should give them all a raise."

"Do you know how much you presently pay them?"

"No. Good point. I'll start there. Reggie manages all that. I'll ask him."

"How *is* Reggie?" The affection in Rachelle's voice rang sincere.

"Same as ever. I don't know what I'd do without him."

"He's a good friend."

"Yes, he is. How is married life?"

"I love it. Although I'll probably never get used to being called Princess. I still look around for one every time I hear it."

"Do you ever miss your old life?"

"I thought I would, because it's a very public lifestyle, but there's a town here where we can go to simply be ourselves. Magnus was raised there, and I'm glad our children will have the same opportunity. He has friends there, and now so do I. Don't get me wrong, having a title and the responsibilities that come with it is an honor I welcome, but it's nice to be able to step outside of it now and then to just—breathe."

"Exactly. We all need that." She understood. He was tempted to share about his sanctuary. He trusted her, but the risk was too great. Later, when his life was running smoothly, he'd tell her.

There was a pause in their conversation—enough time for Eric to remember Rachelle's question about Delinda. "I'm surprised Delinda is still in London."

"Make time to see her, Eric. She just needs to know you're doing okay."

Eric groaned. "By her definition or mine?"

Rachelle made a sympathetic sound. "I know she's not an easy person to talk to, but you're the only reason she's in London."

"I'm happier when she's not part of my life, Rachelle. I know that sounds cold."

"No, just honest. Do you want me to talk to her? See if I can get her to give you some space?"

Had she been beside Eric and not simply on the phone, he would have hugged his sister—not because he was going to take her up on the offer, but because she had once again proved her loyalty to him. One day he might even deserve it. "I'll call her, but thanks, Rachelle." His voice tightened with emotion. "Seriously, thank you for everything."

"That's what family is for, Eric. Yes, we make mistakes, drive each other crazy, but when it matters, we're there for each other. Even Grandmother. She loves you so much."

"I know," he said, more for Rachelle's benefit than because he agreed.

"If you're serious about a second visit to the children's hospital, I'll start making arrangements."

"Yes, I'm in."

"Great. I'll call you tomorrow with information."

"Talk to you then."

"I love you, Eric," Rachelle said.

There was a time when those words would have rung false to him, but he wasn't that man anymore, and he didn't want to see the world through those eyes again. "Love you, too. Stay safe."

Rachelle hung up. Eric shuddered as he remembered how close he'd come to losing her. It would be easy enough to blame her association with Prince Magnus for what had happened, but the truth stared Eric in the mirror each morning. Rachelle had traveled to London out of concern for Eric. He hadn't pulled his head out of his ass long enough to ensure her safety. There was nothing he could do about what had already happened, but he was determined to be a better brother to her.

He scarfed down his breakfast with enthusiasm. Amazing how much better he felt now that he wasn't using one pill to sleep and another to get him out of bed the next day. Slowly his life was coming around. He called his publicist and announced that he would be pushing back the production of his next movie. Not forever, just a few months.

On impulse, Eric took out his flip phone and dug Sage's business card out of his wallet. He punched in the numbers and held his breath. "Hey, it's me."

"Wayne?"

"Yes." It was a little disappointing that she didn't recognize his voice.

"Why does caller ID say Tim Toadhill?"

Oh, shit. "He must have had the number before me." The lie rolled off his lips with ease. He didn't feel guilty this time, though. To be with her, he was willing to give this persona life. If things worked out with her—well, he'd face that hurdle later. He hadn't wanted to start anything with her when he'd thought he might be pulling out of her world at any time, but now he had a plan that would allow him to stay in both lives. "What are you doing today?"

"You said you didn't want to see me anymore."

He smiled. "What I said was that it was impossible to without wanting to sleep with you."

"Oh yes, because it would be devastating for me when you move on."

"I said that?"

"You did."

"I'm an ass sometimes." When she didn't jump in to deny his claim, he said, "Come out and play with me today. I'll make it up to you."

"Oh, I don't know—"

"Yes, you do. Listen, I like you. I want to see you today. I'm 95 percent positive I won't be an asshole today if you agree to give me one more chance."

She laughed at that. "So there's a 5 percent chance you might?"

Hooked her with humor. All he had to do was close the deal. "I'm a work in progress."

"Apparently. Where exactly would we go . . . if I agreed to go anywhere with you?"

He thought about what she'd enjoy and took a shot. "Have you been to Stonehenge? It's drivable from London."

"I've always wanted to but haven't made it out there."

"It's settled, then. I'll pick you up. There's not a lot out there, but we can walk around, check out the visitor center, then drive over to Bath for a late lunch. Have you gone to the Roman baths?" Although he could afford to fill the day with luxurious perks, he decided to keep it simple. Sightseeing had become nearly impossible for him to enjoy once he became famous. Frankly, not much was worth the production involved. As Wayne Easton, though, he could experience both, as anyone else would. "Where do you live?"

His heart beat double time as he waited for her answer.

◆ ◆ ◆

Sage sat on the arm of her couch and fanned her face nervously. She knew what Bella would say if she asked her opinion. Stonehenge and the Roman baths had been on her bucket list well before she moved to London. Funny how knowing something was close enough that she could go at any time had led to putting both off on so many occasions. Since the man from the park had not yet called her back, there was no reason she couldn't go with Eric.

But should I?

He was an exciting unknown. One minute he was moody, the next sweet, then surprisingly arrogant. Which would he be that day?

The memory of his lips on hers returned, bringing warmth to Sage's cheeks. She wasn't a virgin. She understood desire—but this was more. This was intense. He'd been on her mind last night when she'd gone to sleep and right there to greet her when she'd woken.

How could she feel so much for someone she hardly knew?

How will I ever know him if I don't spend time with him?

"Are you married?" she demanded.

"No."

"You keep saying your life is *complicated*. What does that mean?"

"I'm not ready to tell you, but I will one day."

"You're not on the run from the law?"

"No."

"Is your real name Tim Toadhill?"

He chuckled. "Absolutely not."

She wanted to trust him, but her instincts were off lately. Bella's warnings echoed in the back of her mind. "Stonehenge, Bath, then home. That's all I'm agreeing to."

"That's all I offered," he answered with humor.

"You—I—whatever, you know what I'm saying."

He laughed again. "Yes, I do. I'll pick you up in an hour."

An hour. "Okay."

After hanging up, Sage rushed to shower and dress. She changed her outfit several times. She wanted to look nice for wherever they went to dinner, but eventually she settled on jeans and a buttoned shirt. Stonehenge was outdoors, and she didn't want to look like she was trying too hard.

A short time later, she met him on the street. As she slid inside his small, dilapidated car, she was glad she'd chosen as she had. She manually rolled down the window on her side. "It's muggy today. No air?"

He looked at the panels as if he wasn't sure, then shrugged. "Nope, sorry. Once we get on the road, it cools off." He pulled out into the traffic.

The car supported her initial impression that he was on a limited budget. It was clean, but definitely a car of last resort. She pulled her hair up into a messy ponytail to stop it from blowing in her face and turned to study his profile. Outside of his scar he was a dead ringer for the movie star she'd compared him to the night before. She almost said it but held her tongue. She'd already nearly interrogated him, and that wasn't the tone she wanted the day to have. "So, you haven't been to Stonehenge, either?"

"By the time I moved to London, I wasn't comfortable being in public anymore."

Because of his scar? She didn't want to push for more than he wanted to share. "But it's getting easier?"

He glanced over at her. "Lately, yes."

In an instinctive act of comfort, she touched his arm. "I'm glad."

He took her hand in his. "Me too." A small smile came and went on his face. "I haven't always been someone I was proud of."

Her heart fluttered from that simple connection. She'd tried and failed to explain this to Bella. Wayne could be dismissive and defensive, but it was how he protected himself. He didn't want to be that person; she would have bet her life on that.

A man trapped within himself—reaching out to her.

What happened to him?

Normally bearing witness to such pain would have her instantly putting him in the client category, but Sage didn't want him in that role, and that confused her more. She didn't want to help him and walk away. She didn't want either of them to *move on*. "I could say the same about myself. When you were a kid, didn't you think you knew everything? Why is it that the older I get, the less I'm sure about anything?"

"That's not true. You were sure that man would call you. Did he?"

Ouch. "Not yet."

"He will."

Her eyes flew to meet his before he turned his attention back to the road. "I thought you doubted he would."

"I did. I don't believe in fate or the supernatural, but I do believe in you."

"You do?" *Whoosh.* Sage tightened her hand around his.

He glanced her way again and brought her hand up to his lips. "You make the world a better place, one random act of kindness at a time."

Warmth spread through Sage, and her ability to speak dissolved. She'd let him in, and he understood. She was used to hiding what she did from the men she dated. She'd always believed that one day she'd meet one she could be herself with, and she finally had. "Thank you," she finally croaked.

They drove along for a few minutes in the quiet that followed. He would shift, then take her hand back in his as if it belonged there. Sage studied his strong profile. Was this how forever looked?

"So, I read up about Stonehenge. The monoliths are roped off. To actually go between them, we would have had to sign up for a sunrise tour."

"I don't mind. It'll still be interesting to see them."

"You were raised with money. Do you ever miss the privilege of it? Skipping the line? Being treated special?"

It was an odd question that from some might have sounded envious or sarcastic, but instead he seemed genuinely curious. "Privilege comes at a cost I'm not willing to pay. I know having money sounds amazing, but the reality of it often isn't. People treat you differently when they think they can get something from you. Or they use money to control you. I freed myself when I walked away from my inheritance."

He pulled over along the side of a back road. "You're serious?"

"Absolutely. I also believe money is an addiction, at least at a certain level. At first, all a person wants is enough to pay their bills. Then to buy a few nice things. They might take care of the people around them. But something happens when they reach a certain level of wealth. It starts to take over their lives. They become obsessed with making more or keeping what they have. No matter how much they have, it's no longer enough. I feel bad whenever I hear that someone has won the lottery, because I know their life is about to change, and I pray they won't lose themselves and everyone they love because of it."

He turned the engine off, unbuckled his seat belt, and turned to face her. "That's not a popular modern view. Isn't more always better? Life is competitive, and no one wants to come in second." He wasn't actually debating the point with her. He seemed to be searching for an alternative to what his experience had been.

"Who says that's the way it has to be? Rules only apply when you're playing the same game. I rejected that life. I don't have an impressive bank account, and my parents think I've wasted my potential, but I like my life. There are parts I'm still working on, but I'm not in competition with anyone. I'm living the way I want to. Is skipping to the front of the line worth giving that up? I don't think so."

"Do you know how beautiful you are?" He leaned forward, cupped her chin with one hand, and kissed her.

She undid her seat belt so she could move closer. Their kiss deepened, and she gave herself over to the desire rushing through her. His seat jolted backward, allowing room for her to straddle him. His hands went to her hips, his thumbs caressing the bare skin beneath her shirt. She arched against him and ground herself intimately against his bulging cock.

It felt good, so damn good.

Her hands went to his face. He froze and took both of her hands in his. "Don't," he ordered huskily. "Don't ever touch my face."

She would have promised not to, but as he began to kiss her neck, it felt too good. Slowly, he worked his way from below her ear down to the collar of her shirt and back. She writhed against him.

He raised his head and met her gaze. Their ragged breath mingled. "We need to take this slow."

She chuckled, still breathless. "Isn't that my line?" Her eyes fell to his scar. Up close it almost looked—

He released her hands, shifted her off him, and angled his face so his scar was hidden. "This wasn't why I asked you out today." He started the car again.

No? Damn. Sage settled herself back into her seat. He pulled back out onto the road as she tried to collect her scattered thoughts. Of course slow was better. That he didn't want to rush her was actually refreshingly respectful. Or was his withdrawal for another reason? "It's not repulsive. Your scar. I actually like it. It gives you character."

"I don't want to talk about it."

"I think you should. Maybe then you'd see—"

His hands tightened visibly on the steering wheel. "This isn't going to work, is it? What the fuck was I thinking? I thought if we didn't—if we could simply spend time together and not take it further—that it wouldn't be an issue."

"It's not an issue for *me*." Sage clasped her hands on her lap.

He grimaced, and her heart broke for him.

She touched his arm again, but this time he didn't reach for her hand. "But it is for you, and I can respect that."

He groaned. "Why do you want to be with me?"

She squeezed his arm. "Why wouldn't I? Because you're not perfect? News flash—no one is."

His eyes flashed with a defensive anger she was beginning to recognize. "Am I just like the man in the park? Is that why you're with me?"

"You're right. How did I not see it? This is exactly the same. Do you remember how I climbed right on his lap to comfort him?" She let go of his arm. "No? *Yeah,* because I didn't. I'm not with you because I feel sorry for you, but if you can't see that, maybe you should turn the car around and take me home."

He didn't.

They drove without speaking for a mile or so. Then he added, "Do you want to go back?"

She relaxed. "No. I'd like to see Stonehenge, and I was looking forward to a dinner in Bath."

He glanced at her, then back at the road. "I don't know why I say some of the shit I do."

"Everyone reacts differently to being afraid."

"I'm not—" He stopped. His hands clenched again on the steering wheel. "I don't want to fuck this up."

His pain was palpable.

She said, "So, let's go slow—just like you said."

They talked about what they both were excited to see at Stonehenge, then about nothing in general for several minutes. The tension from earlier fell away.

A small smile lit his face. "Don't hate me, but all I can think about is how much I want you."

Sage ran her hand from his knee up to, but just shy of, the bulge in the front of his jeans. It was a brief, teasing touch. Then she sat back and said, "That's just awful."

A flush spread up his neck and across his cheeks. "Slow might kill me," he said in a strangled voice.

She laughed, and he joined her. He reached for her hand, and their fingers intertwined as naturally as if they were a longtime couple. Sexual tension sizzled between them, but there was also an underlying friendship building.

"Hey," he said, "tell me about this life you enjoy so much. Who are your friends? Do you have pets? What do you do for fun? I want to know everything."

Her own smile was wide and steady. "Well, my best friend, Bella, is a lawyer. Very serious. We have practically nothing in common, but somehow it works. She gets me, and that's what matters most."

He nodded. "I have a friend like that: Reggie. I can't imagine my life without him."

Yes. "It makes all the difference, doesn't it? No matter how bad a day I've had, I'm okay because I know there'll be at least one person in my corner."

"I've never found that in a partner." He gave her a heated glance.

Her heart thudded in her chest. "I haven't, either."

"I want that," he said simply.

"Me too."

"Is it even possible?"

"I'd like to think so."

He released her hand, returning it to the steering wheel. His other hand went to the side of his face that was hidden from her. "Sage, there's something I should tell you." He looked at her. "My scar—"

"Wayne!" Sage screamed and pointed at a car that had veered into their lane. "Look out."

Eric swerved to avoid the vehicle just in time, missing it by inches. His hand came out to steady Sage as he maneuvered back into his lane after the danger had passed. He swore and kept on swearing. In the past he might have questioned the value of his own life, but he'd be damned if another person he cared about was hurt because he failed to protect them. "Are you okay?" he growled.

"I'm fine," she said breathlessly, "but maybe we should hold off on talking about anything important until we get there."

"Sorry, I—"

"Don't be. It wasn't your fault that guy doesn't know how to drive." She took several audible deep breaths. "Well, that woke me up."

Eric hated that his need to clear his conscience had almost gotten Sage hurt. *Because I'm turned on and turned inside out.* He'd gotten stupid drunk on their kiss and nearly forgotten that all it would take was one touch for her to realize his scar was fake.

One touch could end it all before he had a chance to explain it to her.

Every time she looked at him, he saw the flaw in his plan to keep his two lives separate. What neither he nor Reggie had taken into account was that he wanted Sage to be part of his other life as well. There had to be a way to tell her that would make that possible. *She's right, though—this isn't the time or place for that conversation.* "We're almost there."

She laughed nervously. "Good."

He didn't like the worried look in her eyes, nor the knowledge that he'd put it there. "At this time of year, the fields around Stonehenge should be colorful. Beyond the surrounding grassland, there are pink pyramidal orchids, sainfoins, even a field of blue scabious."

"How do you know that?"

"I googled it," he said with a shrug and glanced at her quickly.

Her smile returned. "Thank you. Did you read how volunteers planted seeds by hand?"

"I didn't get that in-depth."

"Reintroduction of native plants was a labor of love for the local preservationists. The ground had been overfarmed. The soil was dry and blowing away. Once the chalk grass took, wildlife began to return to the area. You know you're doing something right when the birds return. And the insects. The Adonis blue butterfly hadn't been seen in decades but was sighted there once again in 2008. Although some credit that to the reintroduction of some of the wildflowers. No one knows for sure, though, because nature is all about balance. We often don't see how, but everything works together in harmony if we let it. Livestock can graze there again because locals took the time to understand and address the real ecological issues. It's a success story for both humanity and nature." She paused. "You probably don't find this as interesting as I do."

Eric pulled into a spot in Stonehenge's parking lot. "Sage?"

"Yes?"

Try as he might, he couldn't *not* touch her. He ached for her—ached like some smitten teen. Being with her was bringing him back to life, and it felt damn good. He traced her open lips with one of his thumbs. "You are the least boring person I've ever met. I love your passion and to look at things through your eyes. Anyone else would have come here and focused on the mystical history of it. You see more."

"I'm interested in that aspect as well, at least as far as what it says about the people who built it and those who come to see it. I wonder what they were seeking—what visitors still are." Her breath was a tickle on his skin. "There are skeletons buried around and under the stones. I wonder if they found what they were looking for."

If anyone had told him that he could be turned on by hearing a woman talk about ancient bones, he wouldn't have believed it, but she was mesmerizing. Her voice was a soft caress of its own. "What are you hoping to find here?"

She blushed but held his gaze.

He could barely breathe. He knew what she wanted, because his body was throbbing and hungry for the same. He would tell her the truth, but couldn't it wait until after they had this day together? "Come on, let's go check out what's here, then we'll head to Bath."

She nodded.

It wasn't easy to pull away from her, but he sprinted over to the passenger side to open her door. Her hand was back in his a second later. They stood there for a moment simply looking into each other's eyes.

She licked her bottom lip. "Are you ready?"

Eric lost the battle raging within him and pulled her to him for a rough, deep kiss that left them both shaken. "I am now."

Hand in hand, they followed the crowd toward a path. As he always did, he kept her on his side without the scar. She was too smart to not realize what it was if he let her have an extended look. "Even if the stones fly up and start circling us, it wouldn't compare to how good kissing you feels."

"I agree." She laughed and leaned against him as they walked. "However, full disclosure: if the stones start flying around, I'll probably piss myself."

He echoed her laugh and hugged her closer.

Chapter Eight

Later that day, Sage waved away a waiter's offer of another glass of wine. Wayne wasn't drinking, and she was already laughing so hard her sides hurt. He had a way of describing a scene and mimicking the voices of the people involved that brought his stories to life. After a while their conversation grew more serious. She asked him about his family. At first he looked as if he would tell her he didn't want to talk about them, but then he seemed to change his mind.

"I have two brothers and two sisters. Brett is the oldest. He's ultra-responsible. He'd drop everything to help any member of the family, but there is a price for his assistance—a long, mind-numbing lecture meant to ensure you don't make the same mistake again."

"And your other brother?"

"Spencer is a carbon copy of Brett but in denial about it. Not as helpful. No long lectures, but every bit as determined to prove he is king of the hill. It was exhausting to watch."

"Sounds like you don't get along."

"I don't see them enough to feel one way or the other."

"Never?"

"Weddings, funerals. That kind of thing."

"What about your sisters?"

"I have two: Nicolette and Rachelle, but only one that I see lately—Rachelle. You'd like her. She reminds me of you in some ways."

Sage held her breath. This was an entirely new side of Wayne; she didn't want to say anything that would close a door to it.

He continued, "She sees good in everyone—even when there isn't any there."

"Did the two of you get close when—when . . ." Sage left the question unfinished when Wayne turned the scarred side of his face away from her again. She sat back in her chair and decided to lighten the mood. "This was the most fun I've had on a date in a long, long time."

The corner of his mouth twitched with humor, and his eyes narrowed. "Not ever?"

She would let him wonder. A little challenge would be good for him. "Well, Allen Bickerby did take me frog hunting."

"That's my competition?" He turned her hand over, caressing the inside of her wrist.

"It was really entertaining. We released them all at the end, but we counted our stashes first. Of course, I caught more."

"Bastard. He let you win just to soften you up." Wayne leaned in until his lips hovered over hers. "Tell me you didn't kiss him."

"Is that any of your business?" she asked playfully, although when he looked at her that way, it was difficult to remember what they were talking about.

His grin was wide and irresistible. "I'm beginning to think it should be." He traced the line of her jaw. "I don't like the idea of you with anyone else."

"I was twelve. And I wasn't *with* him."

He bent closer still. "I still don't like it."

"I hear he's married now and already starting to bald."

"How bald?" he asked with a twinkle in his eyes.

She laughed. "You're bad."

"You brought it up. Married, huh? I bet he can't bounce a quarter off *his* abs."

"And you can?" Sage rolled her eyes. This was another side of Wayne—the strutting-peacock one. Was that who he was before his accident? In an attempt at humor, she gave him a once-over, but as she did she realized that he kept the scarred side of his face angled away from her.

"You're welcome to try later." The purr was back in his voice.

Rather than answering, she picked up her glass of water and gulped some down. *Slow. We're taking it slow.* Her body had other ideas. It was humming for his touch.

A waiter cleared away their plates and offered a dessert menu. They both declined. When the check came, Sage reached for it. Yes, she was short on rent money, but she did have a credit card she kept with her for emergencies.

He took hold of the check. "I have it."

"No," she said, not releasing it to him. "You paid for Stonehenge and the Roman baths. Let me get this."

"*Sage*, I asked you to come out with me today—I'm paying for the meal."

"*Wayne*"—she said his name in the same tone—"I had a great day, and the food was incredible. I want to contribute." When he still didn't let the check go, she added, "It's important to me."

He lowered his hand then. "Despite how I appear, I *can* afford it."

His mood seemed to deflate, and Sage worried that she had embarrassed him. She hadn't meant to imply he didn't have the money for the bill. Some men were proud about things like that. She put her credit card down on the check while hoping to think of something to say to make him feel better. "I didn't warn you about the 5 percent chance that I might be bullish about paying for my meal. This isn't about you—it's about me. I don't like accepting too much from other people."

He placed his hand over hers. "Because you see it as a form of control."

Her eyes flew to his. How did he understand her so well? "Yes. My freedom is important to me."

"I would never clip your wings, Sage. I'd rather fly with you."

Tears filled her eyes. "I'd like that." Believing him would mean opening herself up to potentially being hurt deeply. Was she ready for that?

The waiter took the bill, then returned it a moment later. Sage released Wayne's hand long enough to sign the slip and return her card to her purse.

The drive back to her apartment was comfortable and full of light conversation. It was as if neither wanted to risk ruining what had been a perfect day together. He walked her inside, all the way to the door of her apartment. She unlocked the door and held it open behind her.

He leaned in. Sage licked her bottom lip in anticipation. One moment stretched to two. She was tempted to throw herself into his arms. Wasn't it what they both wanted?

Their ragged breaths mingled.

"Do you want to come in?" she asked, giving in to the temptation of him.

He frowned. It wasn't the reaction she'd hoped for. "Of course I do, but I can't do that to you. I'm not the man you think I am." His hand went back to the side of his face he still had slightly averted. "I'm not yet even the man I want to be, but I'm working on it."

"You're already pretty damn wonderful in my book." She stepped forward and hugged him then, in the same way he'd held her when she'd told him about her parents. His arms wrapped around her tightly. She'd been with men who had seemed to have their lives together, but being with them had lacked the level of connection she felt with Wayne. She felt his confusion and his pain as clearly as her own.

They were two lost souls who found acceptance and comfort in each other. Only with him could she admit to herself that her family's rejection had left her with a real fear of being abandoned again. A real fear—one that affected how she lived her life and how many people she let into it. Bella had once asked her why she didn't stay in touch with any of the people she helped. Sage had claimed it was part of the process, but the truth was she walked away from them so they couldn't walk away from her. In Wayne's arms, she could face that side of herself without shame. They were both works in progress.

She raised her face from his chest to look at him, and the nature of the embrace changed. Desire darkened his eyes. Evidence of his excitement nudged against her.

"Sage. I'm—"

She placed two fingers over his mouth. She didn't want to talk anymore. So much of her life had centered on how other people felt and trying to make them happy. She wanted to be selfish just this once. She'd encouraged countless others to take risks and follow their hearts. Her heart told her that this chance might not come again and she would regret not being with him more than whatever consequence the next day held.

He met the kiss halfway. All thinking, doubting, justifying stopped, and there was just him and the way he made her feel. He claimed her mouth like a man who had waited his whole life for the taste of her. She kissed him back with matching fervor.

His hands sought hers and raised them to her sides while he backed her up against the wall just inside her door. She writhed against him, desperate to feel more of him.

Just when she thought they were at the point of no return, he raised his head and pushed back from her. She was grateful for the support of the wall.

"I have to go," he said, then strode out of her apartment.

She moved away from the wall to the doorway just in time to see him disappear around the corner. She closed the door slowly and hugged herself.

Frustration and embarrassment battered her. She'd never thrown herself at any man. His refusal cut her to the core.

Just as his departure did.

I'm a woman with abandonment issues chasing a man who keeps running away. There is something seriously wrong with me.

◆ ◆ ◆

Eric was still cursing himself when he parked in his hidden garage. He stormed to the changing area and tore the fake scar from his face, flinging it to the ground. He met his eyes in the mirror and hated the man who stared back at him.

He stripped and stood before the closets of clothing. He didn't want to be a fucked-up rich man with a fake scar. He put his fist through the door of the dresser that held his nice clothing. In disgust, he began to throw his makeup and prosthetic scars into a trash barrel that he then sent flying with a kick.

"Bad day?" Reggie asked as he walked toward him.

"Who the fuck am I, Reggie?" Eric growled. "I don't want to be any of these men."

Reggie looked at the broken door of the dresser, then at Eric's bloodied knuckles. "I take it your date didn't go well."

Eric covered his face with both hands briefly. "It was fucking fantastic."

"Okaaaay." Reggie drew out the word. "So, what's the problem?"

"I'm the problem. How the fuck do I tell her the truth? Which part of the real me could any woman love?" When Reggie opened his mouth to say something, Eric growled, "If you fucking say my money, I may punch you."

Reggie held both hands up in mock surrender. "Want my opinion?"

Eric sighed and sat on the corner of the sink. "Sure."

"I don't think you're ready to date. You're still too messed up."

Rubbing his throbbing temple, Eric said, "Thanks," with a hefty dose of sarcasm.

"I'm just saying your moods are all over the place. This morning you were all smiles. Now"—he gestured to the broken furniture—"you're making extra work for me. You might need a little more time to figure this out."

"This morning I thought I could be with her as Wayne and then, I don't know, explain everything to her when I was ready. Then we had a perfect day together and I realized how many ways this could go wrong. I don't want to lose her. I think she's *the one*, Reggie."

"Oh, shit."

"I've never felt so sure of anything—not even with Jasmine. How long did it take you to decide your wife was the one for you?"

"Not long. I still have no clue why she chose me, but I'm not buying her glasses."

Eric looked at the three wardrobes in front of him. "How the hell do I explain this to Sage?"

"Didn't you say she's a plant psychologist?"

"Yes."

Reggie made a face. "So she's already a little—out there."

Eric tensed. "No, she's not. She studied botany and uses that knowledge to help people."

"By cheering their plants up."

"Fuck you."

"Hey, I'm not putting her down. In your case, normal probably wouldn't work. She's an odd duck. You're an odd duck. I've seen worse matches."

Eric stood. He was done with the conversation. He opened the broken door of the wardrobe, pulled out a pair of slacks, and stepped into them. "Anything I should know before I head in?"

"Your grandmother came by. She'd heard you were back."

"Of course she did."

"I told her you'd call her tonight."

Eric stopped midway through putting his shirt on. "Why the hell would you tell her that?"

"It's time, Eric."

He was right, but that didn't make the idea of adding a conversation with Delinda to the day sound any more appealing. "I'm already in a shitty mood. I guess this is as good a time as any."

Reggie pocketed his hands in the front of his jeans and made a face. "I can't believe I'm going to say this, but go easy on her."

Eric stepped into his shoes. "Keep talking like that and I'm going to start to think you're on her payroll."

"I don't need money. Living here costs nothing, so I've invested my salary every year. And you pay me well. I mean, really well. You're generous to a fault."

"Whatever." It was difficult to tell if Reggie was joking, and, honestly, Eric didn't care. Reggie could have it all if he wanted. "Anything else I need to know?"

"You now officially have a searchable background story as Wayne Easton. If anyone asks, your parents disappeared during a trip to Thailand when you were a baby, and you were raised by a priest in the mountains of Connecticut."

"Does Connecticut even have mountains?"

"I don't know. Anyway, you dropped out of college to follow your dream of juggling in a traveling circus, which was how your face got messed up."

"In a juggling accident?"

Reggie shrugged. "Bar fight with a clown."

"You're not serious."

"Hey, next time write your own life history if you're going to be picky. I thought a clown fight was cool. Besides, someone would have to do a background check to know any of that crap. According to you, you don't even talk to anyone."

"True." He went over the life Reggie had created for him and smiled. "You're a real ballbuster, you know that?"

Reggie smiled back. "You can take the reins back anytime you want."

Eric nodded. One day. "On that note, what do you think about me buying the building my apartment is in?"

"Why?"

"I'd like good things to happen for the people who live there. I don't want them to know it was me, but they work hard, and I'd like to see them have more opportunities than they do."

"I like the idea, but don't look at me for fairy-godmother shit. I've got enough on my plate here. I do know, though, someone who would love to help you with that."

"Really?"

"Your brother Brett. He calls all the time as well. Didn't he do something similar for the half of your family that went with your mother?"

"He did."

Reggie brushed his hands together. "Another problem solved. Damn, I'm good."

"I haven't talked to Brett in a while. You know I don't get along with my family."

Reggie's expression grew more serious than normal. "Listen, I don't have anyone outside of my wife and kids, so I'm no expert when it comes to family, but you're clearly not happy with things as they are. Let the past go. They made mistakes. You made mistakes. Move on. You've given bitter and alone a chance, but it's not a good look on you."

Every word rang true to Eric. "You're as good as anyone I spoke to at the clinic."

Reggie smiled. "And I don't even like people."

Eric chuckled. "I'm heading back to the main house. I have a few phone calls to make."

They walked out of the garage and headed across the lawn toward the house. He wasn't proud of his behavior back in the lair. *Bitter and alone? Is that the life I've chosen by default?*

Is that who Sage sees when she looks at me?

Just before they entered the back door to the house, Eric asked, "Hey, how much *do* I pay you?"

"Wake up and find out." For once Reggie was absolutely serious. "You also employ a competent accountant who justifies his high salary by documenting where every penny of your money goes."

It was an uncomfortable conversation to have. "It doesn't matter."

"It does to me." Reggie shook his head as he walked away. "It should to you. I hope one day it will."

His words stayed with Eric long after he'd left. Eric *had* withdrawn from his family and everything he associated with them because he didn't want to play by their rules. Sage had echoed the same. He'd stopped playing their game, but unlike Sage, he hadn't replaced it with anything better—he'd simply shut down.

He couldn't change his family. He couldn't go back in time and undo the mistakes he'd made, but, as Sage had once told him, he could control how he behaved from now on. Reggie didn't pull punches. He also didn't usually care about who Eric slept with. For him to intervene and suggest that Eric wasn't ready to date yet meant he cared about the outcome.

Because I'm an odd duck, and so is she. Eric smiled. He liked every little thing that made Sage unique. He admired her for choosing her own path. He loved that the career she professed having was really a ruse to get her close enough to help the people she saw in need. From the way she looked at every issue through a humanitarian lens to the sweet passion of her kiss—she was perfection.

Sage might be different, but she was gloriously so. *My life is not mainstream, but if I can pull my head out of my own ass, I could be someone she sees in the same light.*

If anyone could understand the difference between lying and playing a role, it would be Sage. Her whole career is based on that very idea.

Now—as Reggie suggested—I just need to get my shit together.

The first call he made was to Rachelle's husband, Magnus, to confirm that Eric would indeed be available to visit the children's hospital in Vandorra. Rachelle had already spoken to him about the possibility, so they planned it for a few days from then. Magnus's only warning was that if Eric attempted to back out of the visit, he would personally fly to London and drag his ass to it.

Eric assured him he would be there. Magnus wasn't joking—he'd nearly kidnapped Eric for his first visit to the hospital. Eric wasn't proud that it had taken that much to get him to do something he should have instantly agreed to. The visit had been an eye-opening experience for Eric—just as he was sure his second trip would be.

Every life is worth fighting for. Even mine.

He remembered what one of his counselors had said about forgiving himself being as important as forgiving others. It was difficult for Eric to go there, because it meant facing everything he hated himself for.

Or *had* hated himself for—he was slowly letting some of it go. Maybe he wasn't the perfect son. He could have tried harder to patch things up with his family. He could have spent less time running from his demons than trying to numb them with drugs.

I could have been kinder to everyone—even me.

He remembered his first visit to the children's hospital. He hadn't wanted to wear the spandex costume from his movies, because back then his concern had still been all about himself and how he felt. *But that's not me anymore. I am looking outside myself.*

That realization gave him hope that he was worthy of another chance with Sage. He wasn't looking forward to trying to explain his triple life to her, but as long as he knew he could be as good for Sage as she had been for him—he'd explain it as many times and in as many ways as she needed to hear it.

Before that, though, Reggie was right that he needed to get his life a little more under control. His second call was to his brother Brett.

"Brett, it's Eric."

"Hang on." His brother called to his secretary to hold his calls. "What do you need? Did something happen? It's not Grandmother, is it? Is she okay?"

"Everyone is fine." It was somewhat sad that Brett assumed Eric wouldn't call unless there'd been a catastrophe of some sort. "How is Alisha?"

"Good. Really good."

"And the baby—" *Fuck, I know it has a name.*

"Linda is walking now, but mostly at night. None of us are getting enough sleep, but we just found out we're expecting a second child, so we're signing on for a few more years of that lifestyle. How about you?"

"Better." He paused. "Sorry I haven't been returning your calls. I've been off the grid for a while."

"Well, it's good to hear from you now. How are you surviving having Grandmother in London?"

"I haven't seen her in weeks."

"I know," Brett said quietly. "I tried to explain to her that you might need time, but there is no crowbar strong enough to tear her away from you. She's convinced you need her."

Eric made a pained sound in his throat.

Brett added, "The two of you were once very close."

"A long time ago."

"Did you know I used to envy your bond with her? She was always serious with me, but I'd walk into a room when you were with her, and she would always be laughing. You could always bring out that side of her."

"Not always." Eric sighed. "Anyway, that's not why I called. There's a project I'm interested in initiating, but it's one that requires—discretion."

"Okay." Brett had never been a man of many words, nor had he ever seemed to want to discuss how anyone felt about anything. He was all business, all the time. Asking him for something personal required a leap of faith for Eric.

"I was hoping you could advise me on how to navigate it."

Without missing a beat, Brett said, "I can be on a flight to London tonight if you need me to be."

"Oh no. That won't be necessary. This isn't anything that can't be handled over the phone."

"What do you need?"

Eric was momentarily surprised by the forthrightness of Brett's support. In the past any offer of assistance would have been accompanied by a list of criticisms and likely a judgment on whether or not the project had merit. Rachelle had said Brett was different, but now Eric saw it. He didn't want to get his hopes up. His relationship with Brett had always been more confrontational than brotherly—as if having a hypercritical father and grandmother wasn't enough, Brett had added a whole new level of judgment. Feeling that they were on opposing sides had stopped them from ever being close.

I made mistakes.

He made mistakes.

It's time to move on and try again.

"If I tell you something, Brett, it can't go further than us. No one can know."

"You have my word."

Eric believed him because, regardless of what other flaws he might have, Brett wasn't a liar. In fact, if anything, he was brutally, painfully honest. "You know I was in a rehab clinic until a few months ago."

"I do."

"I took a good look at my life while I was in there and didn't like what I saw. So I'm making changes."

"Okay." Brett's tone was cautious. Eric couldn't blame him, since this was the most civil conversation they'd had—possibly ever.

"My life had become all about everything I thought I had been cheated of, but visiting the children's hospital was eye-opening. I'm starting fresh, and I want to do more for people."

"That sounds healthy." His tone was relieved.

"But I don't want them to know I'm the one who helped them. I want to do it in a way that they can feel they played a part in their own windfall. Can you understand that?"

"Actually, I understand that very well."

"You've done a lot for Spencer, Rachelle, and Nicolette—probably more than I'm even aware of. Somehow you kept it secret. I'd like it if you could show me how to do the same for some people I've come across."

"Absolutely. You'll need a lawyer and an assistant with a strong nondisclosure contract as well as a good salary. May I ask who it is you'd like to help?"

Eric hesitated. Old family patterns were hard to break. There was no profit in what he was doing—therefore no reason to expect anyone in his family would understand his motivation. Had Eric not been fresh from a conversation with Reggie about giving his family a second chance, he would have told Brett it was none of his business. However, for this to be a true fresh start, he needed to put his expectation of being disappointed aside. "I rented an apartment near the theater district. I needed a way to step outside my life for a bit. No one knows who I am there."

"That's hard to believe. I thought everyone knew your face."

"I cover part of it with a scar while I'm there. People in my building accept it as part of me, so I haven't had a problem." He went on to describe the people who lived nearby as well as how run-down the place was. "I'm so used to people treating me in a different way because they want something from me. I came home the other day and my neighbor invited me to her place for dinner. She's seventy if she's a day, but she is an excellent cook. And that woman can talk, even though I have no idea what she said. She doesn't need words to make a person feel welcome. I'd like to find out what she needs and make sure she gets it. I want to do the same for the others who live there. They're good, solid people."

Eric ended it there and waited. If Brett refused to help him, he'd find another way.

"I have some people on my payroll who excel at finding out what people need, and they're discreet. I'll fly one of them over. They can set you up with everything you need to make this happen."

"Thanks. I'll put them up in a hotel. No one on my staff knows about my double life—except Reggie."

"I've heard a lot about your electrician lately."

"He's more of a friend than an employee."

"That's what I heard. I'm glad you have someone in your life you can trust. That's important."

"I've also met someone." Never, never in the past would he have shared so much with Brett, but if they were starting over, he wanted it to be an honest start. "I've never met anyone like her before, and I know I never will again. She gets me, even the parts I haven't yet told her about. When I'm with her, I feel like I can be a better person. She gives me hope." *And it scares me shitless.*

"Is she a Water Bear Man fan?"

In for a penny, in for a pound. Eric walked into one of the house's large parlors and looked out the window, standing in one life, wishing he were already back in his other. "She doesn't know my real name."

"Sounds complicated."

"More than you know, but I will sort it out. I don't want to lose her. She's probably everything you wouldn't approve of, but—"

"Eric, this may be coming too late, but I understand why you left for Europe. I understand why you don't call. It took meeting Alisha for me to understand how I was repeating the same mistakes Dad did, the same ones Grandmother did. I was harsh and critical of your choices. I'm not excusing my behavior, but I do apologize for it. I see now that there's a better way, and slowly I'm rebuilding my relationships with our siblings. Rachelle was easy."

Eric could see that. "She has a huge heart."

"Yes. Spencer was more of a challenge. I had to prove to him that he could trust me, but things are better between us now. Nothing is overnight, but I want you to know that I'm here for you. I can't tell you how glad I am that you called, because I know exactly how justified your self-exile was. I see it now, though, and I won't ever be that man again."

There was a humility to Brett that hadn't been there before, and it was reassuring. Maybe reuniting with his family was not impossible after all. It also gave him hope that his talk with Delinda might not be as dreadful as it might have once been.

When he looked at his relationship with Brett through fresh eyes, he felt compelled to say, "I accept your apology, but I have my share of regrets as well. I didn't try to see your side. It was all about me and how I felt. That's something I'm working on."

They fell into a short, awkward silence.

Eric finally said, "I should go. Delinda is expecting a phone call from me tonight."

"She loves you, Eric. No matter how she frames it, that's what she's trying to say."

"I know."

"Be honest with her. If she crosses a line, tell her. All she wants is to be part of our lives. Show her how you want her to fit into yours—if you do want that."

Eric's hand clenched around the phone. He'd given up on ever repairing his relationship with his grandmother. A few months ago, if someone had told him that he would be talking to Brett about how to reconcile with her, he would have scoffed at the idea. Admitting that he missed his grandmother didn't mean he had to open the door as wide for her as he had for Brett. Baby steps. "I would like to get to a better place with her."

"Then tell her that. And remember, I'm only a phone call away if you need backup."

"Thanks, Brett. And I appreciate the offer of sharing your staff. I'm going to head to Vandorra in a few days for a visit, so if they can hold off until I return, that would be perfect."

"I'll plan for that. Say hi to Rachelle for me."

"Princess Rachelle," Eric joked.

"Ha. Yes. Call me when you get back."

"I will." And this time Eric meant it.

Eric paced the room a few times after hanging up with Brett. There was no more putting it off. He looked down at his phone and took a deep breath.

What time do women in their eighties go to bed?

I'll call her tomorrow.

◆ ◆ ◆

The next day after returning from meeting Bella for dinner, Sage returned home and began to restlessly clean her apartment. There was something soothing about washing dishes and organizing her things. Some people assumed that since she was "flighty," it meant she was messy as well, but she kept a tidy house. Away at school, her room had been all that was really hers, and she chose every aspect of it carefully.

If she had to label her style, it would be comfortably contemporary. Nothing expensive or too exotic. When it came to her home, she liked simple.

After a quick shower, Sage put on pajamas and flopped on her bed. *What a day.*

In an attempt to keep her mind off the fact that Wayne hadn't called her, Sage had forced herself out into the world early. Normally her radar led her somewhere, but that day she walked without feeling guided. She'd started heading toward the coffee shop and changed her mind countless times. Wayne had her number. If he wanted to see her, he knew where to find her.

Deciding that she'd put it off long enough, she'd taken the Tube to see Mrs. Westerly. She'd almost called ahead, but her gut told her things would go better if she didn't give the woman too much time to think before they spoke.

She'd been wrong.

Mrs. Westerly's home was impressive, or would have been if Sage cared about such things. She was obviously a woman with high standards. Everything from the perfectly manicured front bushes to the plaque beside the door that denoted the historical importance of the building screamed old, stuffy money. She doubted there was a weed in the garden—none would dare.

In Sage's experience, the wealthy fell into one of two categories: those who desperately wanted to be important and those who were born believing they were. Mrs. Westerly was the latter.

A butler answered her door with a surprisingly welcoming smile. "Miss Revere, what a pleasant surprise. I'll announce you to Mrs. Westerly."

How did he know? "Thank you," Sage said. People in her mother's circle and above dissected each other, always weighing if the other was worthy. *Mrs. Westerly probably knows more about my life and family now than I do. I should ask her how my stepmother's trip to London went.*

It wasn't more than a moment or so before the butler was back. "Please follow me."

Sage did. He led her to the doorway of a large library.

"She's right inside. My name is Michael if you need anything."

"Thank you, Michael."

Sage spotted Mrs. Westerly almost immediately. The birdlike older woman was dressed as if she were ready to take tea with the queen. "Come in. Come in," she said brusquely. "Don't just stand there in the doorway gawking at me."

Sage took a deep breath and stepped inside. "Thank you for seeing me without an appointment."

"Of course. Anyone with manners would bend their schedule to accommodate the needs of another."

Nice dig, but I've received better from my mother. Sage had come with a purpose, and she refused to be sidetracked—Delinda Westerly would get her apology even if Sage had to sit on her while she delivered it. "I feel like we got off on the wrong foot."

"We certainly did."

Sage stepped closer. "I wasn't having the best day, and my mood might have spilled over into our conversation."

In cultured, perfect French, Mrs. Westerly said, "Not your fault. You can only behave as you were raised."

Oh, so that's how this is going to go? Confident in her own French, Sage responded in kind. "We all do the best we can. I am, however, sorry for any inconvenience I caused."

Mrs. Westerly's eyes narrowed. Her next words were in Spanish. "Regretfully, I haven't had the time to meet your mother."

Sage seamlessly switched to that language. "A shame. I believe she would have enjoyed the visit." Then, just because she was tiring of the game, Sage asked in Japanese, "How many languages do you speak? Because I speak four."

Mrs. Westerly rose to her feet and switched to English once again. "Impressive, but no level of education can replace a poor pedigree."

"Clearly," Sage muttered. She'd come. She'd apologized. Some people didn't want to be happy, and those were the ones she couldn't help.

"Pardon? If you are tossing insults, at least have the decency to make them audible."

Tempting as it was to release some steam on this haughty woman a second time, Sage kept her temper in check. She decided to leave while she still felt good about her own contribution to the conversation. "Thank you for seeing me, Mrs. Westerly. I've said what I came to say. I should not have blown up on the phone as I did, and I regretted it as soon as we hung up."

Sage was turning to leave when Mrs. Westerly called out her name.

"Miss Revere."

"Yes?"

"I don't like you, and I would appreciate it if in the future you would stay away from both me and my family."

"Okay." It was a strange warning coming from a woman who had invited her to dinner. It was also an easy request to honor, since Sage was reasonably certain she'd never met another Westerly. "It was a pleasure to see you again, Mrs. Westerly."

Mrs. Westerly walked over until she was just a foot or so away. She squared her shoulders as if facing an adversary. "I do not make idle threats, young lady. You may be able to fool some people with that sweet smile, but I know too much about you. Your parents cut you off, so now you make a living swindling people. If I had my way, you'd already be in prison, but trust me, that is something I will remedy if I see you again."

"You don't know anything about me or what I do." Sage leaned forward and said, "I came here because I felt I owed you an apology, and although you are tempting me to tell you what I think of you once again, I will not. You are clearly a very unhappy woman, but I wish nothing but the best for you and your family. I cannot imagine another occasion when our paths would cross."

Sage didn't give the older woman a chance to respond. She didn't see how that would have taken the conversation anywhere better than where it was ending. Michael was beside her in an instant.

"Leaving so soon, Miss Revere?"

"You mean I wasn't in there for hours?" Sage joked, then felt bad, because he had been nothing but polite to her. "Yes, I have somewhere else I need to be." *Anywhere but with her.*

"Mrs. Westerly sometimes comes across as harsh, but—"

"I'm sure she's a lovely woman once you know her." They reached the door, and when he didn't immediately open the door for her, Sage said, "Thank you, Michael."

He looked as if he wanted to say more but nodded and opened the door. "I hope we see you again, Miss Revere."

He apparently had not been eavesdropping on the conversation. However, no purpose would be served by telling him what she thought of his boss. So Sage said, "I hope so, too."

Sage had been on her way home when her phone rang with a number she didn't recognize. "Hello?"

"Miss Revere?"

"Yes."

"I met you in the park the other day. You and your friend gave me your card."

"Oh yes." Sage's mood instantly improved. Life had a way of balancing out. "I'm so glad you decided to call."

He cleared his throat. "I've been thinking about what you said about houseplants. I'm considering getting some. What exactly do you do?"

"It depends on what you need, but I can help you pick them out. I'll arrange them to be delivered to your place, or I can deliver them myself. Usually I do a consultation on care on the first day, then it's up to you if you require more. Some plants adapt easily to a new place. Others need a period of adjustment."

"And your fee?"

"To spend a few hours choosing and purchasing plants, I charge one hundred dollars. Consultations are fifty dollars."

"Do you require usage of my credit card?"

"Oh no. I wouldn't want that responsibility. If you don't have time to go with me, I can purchase them and you can reimburse me, but you'll be much happier if you choose them yourself. You'll be caring for them—you should choose the ones you'd like the most."

"And that's it? No contract? I don't need to sign up for anything? How do you want to be paid? Cash?"

"You can pay me in cash. I have a list of prior clients if you'd like a referral from one or more of them."

"I'd like that. If I say yes, when and where would this happen?"

"Do you know Columbia Road Flower Market? We could meet there later this week. I'll text you some names and numbers. Take a couple of days to contact a few. If you have a change of heart and decide you don't require my services, send me a text. Otherwise, we'll meet up later in the week."

"That sounds perfect. My name is John Kirby."

"I look forward to helping you make some greenery friends. I've never met someone who regretted adding a plant to their home."

"Good to know. Thank you, Miss Revere."

"You're very welcome, Mr. Kirby."

I knew it. I knew he'd call. With her phone still in her hand, Sage was tempted to text Wayne the news. He'd said he wanted to be there when she met with the man. *No. If he calls me, I'll tell him; if he doesn't—he didn't really want to know.*

Instead, Sage called someone she knew would care. "Bella, you are never going to believe who just called me."

"Wayne Easton?"

"No. Mr. Kirby. The guy I met in the park with Wayne. I'm going to meet him the day after tomorrow. I know I have to get the details on him, but I have a really good feeling about him. He's lonely. Your neighbor is lonely. We'll be invited to a wedding by Christmas. I just know it."

"Oh boy."

"You're still going to help me set them up, right? You haven't changed your mind? Wait until you see him. He's adorable. I can easily imagine him helping her dress those little dogs."

"I would tell you you're nuts, but instead I'll just buy a new dress for the future event. I don't know how you do it, but I'd put money on that wedding happening—as implausible as it sounds."

Sage smiled happily. "Want to get together tonight? I have quite the story for you."

"Can you come to this side of town? I won't be able to leave the office until late."

"That's fine. Our usual place?"

"You're on."

"If you're there before me, order me an apple martini. It's been a long day."

"Oh no. Anything you want to talk about now?"

"No. I'll catch up with you later."

"Sounds good."

"Hang on, Sage. Before I forget. We finally got a hit on a Wayne Easton, and I don't like it. I know what happened to his face."

Sage stopped midstep. "What? Tell me."

"Bar fight."

"Was he attacked?" He didn't seem the type to start something like that.

"The report didn't say, but my instincts were right about him. He's violent."

"Or a victim."

"Not likely. It sounds more like a situation where your friend gets drunk and starts harassing another man."

"Does the report say that?"

"No."

"Then what does it say?"

"His face was injured during a bar fight with a clown."

Sage burst out laughing, then felt bad as soon as she realized Bella was serious. "There's no way that's how it happened."

"That's what my guy told me."

"Well, your guy must be wrong. You're a barrister. You know if something doesn't sound right, it probably isn't."

Bella sighed. "I don't like this guy. He's hiding something. Are you seeing him again?"

"I don't know. He hasn't called me since our date yesterday."

"Sage, your instincts are usually spot-on, but they're not with this one. Could you do me a favor? The next date you go on, take me with you."

"That won't be too awkward."

"Please. Promise me."

"Fine. But I may not ever see him again, anyway."

"I've got to run, Sage, but we'll talk more about this over dinner."

"Then it looks like a martini night for me as well," Sage said, but she laughed.

"I just care about you."

"I know. I know. Go. We'll chat later."

Dinner had been wonderful, but it had concluded without Bella or Sage in agreement over Wayne. Since Bella was so wound up, Sage glossed over how her apology to Mrs. Westerly had gone. She left off the part where the woman had threatened to have her jailed. That kind of talk made lawyers nervous.

She also didn't mention the reason behind the threat. Sage didn't know any of the Westerly family unless—and she almost dismissed it as impossible as the idea came to her—Wayne was more than that famous actor's doppelgänger.

Ridiculous.

Still—a clown bar fight?

It sounded like the punch line of a joke.

Bella was correct about one thing . . . something about Wayne wasn't right.

Is he lying to me?

I'm getting as paranoid as Bella.

But without the scar, Wayne was a dead ringer for the movie star.

He looks so much like Eric Westerly. But if he is . . .

Everything he'd said to her, every experience they'd shared, would have been a lie. All she thought she knew about him—from his shame about his appearance to his struggle with money—wouldn't be true.

She didn't want to believe it.

He would be just another rich, unhappy soul she was meant to help in some way.

Not a man I could spend the rest of my life with—just another client I confused with more.

She tossed her phone down on the couch beside her. *I need to stop. I'm not going to resolve this tonight—all I'm going to do is upset myself. When I see Wayne, if I see him again, I'll ask him. Face-to-face.*

Chapter Nine

Eric closed his eyes briefly as he waited for his grandmother to answer her phone. One ring. Two rings. He half hoped for the reprieve of having his call go to her voice mail.

No, I've got this.

"Eric, are you all right? When you didn't call me last night . . ."

"I'm fine, De—" He stopped before calling her by her first name, because he knew how much it bothered her. "Hello, Grandmother."

"It is so good to hear your voice, Eric."

There was a vulnerability and emotion in her tone he hadn't expected. Although she wasn't English, she maintained a stiff-upper-lip coolness, even with her family. He'd once known how to break through her tough exterior but hadn't seen the softer side of her since he was very young. "How are you?"

"I'm well. I heard you're returning to Vandorra to visit the children's hospital. What a wonderful way to use your celebrity status to help people. I'm proud of you."

Whoa. I was not expecting that. "Thank you." There was a long, awkward pause before Eric asked, "Is it true you're dating King Tadeas?"

She tsked. "Dating? We're not teenagers. We spend time together, that's all. Now that Rachelle and Magnus are married, it makes sense for us to attend the same events."

"I like him, Grandmother. My impression of him was only good."

"He likes you, too, Eric. In fact, he's been spending a lot of time in London, in case you—"

"I'm fine, Grandmother."

"I know you are, but if there is anything you need—anything—I'm here."

He waited for her signature judgmental zinger, but none came. If this were one of his movies, Water Bear Man would reveal her then and there as an impostor. A switch had certainly been made, because this was not the grandmother he knew. "I appreciate the offer, but as I've said, I'm fine."

When she spoke again, her voice was thick with emotion. "I know I'm not always easy to talk to, but I do love you, Eric. You have no idea how much. I have failed you and my other grandchildren in so many ways, but if you give me another chance, I want very much to be a part of your life."

It was a moment of choice for Eric. There was no law that said he had to agree to let her back in. Any control she'd once had over him had dissolved when he started making his own money. Saying no would keep her out of his life, out of his business. It was the safer, less frustrating of the two options. Was it what he wanted, though? Distancing himself from his family hadn't made him a happier person.

He thought about Sage and the kind of man she belonged with. He'd told her he wanted to fly with her—not clip her wings. Those hadn't just been words designed to impress her. He'd meant them.

Still, Delinda didn't do things halfway. He didn't want to go back to when she'd felt she could comment on every aspect of his life. So where did that leave them?

Could he—as Brett had suggested he should—establish boundaries? Was she capable of respecting them?

A memory of sitting beside her in her garden in Massachusetts came back to him. He'd been doing an impression of his headmaster, and she was laughing right along with him. Where had that part of their relationship gone?

"Would you like to accompany me to Vandorra?" Really, there was no better test of this softer side of her than standing beside her while dressed in his superhero costume. The grandmother he missed would see the humor and value in it. If she could put aside her pride and stand beside him for the benefit of the children, Eric could see a real chance for them working things out. If she couldn't, he'd have his answer.

"I would like that very much, Eric. Very much. Would you be comfortable with Tadeas accompanying us? It would mean a lot to him to see you bring joy to his people."

Not only did she say yes, but she's asking me what I want? Asking? Who is this person? "It would be an honor."

"Thank you, Eric. Do you have a set plan yet for your arrival, or would you like to travel with us and the royal guard?"

Eric hesitated. In general he preferred to leave himself an escape route, especially when it came to family, but he took a deep breath and told himself that was no longer how he operated. This was about breaking old habits and replacing them with healthier ones. No drugs. No withdrawing. He was stronger than that. "I'd love to fly over with you and King Tadeas. Tell me where and when to join you, and we'll make the trip together."

Something caught in Delinda's voice. "I'll do that. Would you like me to text the information to you?"

"You text now?"

"Spencer assures me it's the way of the world. I don't understand half the technology he has filled my home with, but I humor him because it seems to make him happy. Everything in my home is now either talking, listening, or attempting to entertain me. To me it's like an overeager houseguest, but Spencer is convinced I'll grow to love it."

"I'll have to keep Reggie away from Spencer or my house will be the same."

"You rely on your friend Reggie for quite a bit, don't you? Are you sure you can trust him with the level of responsibility you've put upon him?"

Eric tensed. In the past he would have felt he needed to defend his decisions to her. He wouldn't have changed her opinion, but the conversation would have been heated and frustrating for both. It was time for that to change as well. Like Sage, it was time to forge his own path. "What I do with my friends and the decisions I make for my household are my business. I would appreciate it if you respect that I don't want to discuss them."

Delinda was quiet for a moment before adding, "Of course." She wasn't happy, but she didn't say it. Even that was an improvement.

"So, I'll watch for your text and meet up with you day after tomorrow."

"Yes. Good night, Eric."

"Good night, Grandmother."

Eric wandered through the halls of his large home for quite some time in thought after he hung up with Delinda. The jury was still out on whether inviting her to join him in Vandorra was a good idea, but he was glad he'd suggested it. Regardless of how it turned out, he felt good about how he was moving forward.

He wished he could share these successes with Sage. He would have loved to call her and tell her about his conversation with Brett and the possible insanity looming ahead of him that week.

He thought back to the last time he'd seen Sage. Their last kiss had almost been his undoing. He'd wanted nothing more than to slam her door and carry her off to her bedroom. The man he'd been would have done just that. He'd been a selfish bastard, not caring about anyone else's happiness because he himself had been miserable.

It was different with Sage. He didn't want to sleep with her before she knew the truth about him. The problem was, he wanted the truth to be a little bit better before he shared it with her. He didn't want his confession to be that he was a constant fuckup with no clue how to be any different. He wanted to be able to tell her the worst was over.

I should have called her today.

She probably thinks I don't care, when the truth is the polar opposite.

I'm falling for a woman who may want nothing to do with me when she discovers who I really am.

He took out his smartphone and wrote: Hey. He was about to send it when he realized it was the wrong phone. *Shit.* He deleted the message and took his flip phone out of his pocket.

He decided to call rather than painstakingly try to input the letters on the older keypad. She picked up on the first ring.

"Wayne?" she asked breathlessly.

"It's me," he answered in a pathetic attempt not to lie to her more than he had. God, it was good to hear her voice. "I would have called you earlier, but it was a busy day. How was yours?"

"Confusing. I honestly had no idea if I'd ever hear from you again."

"I know I've been acting kind of weird, but I'll explain everything to you soon. Not tonight, though. Not on the phone. Are you free tomorrow?"

"No," she said with a touch of defiance in her tone.

"Are you upset with me?"

"Yes. Listen, I know you're dealing with something, but I'm getting really tired of being left standing there wondering what I said or did to make you sprint away. I don't need another person in my life who makes me feel like nothing I do is right."

"You're not the problem, Sage. You never have been."

"Still, I'm busy tomorrow."

"Because you actually are or because you don't want to see me?"

"I don't want you to think that you can do and say whatever you want and I'll just accept it. I waited all day for you to call, and it wasn't fun. I don't like the way it made me feel, and I need time to think about if I'm willing to risk feeling that way again."

"I'm sorry, Sage. I didn't mean to hurt you. Leaving when things get difficult is not my finest quality. I won't do it again. I promise. I wouldn't blame you if you said you never wanted to see me again, but that's not what I want."

"It's not what I want, either," she said. "Do you remember how you said you wanted to be there if I met up with the man I gave my card to in the park? He called. I'm taking him flower shopping day after tomorrow. You could join us if you'd like."

"Day after tomorrow? Shit, I wish I could. I have something planned for that day that I can't get out of. It's really important or I would cancel it."

"What are you doing?"

Fuck. Fuck. Fuck. "Something with my family that involves travel."

"Where to?"

"How about if I promise to sit down with you and tell you all about it when I come back?"

"Let me get this straight. You're going somewhere—you can't tell me where. To do something—you won't tell me what. And you want me to be okay with that because you'll explain it all to me later?"

"Yes?"

"No," she said, and hung up.

Fuck.

◆ ◆ ◆

Wayne called her back, but she silenced her phone. Bella had told her to demand that people treat her better, and Sage was beginning to do just that.

Wayne, if that really was his name, could either tell her whatever it was he was hiding from her or he could find another woman to frustrate. Just because he had eyes she could get lost in and a body designed to tempt any woman didn't mean he could do as he pleased.

The next morning Sage woke up to a bouquet of wildflowers being delivered to her door with a card that simply said, "Call me."

"No," Sage said to the deliveryman as she handed it back to him. "Tell him they were refused."

A short time later, her doorbell rang, announcing the delivery of coffee and her favorite pastries from the café where they'd met. It was accompanied by a note saying, "I'm sorry."

It was harder to pass them up, but she did. "No," she said to the delivery person. "Not good enough. Thank you, but no, thank you. Please take them for your coworkers. I hate to see them go to waste."

Sage was dressed and ready to walk out the door of her apartment when a third delivery arrived. It was matinee tickets for a show at the theater she'd once asked him to go to with her. What had been the reason he hadn't been able to go that day? She realized he hadn't actually told her. He'd avoided answering her questions then, just as he was still doing. She handed the tickets back to the delivery person and simply shook her head.

Sage filled her day with all the things that made her happy. She walked around London and people-watched. All the while, she told herself she'd done the right thing. Hadn't Bella said that one of the reasons she worried about her was because Sage was a pleaser? *And that I make excuses for people's bad behavior because I can't walk away from someone in pain? Well, everyone has their limit, and I've reached mine.*

When she returned to her apartment, she read a book and went to sleep early. If he had called that night, she wouldn't have picked up, but she was still disappointed when no call came.

Where was he going the next day? What did he feel he couldn't tell her yet? Did he understand that while he was figuring stuff out, she was slowly going insane?

Sage wasn't a conspiracy theorist. She didn't look for hidden agendas or lies. She preferred to believe that good triumphed if one had faith in it. People were inherently good, even those who didn't appear to be at first glance. Once they found something that made them happy, they blossomed like flowers in the sun.

Still, Sage was reluctantly beginning to wonder if Bella's more cautious view of people didn't make more sense. There was a very good chance that Wayne Easton was a big, fat liar. Sage didn't know how big or what his motivation was for not being honest, just that her radar had let her down. It shook her confidence in a process she'd come to trust.

She had a fitful night of sleep, full of dreams of being trapped in a glass-walled maze. Every decision she made was wrong, every path she chose led her back to where she started, and she could see Wayne on the outside of the maze, mocking her for not being able to find her way out.

When she woke late the next morning, she wasn't in a good mood. She showered, dressed, and gulped down a coffee without smiling. She hated that on her first day with Mr. Kirby she felt like she had nothing to give him. She should have been radiant, bouncing with enthusiasm. Instead she was fighting a headache and wondering if she should cancel.

Her phone rang. For just a heartbeat, she thought it might be Wayne and chastised herself for being disappointed that it wasn't. "Hi, Dad."

"I had an interesting lunch today with one of my investors. He wanted to know if you and I speak. I told him of course we do. Then he asked me to talk to you regarding the nature of your business. You don't run a business, do you, Sage?"

"I do. I'm a plant psychologist, remember?"

"Oh my God, I thought that was a joke."

"Wow, look at the time. I have to go, Dad."

"No, hold on. Whoever you're working with right now—I want you to call them and tell them you can't see them anymore."

"Why do you care who I'm working with?"

"I don't, but some very powerful people do."

"I don't understand."

"You don't have to. You just need to tell your . . . What the hell do you call someone you work with?"

"Clients?"

"You need to tell whatever clients you have that something has come up and you'll need to terminate your association with them."

"No. I'm not going to do that."

"If it's about the money, Sage, I'll wire you some."

"I don't want your money."

"Fine. Play hardball. Name your price."

"What are you talking about? I don't have a price. I'm not shaking you down for more. I'm saying I refuse to let someone I don't even know tell me what I can or can't do." *Why would anyone want to stop me from having clients?* "This doesn't have anything to do with Mrs. Westerly, does it?" Her name kept coming up, and she'd already warned Sage to stay away from her family. Did she believe Sage knew one of them?

"I'm your father, and although I've always tried to respect that you're a little odd, this time it's affecting my business. Stay away from Eric Westerly. Is that clear enough for you?"

"First, I don't know any Eric Westerly. Second, what will you do? Cut me out of your will? Stop treating me as well as you do? Even if you threaten to stop talking to me, I'm beginning to think that might be for the best." With that, Sage did something she'd never done before—she hung up on her father.

Stay away from Eric Westerly.

Sage turned on the television and was about to hunt for a video of Water Bear Man when she saw him on a news clip. Eric Westerly was in Vandorra visiting a children's hospital in his superhero costume. The media couldn't get enough of it. Sage flipped through the channels and found Water Bear Man everywhere. Some stations spoke of how exciting it was to see him doing a public appearance. Other stations focused on his family tie to Vandorran royalty. King Tadeas. Crown Prince Magnus. Princess Rachelle, granddaughter of Delinda Westerly of Boston.

Rachelle. Wayne's sister's name is Rachelle.

As the camera did a close-up of Water Bear Man's face, Sage's heart began to thud in her chest. *Wayne is Eric Westerly. On a trip with his family.*

It was the worst of what she'd feared—not only had Wayne lied to her, but everything they'd shared had also been a lie. The only thing Sage was certain of was that Delinda Westerly didn't want her around her grandson. She'd thought she'd gotten to a point where nothing could embarrass her anymore, but seeing Wayne/Eric on television, smiling and laughing as if he didn't have a care in the world, tore at her confidence. *Am I a joke to him as well?*

She turned the television off and reached for her phone. "I'm sorry, Mr. Kirby, but I can't meet you today."

"Oh." He sounded disappointed. "Do you want to reschedule?"

Tears entered Sage's eyes, and her voice became shaky. "I don't know. Maybe it's for the best if we don't."

"Did something happen? Are you crying?"

That's all it took for Sage to burst into tears. She cried for the little girl who was finally facing the fact her parents were not coming back for her. She cried for the woman who was no longer sure she could trust her instincts. She even wept a little for the man on the phone who she hoped would find his way to happiness, because she no longer had what it would take to help him. "No," she croaked.

The man was quiet, then said, "I've done enough of it myself to know what it sounds like. Did you lose someone?"

"He was never actually mine," she answered with a loud sniff.

"That doesn't make it easier, does it?"

"No, it doesn't."

"Do you have anyone you can call?"

Sage glanced at the time on her phone. She didn't want to bother Bella with this. Honestly, it was nothing more than what she'd said would happen. "Not at this hour, but I will later."

"I know you don't know me, but if you need to talk to someone—"

Sage teared up again. "I'm sure you have enough troubles on your own without listening to mine."

"That's the thing—I don't. My wife passed away a year ago. I retired early to take care of her, and my life became all about Rita. I've been lost without her. I don't regret one moment with her, but I don't know who I am now. When my dog died last week, I started to wonder what the hell I was still doing here. I was pretty damn close to finding the nearest bridge and jumping off. Just to get the waiting over with. I asked for some kind of sign that I shouldn't—anything. And you and your friend walked over. I don't believe in miracles, but I'm still here, and I feel like someone heard me. So, if you need a friend today, I'd love to go plant shopping with you."

Sage wiped her tears away and took a deep, steadying breath. "I'd like that."

They made arrangements to meet thirty minutes from then. Sage quickly freshened up her makeup without looking herself in the eye. She was a tangle of emotions—some good, some bad.

She hadn't expected to enjoy her day with him, but John Kirby was an incredibly sweet man who turned out to be a really good listener. He was an opportunity for a fresh perspective. As they picked out plants for his home, she told him about Wayne. Not everything. She didn't tell him who he was, but she did say that he'd lied to her.

He didn't tell her she shouldn't ever see him again or that she shouldn't have trusted Wayne. He nodded in understanding.

Reeling from Wayne's deception, Sage confessed the true nature of her own business. She had no idea how he would take it, but he seemed more curious than upset.

"So, do you actually know anything about plants?"

"Oh yes. I have a degree in ethnobotany."

"But the real reason you offer to help people with their plants is because it gives you a way into their lives while you help them?"

"Yes."

"Do you ever tell them that?"

"No."

"Then why tell me?"

"Because I don't want to lie to you. Not today. Not when I've just discovered how much it can hurt to learn that something isn't true."

He picked up a small flowered plant. "Lies come in all sizes, and some hurt no one at all. I used to tell my wife she was beautiful every day—even at the end, when she was only a shadow of the person she'd been. Was that a lie? She was beautiful to me, and she needed to hear those words. I talked to some of your old clients. They all said that bringing plants into their homes was a catalyst to a happier time in their lives. Your lie didn't hurt them."

"I hope not." Sage hugged the potted plant she was holding closer. "I'm so sorry about your wife."

They went to the stall owner. John paid for the plants they were holding. "Funny thing is, I feel like she's with me today and smiling. I've been so sad for so long. It has only been since meeting you that I've begun to feel like I might be ready to start over. Maybe get a new job, although I don't need one. I'm ready to start caring about something again. Does that sound crazy?"

"No, it sounds beautiful."

They placed the plants in the trunk of his car. "How did you plan to help me?"

Sage tucked her hands in the back pockets of her jeans. "I was going to play matchmaker."

His eyes lit up. "Really? Who did you have in mind?"

Sage described Bella's neighbor's dogs, and how she was eccentric but in a beautifully fun way that Sage had hoped would make him smile.

"She dresses them up? Seriously?"

"You should see how adorable they look. Her grandchildren think it's hilarious. All the pictures on her walls feature them laughing and holding them."

"And how were you going to get us together?"

"My friend is her neighbor. We were going to introduce you."

"That's it?"

"When it's right, that's all it takes."

He nodded. "I'd like to meet her."

"You would?" Sage's eye popped.

"I've never seen a dog in a dress, and it sounds pretty damn amusing. I want reasons to laugh again."

"You will find them," Sage said, "and if you're serious, I'll set up that introduction."

"I am. Would you like a ride back to your place?" he asked.

"No, I like to walk."

"Sage."

"Yes?"

"Good luck with your man."

"He's not mine. He's not even who I thought he was."

Her client shrugged. "He looked at you the way I used to look at my wife. That's not easy to find. Maybe he deserves a second chance. Maybe he doesn't. But I hope you find what you're looking for as well."

Sage gave in to an impulse and hugged him. “Thank you. Tell me if you have a problem with any of your new friends.” She pointed to the trunk.

He stepped back and chuckled. “I will. After I settle them in, I think I’ll go shopping for a new suit. I hear I might have an occasion to wear one soon.”

Sage smiled. “I’ll call you when we have something set up.”

He waved.

She waved back and turned away. The day had not gone at all the way she’d expected, but she felt better than she had that morning. Wayne . . . Eric . . . whoever he was would probably call her when he returned to London.

She had no idea what she’d say when he did. Would he finally be honest? Would he try to explain his lies away with more? *Usually I’m drawn to help people I understand. I don’t understand Wayne . . . Eric . . . no, I don’t understand him at all.*

Chapter Ten

Still dressed in his formfitting gray spandex outfit, Eric flexed before placing his hands on his hips and smiling down at the eleven-year-old boy at his side. "Finn of Vandorra, we have successfully given out all of the plushies and met with every child. You are indeed a worthy assistant."

Finn smiled proudly. His parents stood nearby, beaming.

When Eric had heard that Finn had not only received his heart transplant but was home again and doing well, he'd requested that the boy be invited to the hospital to help with his visit. It was, after all, at Finn's urging that Magnus had sought to bring Water Bear Man to Vandorra in the first place. Not every child had the happy ending Finn had gotten, but it touched Eric deeply to see that he had.

Although the media had not been allowed within the hospital, flashes from cell phones were still constantly going off. Rather than withdraw from them, Water Bear Man puffed out his chest for the benefit and amusement of the children.

Eric glanced over and saw Magnus and his father, King Tadeas, looking on in approval. Raising his voice loud enough for them to hear, Eric said, "Finn, what do you call a prince with a bad case of the farts?"

Finn's eyes rounded, and silence fell over the corridor where they were all gathered.

With a huge grin, Eric boomed, "Air to the throne."

Finn giggled behind his hand. King Tadeas laughed, opening the door for others to laugh along.

Eric looked down at a little girl who was standing beside Rachelle and asked, "Young lady, what does a king say when he farts?"

"I don't know," she said, then whispered to Rachelle, "Can he ask that?"

Rachelle hugged the child. "Water Bear Man is just having fun." She smiled at her father-in-law as if to check his reaction, then seemed relieved. "What *does* a king say when he farts?"

Eric waved a hand in the air as if to dissipate a smell, then put on a comically haughty voice. "Royal pardon."

Even Delinda, who was watching the scene from King Tadeas's side, began to laugh at that one. She shook her head as she did, but she looked thoroughly amused. It was a good note to end his visit on.

"Boys and girls, kings, princes, princesses, and whatnots, it is time for Water Bear Man to return to his post on the moon. Sleep soundly tonight—I am watching over all of you."

As Eric and his family walked away, children waved from the doorways and beds of every room they passed. The entire visit to Vandorra had gone better than he'd expected. The trip over with Delinda and King Tadeas had been relatively uneventful. Although a part of Eric thought it was bad for his grandmother's already healthy ego to be courted by a king, Tadeas was a calming influence on her. He might be smitten with her, but he didn't let her dominate him. She was softer when she was with him, as if she was able to let her guard down somewhat because there was someone she could rely on, if need be. It was nice to watch them together.

The only shadow on the day was that Sage wasn't there. Instead she was back in London, disappointed in him and shopping for flowers with the man from the park, who could be a psycho, for all they knew. Thankfully, Reggie had agreed to follow Sage to make sure she was okay. He'd texted updates throughout the day, which brought Eric some peace of mind.

He should have been honest with her before he left. Hell, he should have told her the truth from day one. That train of thought, however, was a dark rabbit hole he would not go down. He'd learned that much from one of the counselors at the clinic. Fixating on mistakes from the past was self-destructive. All he could change from that day forward was himself.

Ready or not, when he returned to London, he would tell Sage everything—the good, the bad, the whole truth. Waiting until he was in a better situation might have cost him his chance with her.

No. He wouldn't let that be the way this played out. They were meant to be together. She was the only thing that made sense to him.

Eric stayed in Vandorra long enough to have a meal with Rachelle, Magnus, Delinda, and King Tadeas at the castle. Rachelle asked if Eric had heard that Alisha and Brett were expecting their second child. She looked over-the-top happy to hear that Eric had received the news during a phone conversation with their brother. There was a time when Rachelle's interest in his interaction with his sibling would have felt oppressive, but he now understood that she cared deeply for both of them. Her interest was based in love, and that put her curiosity in a favorable light.

Rachelle suggested Eric call Spencer to inquire about Skye, his adopted daughter. She retold the story of how Hailey, Spencer's wife, had taken in her niece when the child's parents had died in an accident. Spencer, Rachelle said, wanted his daughter to know all his siblings. The way she said it touched his heart. His family might not mesh well, but they were good people. Could one phone call make things less strained between them, or was that wishful thinking?

When it was time to return to London, King Tadeas remained behind in Vandorra, saying that he would follow in a few days, and Eric flew back with Delinda. He settled into a seat beside her on the private jet, expecting to enjoy the flight.

He knew the mood of the trip was about to nosedive when, after takeoff, his grandmother laid her hand over his and said, "Eric, there is something I need to discuss with you."

Here it comes. What is it that she doesn't see as up to Westerly standards now? My career? My behavior? Something I said or just me in general? "It's been a long day, Grandmother. I'm tired."

She pursed her lips, a sign that she was not pleased with his answer. "I wouldn't bring it up if it weren't important."

Eric rubbed his hands over his face. Boundaries. If she crossed one, he would just redraw them for her. "Okay."

"I'm concerned about this woman you've been seeing—Sage Revere. I have heard nothing good about her or her family."

Eric undid his seat belt roughly and stood. He needed to put physical distance between them while he processed the full implications of what she'd said. "How do you know about Sage? Are you having me watched?"

Delinda's chin rose. "Of course I am. You gave us quite a scare. We were all hopeful when you went to the clinic, but then you began this second, secret life. Yes, I was concerned enough to have you followed."

"But you didn't stop there, did you? No, you wouldn't. What else have you done? Let me guess, since you apparently don't like her—have you threatened her yet? How about her parents? Would you even admit it to me if you had?"

Delinda rose to her feet, although she held on to the back of the seat to steady herself. "Eric, I do what I do because I love you. Do you remember when I warned you about Jasmine? You didn't want to believe me, but she turned out to be exactly what I thought she was. I'm right about this woman, too. She supports herself by targeting wealthy people and milking them for their money. That's why she's with you. Do you honestly believe she doesn't know who you are? That a press-on scar is really that good of a disguise? Of course she knows you're Eric Westerly. She's playing you just like she plays everyone. Only this time, she thinks she hit the jackpot."

Her words cut through Eric's defenses and made fresh Jasmine's betrayal. It fed the fire of every insecurity he had about not being worthy of love on his own merit and every fear he had about people pretending to care about him. He bent over, sickened by both her assertions and his reaction to them.

Am I that much of a fool? Is Sage no different from Jasmine?

Eric walked away from his grandmother, heading to the back of the plane. Unfortunately, there was nowhere he could go that was beyond the reach of her voice. "I know you don't want to hear this, Eric. I don't want to say it. I just love you too much to sit back and watch you make another huge mistake."

"Stop," he said hoarsely. How was it possible that one woman could unravel the very essence of him? He could feel himself shutting down in response.

"Eric—"

"Just shut up." Eric took a seat near the back of the plane. "This is why you're not in my life, Delinda. Right here. This is it."

Her face went white, and her eyes filled with tears. "I lost my husband because I didn't intervene. I won't lose you, too."

"You already have," Eric said, and turned his face to look out the window. "After we land, I don't ever want to see you again. Don't call me. Don't have someone try to convince me to call you. You have a twisted version of how to love someone, and I don't want you in my life at all. I'll be civil for the sake of the others, but in my heart, you're dead to me."

Delinda gasped, and there was silence.

Blissful silence.

He glanced toward the front of the plane. She had retaken her seat and was facing away from him.

He wished he could silence the questions echoing inside himself as easily as he'd silenced her. *Does Sage know who I am? Did she know all along?*

He hated that Delinda's take on Sage's career fit what she did. Sage did seek out certain people, target them, although he hated that term, and manipulated her way into their lives. She said she did it to help them.

What was more likely to be true? That Sage was a Good Samaritan who was happiest when living month to month and had fallen for him the moment she saw him in the coffee shop? Or that she was a charlatan who recognized him instantly and had been playing him all along—because, to her, he was like coming across a winning lottery ticket?

Had he been so desperate to believe in something that he'd blinded himself to the real her, a money-hungry woman no different from Jasmine?

He hated Delinda for planting the doubt in him.

He hated himself for not knowing whether to trust his grandmother, who was often painfully correct—or his heart, which told him she was wrong this time.

He could grill Reggie about everything Sage had done while he was gone. Wealth made anything possible. He could have someone tap Sage's phone and within days know everyone she knew as well as every move she made.

But how would that make him any different from his grandmother?

He tried to reverse his mood, yank his thoughts back to where they'd been before he'd boarded the jet. He wanted to head straight over to Sage's apartment to confess everything.

He wasn't sure of himself or her anymore, and he didn't know how to change how he felt. He was gifted at pulling away, denying something bothered him, turning off his emotions. He could cut Delinda and Sage out of his life and label Wayne Easton a failed experiment—convince himself that none of it mattered anyway.

Anger boiled inside him. He didn't want to slide back to that place, and he hated Delinda for showing him that he was capable of that fall.

She tried to talk to him once as they left the plane, but he walked away from her and the car she'd arranged to meet them.

Instead of waiting for another car to arrive, Eric walked through the airport in search of a taxi line. Distracted as he was, he forgot why he'd never done that. As people began to recognize him, they swarmed him. It started with relatively pleasant, albeit ill-timed, introductions and requests that he pose for photos or autograph something. He signed countless papers, shook hands, even held a baby while the mother took a photo of him with her child. However, without the personal security he normally would have surrounded himself with in public, he was at the mercy of a crowd that grew in size and then in enthusiasm. People began pushing and shoving to get closer to him. This could go south fast.

Airport security arrived and ushered him away from the crowd to a waiting taxi. A few of them asked for a photo with him as well before he stepped into the car. He wasn't proud of the fact that their requests would have once annoyed him. He took the time to thank each of them, pose for their photos, and wave at the crowd behind them. It cost him nothing, and he left to smiles.

"Where to?" the taxi driver asked.

"Just drive for now," Eric said. "I need time to think."

"It might get pricey fast," the driver warned.

"That's fine."

They were quiet for several miles before the driver spoke. "My daughter's a doctor."

Eric made a guttural sound in place of a response.

"Want to see a picture of her?" The driver held up his phone and showed a photo of a beautiful dark-haired woman. "She's a hard worker. Now my son, he'll keep me in this cab another decade. He's taking his time graduating from university." He went on to share much more about both of his children.

Eric nodded, half listening. Even though his head was still spinning, there was something soothing about hearing about normal people living normal lives. The pride in the man's voice as he talked about his children was moving.

Finally, Eric interrupted long enough to give him his address. The man whistled at the size of the gate, then swore at the size of Eric's home.

"What's it like to live in a house like that?" the driver asked when he parked.

"Not as amazing as you'd think." Eric paid his fare with a generous tip, then stepped out of the car, taking his overnight bag with him. "Thank you for sharing that. You gave me something to smile about on a day when I didn't feel I had one."

"There's always a reason to smile. If you can't find one—be one. Have a good day."

Eric walked into his home with those words still with him. He took out his phone and typed in the name of the taxi driver as well as his children. When Brett's assistant arrived, he had another name to add to the list of people who should unexpectedly have something wonderful happen. Full scholarship for his son? A grant his daughter could use to buy supplies for those in need?

Reggie asked him how his trip went.

Eric shook his head and walked away. He was done—for that day, at least.

Chapter Eleven

Early afternoon the next day, Delinda stood outside the door of her library. "Is he here yet, Michael?"

"Yes. I have him waiting in the parlor. Would you like me to bring him in now or give you a few minutes?"

"Is everything ready?"

"I believe so."

"Then give me a moment to settle, but no more."

"Understood."

Delinda walked to a corner of her library where a technician had just finished installing a huge flat-screen television as well as a new computer system. The young man looked proud of himself as he stood beside it. Delinda didn't thank him. Her appreciation would be shown in his compensation. Instead she had him walk her through how it worked again, then dismissed him from the room.

She had sent a text message to several members of her family, along with instructions on how and when to join her. She cued each of them up on different boxes on the screen. Brett and Alisha were in one, Rachelle and Magnus in another, Spencer and Hailey on still another. She smiled when her good friend Alessandro appeared on the fourth.

If it worked as the technician said it would, they would all also be able to see each other.

"What is this about?" Brett asked.

"Is everything all right, Grandmother?" Rachelle chimed in.

"Cool conference setup," Spencer said with a smile. "Of course, I'd like to upgrade you to virtual reality."

"This won't work if you all talk at once," Delinda said. "Patience, please. We're waiting for one more person."

"Mr. Reggie Pines," Michael announced.

Delinda turned toward her guest. "Reggie, come closer so everyone can see you."

Looking like he wasn't sure what the heck was going on, Reggie walked to stand beside Delinda. He scanned the screen and waved at each of them. "Good to see you all. I can honestly say this is a surprise."

Delinda sighed. "It was this or fly everyone here, and I didn't want to inconvenience anyone."

Spencer coughed.

Alessandro chided him to be nice.

Gathering her courage, Delinda raised her chin and said, "I asked you all here because I need your help. This is an intervention of sorts."

Reggie frowned. "Hang on, is this about Sage Revere?"

"It is," Delinda answered.

"Who is Sage?" Alessandro asked.

At the same time, Reggie raised both hands. "I'm out of here."

Delinda grabbed his arm as he was about to turn away. "Wait. You don't understand."

"I understand enough to know that I want no part of this. I have been kicking myself for convincing Eric to see you. One day with you and he looks like he was hit by a Mack truck. Count me out." Reggie tried to shake himself free of Delinda, but she held on.

Rachelle said, "Grandmother, why do you think Eric needs an intervention? He looked like he was doing so well."

Still gripping Reggie's arm, Delinda said, "The intervention is for me." She released Reggie. "I'm the one who needs help."

"What did you do, Grandmother?" Brett asked.

Delinda lowered her eyes. "I was concerned for Eric, but I may have overstepped."

"May have?" Reggie asked.

Throwing her hands up in the air, Delinda said, "Okay, I did. I went too far. I'm not perfect. I don't have all the answers. I'll probably drive all of you away again and die alone." She paused for emphasis. "Or you could help me fix this."

"Why don't you start from the beginning so we know what you're facing?" Hailey asked.

"You know why I'm in London. I know you all think that one visit to a clinic solved Eric's problems, but we don't know what he might still be struggling with. All I wanted to do was make sure we would know if he started to slide—so I hired someone to follow him."

"Not that Alethea woman again," Alessandro groaned.

"No. No. I learned my lesson with her. This was someone who would just follow him and report back about what he did."

"Only . . . ?" Rachelle covered her face with one hand, as if what she'd heard caused her pain.

Magnus interjected, "You had reason to be concerned for your grandson."

"Exactly," Delinda said. "Rachelle, your arrival in London might well have saved his life. I wanted to do my part."

Reggie sighed dramatically. "But you didn't stop there."

"No." If there was anything Delinda hated, it was admitting she was wrong. She'd grown up in a household where weakness was not tolerated. "I found out he was seeing a woman of questionable morals and got involved when perhaps I shouldn't have."

"Grandmother," Brett asked, "this woman you're referring to . . . Eric spoke to me about her. He cares for her."

"He shouldn't. She's after his money."

Reggie shook his head. "No."

"I have it on good authority that she targets rich clients, then fleeces them. She does it all under the guise of being able to communicate with plants," Delinda said.

Reggie folded his arms across his chest. "Your authority is an idiot. I followed this woman before and after Eric asked me to. Everyone likes her. Her old clients have nothing but good to say about her. Trust me, I've spoken to several of them. Tops, they paid her a couple hundred dollars, and in return they say she filled their lives with plants and happiness. I don't know what the hell she tells these people, but they all say they were at a low point before they ran into her. You tell me if that isn't worth a couple hundred bucks."

"Her mother is a horrible, grasping social climber," Delinda snarked.

Reggie shrugged. "We can't choose our family, can we?"

The room was dead silent.

Michael stepped into the room and went to stand beside Delinda. "Sometimes we can and we're better for it."

Delinda's heart swelled. If she were the type to hug, she would have embraced him then. He was very much a part of her family, and she was grateful to have him. That conversation, however, would wait for another day.

Reggie stubbornly held to his opinion. "I don't care who her parents are. I like Sage and who Eric is becoming since he met her. She's good for him."

Delinda searched the faces of her grandchildren and saw only disappointment. She saw the same in Alessandro. The battle went out of her. "I was *wrong*." When no one jumped up to assure her that she hadn't been, she snapped, "So intervene already. I threatened her, her parents, and told Eric she was after his money, just like Jasmine was. How do I fix this?"

In the stunned silence that followed, Magnus asked, "She is joking, isn't she?"

Rachelle shook her head. "No, she is not. Grandmother, how could you?"

On legs that suddenly felt unsteady, Delinda moved to sit in a chair. "I was afraid I would lose him the way I lost my Oliver. I wanted to protect him."

"Who was Oliver?" Reggie asked.

"Our grandfather. He killed himself," Brett said quietly.

"Oh." Reggie went to sit on the arm of Delinda's chair. "Well, no wonder you're all fucked-up. I get it now." He gave her shoulder a pat.

Delinda almost told him to remove his hand from her, but she felt another hand on her other shoulder. She looked up to see Michael standing beside her. Reggie had become Eric's family just as surely as Michael had become hers. She would learn to love him. She gave each of their hands a pat.

Tears filled her eyes. "All I ever wanted was for my family to have better than I did. Maybe I went about it the wrong way, but I never meant to hurt any of you." She dabbed at her tears. "I tried to keep Rachelle safe in Vandorra, and I failed her as well."

"I'm still here," Rachelle said. "You didn't fail me."

"We've all made mistakes," Brett said. "Not one of us is perfect."

"Nope, not one of you is. I've never seen a more messed-up family," Reggie said, then smiled. "No offense."

Hailey added, "Everyone here knows you mean well, Grandmother. It's just sometimes the methods you employ that—"

"I know. I know." Delinda waved a hand in the air. "I go too far. Let's move past that, on to something helpful like suggestions."

Spencer jumped in. "Delinda Westerly, my wife is attempting to make you feel better."

Hailey countered kindly, "She's not upset with me. She's upset with herself."

Alessandro cleared his throat loudly. "If you want my opinion, and since I'm here I'm guessing you do, you should start by apologizing to this Sage woman."

Delinda glanced up at Reggie. "You really think she's good for Eric?"

He nodded. "She's his odd duck."

Delinda blinked a few times. "I don't know what that means, but I'll take that as a yes."

Alisha chimed in, "I think what he means is that she's different, but she's Eric's kind of different."

"That's exactly what I mean," Reggie said.

Delinda took a moment to consider her options. "I could host an event and arrange for her—"

"No," they all said in unison.

"Or I could"—she looked at each of them again and resigned herself to her fate—"apologize to her and promise Eric that I won't get involved in his personal business again." She sniffed loudly. "He said I was dead to him."

"He didn't mean that. He was angry, Delinda," Alessandro said gently. "He had a right to be."

"I wouldn't have actually had her arrested or ruined her father's business," Delinda said.

"*Now* she's kidding," Magnus said with confidence.

"No," the others said in unison again.

Delinda rose to her feet. "Thank you all for meeting with me. I now know what I must do."

Brett said, "Grandmother, would you like to see Linda before you go?"

A smile instantly spread across Delinda's face, and she stood. "Is she awake? I would love to."

Brett held his young daughter up to the camera, and Delinda cooed to her. She said, "Dee Dee," and smiled, reaching her hands out in request for Delinda to pick her up.

Hailey added, "Skye will be sad she missed talking to you. We'd love to sign back on again this evening. Perhaps you could read her a story?"

Tears filled Delinda's eyes once again. "I would love that."

"Do you think now is the time to share our news?" Rachelle asked.

Magnus nodded.

"We're having twins."

Overcome with gratitude and love for her family, Delinda placed a hand over her heart. "We may not be your average family, but I wouldn't change a single one of you."

She waited for them to say the same. When they didn't, she waved them off and ended the connection.

"That's my cue to go," Reggie said.

"Reggie," Delinda said, "thank you for all you do for Eric, and for coming here today."

Reggie nodded. "I hope you sort this out. Family's important."

"Yes, it is." Delinda smiled at Michael. "And I'm very lucky to have the one I do—both the ones by blood and the ones by choice."

Michael flushed, then cleared his throat. "I'll walk you to the door, Mr. Pines."

Chapter Twelve

Sage was gathering up her purse and phone when she heard a horn blaring from the street below. Rolling her eyes at the lack of consideration some people had for others, she almost ignored it, but it was so insistent that she went to her window. She half expected to see a car pileup or a street altercation in progress.

Her jaw dropped when she realized what the honking was for. The street was at a complete stop. People had gotten out of their vehicles to take pictures of Eric Westerly, standing half out of a long white limo with a bouquet of red roses in one hand. It looked like the final scene of a romantic comedy, and not one Sage ever imagined herself starring in. She stepped back from the window.

Was this his idea of an apology? A public spectacle? She didn't want this—she wanted answers. Unable to leave through the front of the building, she decided to slip out the back. She made it as far as the alley before realizing that that, too, was blocked. Eric was at the entrance of it looking up at the fire escape as if he were about to scale it. The crowd surged and ebbed against a small army of security.

He sensed her presence, and the attention of the crowd turned to her. Instantly she was surrounded by people with cameras asking her if she was the reason Eric Westerly was there.

She shook her head while holding his gaze and shouted, "I'm sorry. You have the wrong woman. I don't know him."

He walked toward her with the arrogance and confidence she'd glimpsed in Wayne but without the softer side. "I'm here to rectify that."

She didn't want to have this or any conversation in front of a crowd of his fans. Without his scar, his Hollywood-perfect face looked alien to her. "I'm sorry. As I've said, you have the wrong woman."

He held the flowers out to her. When she made no move to accept them, he threw them over his head toward the crowd. A wild dash was followed by one woman holding the red roses above her head with the triumph of some rabid bridesmaid.

They stood locked in silence while the crowd strained to hear. Several people were desperately trying to get close enough to record it on their phones. "I don't want to do this here," Sage said, breaking the quiet tension.

"Then come away with me. We can go anywhere, do anything. Do you want to talk about this over dinner at the top of the Eiffel Tower? How about while dipping our toes in the water in Fiji? You name the place, and that's where we'll go."

Her heart broke a little as she searched for but found no sign of the man she'd thought he was. "What are you doing here? What is this? I don't understand."

He reached for her hand, but she evaded his touch. "I'm showing you what we could have together. I'm sorry I wasn't up front with you about my real name, but surely you can forgive me for needing to be careful. This is my life, Sage, and you could be part of it. Say yes, and you'll never have to work another day in your life. You'll never want for anything. You and I will travel the world together."

Sage started shaking her head as he spoke. Nothing about the scene rang true. It wasn't a declaration of love, and it didn't feel like an apology. There was something burning in his eyes, but it wasn't the desire she'd seen so many times in the past; it was—anger?

What have I done for you to be angry with me? I'm not the one who lied about who I was. I didn't act like I cared one moment only to ditch you the next.

If she were a vindictive person, she would have thrown her questions at him right then, but even though he was breaking her heart, she didn't want to hurt him. She'd known he wasn't happy from the first time she'd seen him. She'd thought she could help him, but the man standing before her didn't want help—he was there to prove something.

What?

What does he want from me?

She stepped closer and lowered her tone. This wasn't the place or the situation in which she'd imagined them having this conversation, but he wasn't leaving her much choice. "I don't want flowers or gifts. I like my job and my life, so I don't need to be rescued from either. I wanted the truth, but now I'm not even sure I want that. I don't know you—not this you. I don't understand what you're doing here today. All I am sure of is that if you think I want what you're offering, you don't know me, and that's the part that hurts the most."

"I'm offering you everything, Sage."

"Too bad it's nothing I want," she countered. "I'm sorry. Goodbye, Eric."

She rushed away from him and the crowd before either could stop her. Sage ran inside, up four flights of stairs, and into her apartment. Only once she was safely inside, with her back against the door, did she give in to the emotions and questions swirling within her.

He had come to her, and she'd turned him away. Had it been the right choice?

She was still trying to catch her breath when she felt as well as heard a loud knock on her door. "Sage, open up. We need to talk," Eric said.

She counted to ten, took several deep calming breaths, then turned and opened the door. "Wasn't that what we just did in front of all of London?"

Still looking very much like a slick, groomed movie star, Eric walked past her. "Is that why you said no? Because there was an audience?"

She closed the door and hugged herself, trying to make sense of this new side of a man she'd thought she knew. "You lied to me."

"You lie every day. Isn't that what your *career* is all about?"

She gasped. "I didn't lie to you. I let you in."

"I don't know how much of you is real and how much is a fabrication. It doesn't matter, though. I want you in my life."

"Doesn't matter? What are you talking about? Who are you? Where's the man I went to Stonehenge with?"

His hands fisted at his sides. "Wayne Easton doesn't exist. Take a good look—this is the real me. But before you refuse me again, think about everything I could offer you. I'm not looking for a one-night stand. I want to make this work. If that means putting marriage on the table, I'll do it."

She shook her head again. "You don't even sound like you like me."

"But I want you." He reached for her, hauling her against him. She wanted to resist, but her body came alive for him. Every single place their bodies touched sent fire licking through her. She'd dreamed of being his so many times. Sweet and tender sex . . . or rough and angry . . . it all sounded good to her right then. He leaned down and growled in her ear, "You want me just as badly." He trailed kisses down her neck while cupping her ass and lifting her off the floor.

Sage's legs naturally went around his waist even as she told herself not to give in to the desire rushing through her. He carried her through her apartment to her bedroom and tossed her down on the bed. The air sizzled with sexual tension.

"Tell me to go and I'll go." His eyes burned with need. "Or ask me to stay and I will." He stood over her like a conquering pirate from every fantasy she'd ever had—impossible to resist, even though she knew she should.

Her brain argued that there were things they should discuss before going any further. It pleaded with her to slow down. Her body revved louder than those thoughts.

She'd wanted him, had wanted him for long enough that the promise of finally having him outweighed every reason she shouldn't. No one had ever made her feel so out of control. No one might ever again. She was a woman who followed her heart, and it was saying it was willing to risk getting broken if it meant having this. They did have a lot to talk out, but couldn't that happen after she visited heaven?

She sat up on the bed, struggling to maintain control of both herself and the situation. "I—we—" She met his eyes and desire won. "Stay."

He stripped off his shirt, revealing a powerful chest and six-pack abs. He didn't hesitate. In a few efficient movements, he discarded his clothing and tossed a condom on the bed beside her. "Come here."

Her gaze dropped to his cock, fully erect and irresistibly large. If this was a mistake in the making, she couldn't imagine regretting it. She moved to a kneeling position and began to unbutton her shirt. "Why don't you come here?" With him she felt bolder, sexually playful in a way she'd previously lacked the confidence to be. She slipped her shirt off and dropped it beside the bed, then undid her bra and tossed it aside as well.

With a growl, he helped her stand, then removed her shoes and eased her out of her pants and undies. He crawled up onto the bed in front of her and caressed her breasts gently. "So beautiful."

She couldn't resist running her hands down his flat stomach to his eager shaft. "You're not so bad yourself." His throbbing cock jerked at her touch.

When his mouth claimed hers, she gave herself over to the pleasure of it. He took her mouth boldly, as if it were his to have. His touch was just as confident and proprietorial. And she loved it.

There was no holding back for either of them. She hungrily dug her fingers into his muscular back when he moved his mouth down to her breasts. He circled one nub with his tongue, nipped at it gently, then moved his attention to her other. She alternated from caressing his rock-hard cock to running her hands over every inch of him she could reach. It was all equally good.

He lowered her to the bed and ordered her not to move. She could have protested, but she was eager for whatever pleasure he wanted to bring her. He kissed his way down her chest, across her stomach, and settled himself between her legs.

She closed her eyes and gripped the bedsheets as he parted her sex and dipped his tongue into her. She was drowning in the sensations, mewing for him not to stop. He circled her clit, teased it, did a mind-shattering combination of sucking and flicking that had her arching off the bed. Just when she was thinking it couldn't get better, he thrust a finger inside her and worked it at just the right angle to send heat flooding through her. There was no reprieve from the pleasure, though. His mouth was relentless, and he moved his finger in and out of her with increasing speed until the first wave of heat gave way to another, stronger flood of release.

She cried out mindlessly.

He withdrew. She was too dazed to either move or protest. A moment later, he was back and sheathed in a condom. He kissed her again deeply. She opened her mouth and her legs wide for him. He raised his head and dipped the tip of his cock inside her. She bit her bottom lip in anticipation and held his gaze.

"You're mine now, Sage," he growled, and thrust powerfully into her.

She gasped with pleasure and clenched herself around him.

There was no tenderness in this mating. He pounded down into her. She met him thrust for thrust. Her frustration with him, her confusion and heartache, surfaced and added a wildness to her own movements. She pulled his head down and kissed him angrily. How dare he call her his?

Nothing she'd ever shared with a man prepared her for how good and how equally bad being with him felt. Even as she felt her body begin to flush in preparation for another climax, she hit his chest with a clenched fist. This wasn't love—this was something else—and it felt wrong to enjoy it.

Her anger made him even wilder. He thrust deeper and deeper, harder and faster. She clung to him and cried out into his kiss as she had her second orgasm . . . or perhaps her third. He growled something in her ear, climaxed with onc last powerful thrust, and shuddered above her.

He rolled off her, disposed of his condom, and lay there next to her, breathing as hard as she was but not touching her. Neither of them said a word, and she wondered if he was regretting what they'd done as much as she was.

She hadn't thought it was possible, but she felt more rather than less of a distance between them.

Eric just had amazing sex with the woman he couldn't imagine not spending the rest of his life with, and somehow it had left him feeling like shit. He had spent a sleepless night battling his feelings for Sage.

On one hand, she was everything he'd ever wanted—and more. On the other hand, he didn't trust that she could be. He wanted to. He wanted to believe she didn't care about his money or his fame and that she'd fallen for him when she thought he had neither.

He'd made a fool out of himself over a woman before. He couldn't risk doing it again.

If she wanted his money, he'd give it to her. She could have the big house, the status and parties, as long as he could have her. No, he wasn't proud of his weakness for her, but he was jaded enough to believe he could manage it. So, she wasn't who he'd thought she was. Weren't most people a disappointment anyway? At least this time he'd be going into the union with his eyes open.

She'd returned all his smaller gifts, so he'd brought out the big guns and they'd worked. She might have protested in public, but in the end she'd asked him to stay, just as he'd known she would. After all, money made almost anything forgivable.

He flopped an arm over his eyes and sighed. He should be happier than he felt. He could probably say anything to her at this point and she'd agree to be with him simply because he'd dangled marriage in front of her. Even if he insisted on a prenup, she would likely jump at the chance to walk down the aisle with him.

He'd gotten the answers he came for. Disappointment in her, though, wasn't enough to change the fact that he wanted her. He just needed have more realistic expectations.

He turned onto his side and propped his head up on one hand. Gently, he moved a stray lock of hair away from her forehead. She shifted to meet his gaze, looking as miserable as he felt. *That's not a good sign.*

"Why?" she asked hoarsely.

"Why what?"

"Why are you angry with me?"

Her question knocked the wind right out of him. She understood him in a way no one else did, and that realization only confused him more. "How could I be after what we just shared?"

"I don't know." A tear slid out of the corner of her eye and fell silently on the pillow below her head.

He wrapped his arms around her and rocked her against his chest. Had he been too rough? She'd seemed to enjoy it. "Sage, what's wrong?"

She buried her face in his chest. "Besides everything?"

"Talk to me, Sage. Did I hurt you?"

She lifted her face. "Right now? No. No, that was all good. Great, even. But—"

"But?" Relief flooded him that she'd enjoyed herself as well.

She sat up and covered herself with part of the blanket. "Don't you think you owe me an apology or an explanation or something about pretending to be someone you're not?"

He shrugged and said what he didn't want to believe. "You knew who I was."

"I didn't."

He raised a hand to cover one cheek. "So if I do this, I look like an entirely different man?"

Her mouth dropped open in surprise. "I had no reason to doubt you were who you said you were."

That would have been easier to believe had he not seen her face in the alley. "Then it must have been a shock to see me outside your window without my scar."

She frowned at him. "Not for the reason you're implying. I figured out who you were when I saw you on the news."

"Of course you did."

She moved off the bed to stand above him, hands on hips, looking gloriously beautiful even with fury spitting from her eyes. "Enough with the snide little comments. If you have something to say, say it. What exactly do you think is going on between us?"

He moved to sit up on the side of the bed. "Nothing unusual. You're fucking me because I'm rich." She slapped him clean across the face then. He shook his head at the sting of it. "What was that for?"

She retrieved her bra from the floor and put it on, then angrily pulled her shirt on and buttoned it. "Don't say another word. Not one more word." He stood and reached for her, but she pushed away from him and kept getting dressed instead. She'd just finished tying her shoes when she said, "Wait, where am I going? This is my apartment. You need to leave."

She meant it. She started picking up his clothing and throwing it at him. He caught each item easily. "Sage, obviously, I could have expressed that better. What I mean is that I don't care how long you knew my real name. I don't care why you're with me. I enjoy being with you, and I know you enjoy being with me. You don't have to pretend to be upset. Pack your stuff and come home with me."

She picked up one of his shoes and sent it sailing toward his head. He ducked just in time.

"Get dressed and get the fuck out," she snarled.

He put on his clothes, mostly because she looked like she might go homicidal if he didn't. "You don't have to do this, Sage."

She walked out of her bedroom.

He followed as soon as he had his shoes on. She was already at the door of her apartment, holding it open. Her face was flushed. Her breasts heaved in anger. She'd never looked more beautiful . . . except possibly when she'd orgasmed beneath him. She didn't, however, look as if she'd want to hear that observation.

Her voice was tight as she said, "I thought you and I had something special. I thought you understood me like no one else ever had, but I was wrong. I don't care how much money a person has. You know that. Or you should. I shouldn't have slept with you. I thought maybe, somewhere in there was the man I was falling in love with. But Wayne Easton doesn't exist, does he? I'm an optimistic idiot. So, please, go. I don't ever want to see you again."

He stood in front of her, a ball of male confusion. She was kicking him out. Only one other woman ever had, but this was a very different experience. She wasn't Jasmine, telling him she was disgusted by his touch. She'd just said she'd been falling for him before he'd accused her of wanting to be with him for his money.

He didn't want to leave. He didn't put up a fight, though, when she shoved him out the door and slammed it in his face. He needed time to think before he opened his mouth again. He stood in the hallway for a long time wondering what the hell to do next, yet certain of one thing—they weren't done.

Chapter Thirteen

Sage walked away from the door on unsteady legs. Never in her entire life had she struck another person. She'd also never slept with someone she was angry with. *Who am I becoming?*

She went to the window of her apartment and watched the white limo from behind the curtains. Her heart rate accelerated when the man she'd just thrown out of her life and her apartment finally appeared beside it. Despite the excited commotion around him, he wasn't smiling. He looked up in her direction, and their eyes met.

She could still hear him telling her he thought she was with him for his money. If that's what he thought of her, there was nothing to argue about. She'd wasted half her life trying to get her parents to really see her and—she swallowed hard—love her as she was. Only a masochist would look for that in a lover as well.

"I want to make this work. If that means putting marriage on the table, I'll do it."

Fuck you, Wayne or Eric or whoever the fuck you are.

I don't need you.

She stripped, went to the shower, and tried to wash the memory of him away. It was too vivid, part of it too good. She had always trusted her feelings, believing that they always ultimately guided her to where she was meant to be.

I shouldn't have slept with him. How did I possibly think it would make things better between us?

Defiantly, she dressed in her nicest outfit and applied much more makeup than she normally wore. She brushed her hair until it shone, then styled it in long curls that framed her face. Then she grabbed a gallon of ice cream, sat on her couch, and cried her heart out. She cried so long and so hard, she curled up and slept.

She woke several hours later to the sound of her phone ringing. Bella. She let the call ring through.

The phone rang again, so she tossed it on the chair across the room. There wasn't a person she wanted to talk to. Tomorrow, yes. Tomorrow she would pick herself up, dust herself off, and go back out into the world. But not today.

The sun went down without Sage moving from her couch. She didn't bother to turn on a light. How could she feel so heartbroken when nothing they'd shared had been real? Wayne was a fabrication, the creation of a coldhearted actor who was probably doing it for sick amusement.

"Come home with me."

Double fuck you, Eric Westerly. I wish that shoe had hit you right in the middle of your big, fat face.

A light knock on her door was followed by a more persistent, louder one.

"I'm not home," Sage finally called out. "Go away."

The knocking paused, then began again until the pounding crept into her head as well. Sage dragged herself off the couch and made her way to the door. If it was Eric again, he wouldn't like what she had to say to him.

She threw the door open and looked first at where Eric's face would have been. She saw no one. Then went to shut it when she looked down and saw her visitor.

Mrs. Westerly stuck her purse in against the jamb, deftly preventing Sage's action. "Miss Revere, I'd like a moment of your time."

Sage opened the door only to have leverage to push the woman's purse out. "I'm not interested."

Mrs. Westerly stepped forward, placing her body in the doorway enough to block Sage's ability to close the door. "There's something I need to say."

Upset as Sage was, she hadn't yet sunk to the level of shoving an elderly woman. She sighed and rubbed her swollen eyes. "I don't want to hear it."

"Might I come in for a moment?" Mrs. Westerly asked, as if she didn't know how unwelcome she was.

"Sure, why not," Sage said in resignation, letting the door swing wide-open. "It's not as if my day could get worse." Without waiting to see what her guest would do, Sage returned to the couch and looked sadly at the now-empty carton of ice cream.

Mrs. Westerly turned on the light, closed the door behind her, and after inspecting that it was clean, sat on a chair across from Sage. She looked Sage over slowly once, then again. "Are you unwell?"

Sage shook her head.

Mrs. Westerly motioned to her face and grimaced.

Sage ran a finger beneath one of her eyes. It came back smudged with the makeup she had applied earlier. The embarrassment she normally would have felt at raccoon eyes didn't come. She was still in shock from her morning. "Long day" was all she said.

Mrs. Westerly nodded and looked around the room before speaking. "I heard that Eric came to see you this morning."

Great. This is exactly who I want to discuss him with. Just great. "You'll be happy to know it went badly. Whatever we had is over."

"Because of me," the older woman said. "I'm sorry."

Unable to stomach another lie, Sage called bullshit. "You'll have to excuse me if I don't believe you at all. Hey, it's easier this way. Now you don't have to have me arrested."

"I shouldn't have threatened to."

"We agree on that, at least."

Mrs. Westerly folded and unfolded her hands. "I was misinformed regarding your business practices. After closer inspection, I regret that I jumped to the conclusions I did."

Sage waved a hand in the air. She didn't want to have this conversation. "I don't care. I'm used to people not understanding what I do." *The only opinion that mattered was Wayne's—not Eric's. Whoever. God, I hate him.*

"Well, you were big enough to deliver your apology to me in person, so I am here to offer you the same consideration. I'm sorry I thought you were a money-grabbing opportunist."

Sage laughed because it was that or cry. "I forgive you. Now, could you leave? I'm really not in the mood for company."

Mrs. Westerly didn't move to stand. Instead she tapped her fingers on the arm of her chair. "I told Eric what I thought of you, and I fear that has caused problems between you two."

"It shouldn't have. It wouldn't have if he had had any faith in me. So, although I appreciate your apology, it's really only making me feel worse." *Well, at least I know why he changed.*

"Eric had his heart broken once by a woman—"

"I know, he told me."

"It hurt him deeply. You have to understand—since that betrayal, he hasn't been able to trust anyone."

"No. I don't have to understand anything. He was hurt. I get it. But you know what? He's not the only who has ever had his heart broken. He's not the only one who has ever believed in someone who didn't deserve it. But who he becomes because of it is his choice."

Mrs. Westerly went to sit beside Sage. "You're upset right now, but—"

"Upset? No. Disappointed that I let myself fall in love with a man who has no idea how to love back—that's more accurate. Thank you for apologizing, but it doesn't change anything. There's nothing to work through. I met the real Eric Westerly today, and I didn't like him. End of story."

After a moment, Mrs. Westerly said, "I'm sorry to hear that. I was hoping I could convince you to give him a second chance."

Sage shook her head. "I don't see that happening."

Mrs. Westerly stood and hovered above Sage for a moment. "Not a single one of us is perfect. I should know—I'm less perfect than most. Eric shouldn't have believed me, but I shouldn't have planted the doubt in him. I'm sure there are things you've done that you regret. You're angry right now, but it will pass. Don't rush to make any solid decisions until some of it does. Eric is complicated, but you sound like you are, too. I'd like nothing more than to hear that the two of you have worked things out."

She sounded as if she meant it. Sage looked up at her. "I thought you didn't want me anywhere near you or your family."

Mrs. Westerly's chin rose. "I was wrong. It happens from time to time."

Sage would have smiled if her heart weren't still shattered. Instead she simply nodded once.

"I'll let myself out," Mrs. Westerly said, then left.

Sage stayed where she was, hugging herself on her couch. She wanted to believe what Eric's grandmother had said, but she didn't know who to believe anymore.

What a sad thing to have in common with the man I love.

Without a disguise, there weren't many places Eric could go that wouldn't have him under constant public scrutiny, so he did as he often had in the past—he holed up in his house, avoiding even his staff. This time, at least, he had his lair. The whole morning looped in Eric's mind like a tragic movie. It always brought him to the same haunting memory—the one that would stay with him for life—and that was the expression in Sage's eyes when she'd told him to leave.

He hadn't slept at all the night before. It wasn't his excuse, but it was an indicator to him of where his head had been when he'd decided to go to her as himself. Not his whole self. Not his humble side. No, after a night of mentally flogging himself for opening himself up to a woman he knew nothing about and then being shocked when told she wasn't the saint he'd built her up to be—he'd been angry.

Angry with himself for wanting to believe in happy endings.

Angry with his grandmother for pulling him back to reality.

Angry with Sage for shredding the progress he'd made.

He'd hired a limo, gotten the flowers, and headed off to Sage's apartment, not because he thought it would win her over, but because he needed to prove to himself that it wouldn't. Once again, he'd seen a problem as having only two possible outcomes: one, she jumped at the chance to be with him, thus proving her avarice; or two, she turned him away and confirmed her claim that neither wealth nor fame mattered to her.

He hadn't considered the third option—that he was an utter ass and she was kindhearted enough to think she could reach beyond that to the man she saw inside him.

She'd been falling in love with him, and what had he done? He'd thrown all that right back in her face, accused her of fucking him for his money.

One push from Delinda and I'm right back to being who I've always been. Sage dodged a bullet. She deserves so much better.

All I had to do was be honest with her—believe in her.

He looked at his superhero suit hanging in its case. It mocked the strength he didn't have in reality. His gaze drifted to the Wayne Easton wardrobe. Normal. Damaged, but recovering. Socially proactive Wayne. *Also, sadly a caricature of someone I'll never be.*

He met his eyes in the mirror. *Who the fuck do I think I'm fooling? I'm a self-absorbed, entitled narcissist. That's who I am—who I've always been—who I'll always be. People don't change.*

"I figured you'd be here," Reggie said as he entered the area.

"I don't want to talk about it, Reggie. Go away."

"I knew you'd say that, so I've brought reinforcements."

Eric glanced over his shoulder and saw Reggie's wife by his side. Tall, blonde, with classically beautiful features—she could easily have been a model or actress had she chosen either role. Instead, she'd chosen what she said was a more entertaining life with Reggie. "Hi, Alice. Don't mind me, I'm in a shitty mood."

"So, what happened?" Alice asked as bluntly as Reggie would have. They did indeed belong together.

"I fucked up," Eric said. "I know—that's nothing new."

She went to stand on one side of him, Reggie on the other. She said, "Do you know what I hear in my head when I look at myself in the mirror? I hear every child who ever made fun of me when I was an overweight kid, every boy who laughed at me when they heard I liked them, every snicker from the mean girls. Those voices don't go away. And there was a time in my life when they almost won. I starved myself down to ninety pounds. It didn't matter what the scale said. I thought I was still too big. I was in and out of the hospital, frustrating my counselors. I'd lost my job because of so many absences, had stopped paying my rent, and was getting ready to just give up."

"I'm so sorry you went through that," Eric said sincerely. This side of Alice wasn't something they'd ever spoken of before. *Because before now it's always fucking been about me.*

Alice smiled across at Reggie. "It was a lifetime ago. I met Reggie while he was doing electrical work in my apartment building, and he became my guardian angel. He checked in on me, nagged me to eat, dragged me out on crazy expeditions that took my mind off what I was going through."

Reggie's expression turned tender. "It was nothing."

Alice shook her head. "It was everything to me. You didn't judge me, and I needed that." She met Eric's eyes again. "Eventually I told him what I heard when I looked at myself. And do you know what he said?"

"No," Eric said, "but I want to."

"He told me his head was full of horrible things people had said to him, too, but that the trick was to not let those voices rule you. Denying them doesn't rid you of them. Facing them doesn't silence them. You have to embrace them as part of your journey, see them as something that you use to make yourself stronger. I still sometimes hate what I see in the mirror, but then I try to look at myself through kinder, stronger eyes. I strive to be healthy rather than perfect. When that doesn't work, I talk about it just to get it out of my head, and that helps."

Eric's eyes misted, and he looked away, his hands fisting at his sides. "I don't know who I am anymore. I thought I could put everything behind and become someone new but . . . now . . ." He waved at the three areas. "Which one am I?" he demanded of Reggie.

Reggie shared a look with Alice. "They're all you, Eric. You're an angry rich bastard, a natural entertainer, and a good guy at your core."

Alice added, "Maybe it's not about becoming someone new, but about embracing who you are. Yeah, you're angry, but you don't have to let your past win. Sure, everyone thinks of you in that ridiculous spandex suit when they see you, but that doesn't have to define you. Wayne Easton isn't someone you created; he's always been in you—in your generosity with everyone around you. Remember when you didn't want to do another movie as Water Bear Man, but went ahead and filmed another one anyway because you knew it would change the lives of everyone else involved? You employ more people to run this estate than some businesses have on their payrolls, and I've never seen you fire anyone—not even when Reggie suggested it. You're the first one to suggest a person deserves a second chance. That's the Wayne in you."

"She's good, isn't she?" Reggie asked proudly.

"Fucking incredible." Eric wiped a hand down his face. "Alice, I really screwed up with Sage. She was nothing but good to me, and I was horrible to her. I was angry and, if I'm honest, scared. She said she never wants to see me again, and I can't blame her. Even if I ask her for another chance, what kind of husband would I be? What kind of father? I'm a mess."

Alice went over to slip under Reggie's arm and hug him. "We're all a mess. Reggie doesn't talk much about his childhood, but he told me about it, and let me tell you, he's every bit as scarred as the rest of us."

"Hey," Reggie said in playful protest.

"I love you more for it," Alice said, going up on her tiptoes to kiss him on the cheek. "You would be a kind and loyal husband, Eric, because that's the kind of friend you have been to us. You'd be a caring father, because you take care of those you love. Our children adore you, and that says a lot. They don't care how many mistakes you made before they knew you. They only know how many times you've listened to them, remembered what was important to them. You can't fool children—they see your heart."

A spark of hope relit inside Eric. "How much of this should I tell Sage?" He gestured to the wardrobes. "If I get another chance with her . . . Is this something any woman wouldn't run from?"

Alice looked up at Reggie with love in her eyes. "With the right person, you don't have to hide who you are."

Reggie's cheeks flushed beneath her attention. "How much longer until the kids get back from school?"

Alice shot Eric a concerned glance. "Are you okay if we run?"

Eric chuckled and waved them away. "Get out of here. I'm fine."

He smiled as they hurried away, grateful to have them in his life and happy that they had each other. When he looked at himself through their eyes, a kinder view of himself shone back. What had Alice suggested? Embracing even the negative in him because it made him stronger?

He met his eyes in the mirror and thought about how beautiful Alice hated what she saw in her own reflection. He wondered what Reggie hid but now understood why he never spoke of his life before meeting Eric. If two of the most incredible people he knew shared the same struggles he did, then maybe, just maybe, it was time to be kinder to the man in the mirror.

I can be a real bastard.

But I'm a natural entertainer, and I'm determined to be a better person.

That's who I am.

Could that be enough for Sage?

It was time to tell Sage everything and let her make that decision. He took out his two cell phones and laid them side by side on the makeup table. He needed to call her—but as Eric or as Wayne?

Which one would she pick up for?

Something this important couldn't be rushed.

He would probably only have one chance to get it right.

Chapter Fourteen

The next morning Sage was woken by a loud pounding on her apartment door. She rolled over and pulled a pillow over her head. She had every intention of getting up and having a productive day, but not before the sun came up. The banging continued, followed by her neighbor yelling a profanity-sprinkled request for the noise to stop.

Sage hauled herself out of bed and threw the door open angrily.

Dressed in a business suit and pumps, Bella strode past her, then gave her a long once-over. "Never do that to me again. Tell me you're angry. Tell me you don't want to talk. But don't just ignore my calls. I was afraid you were dead."

Sage closed the door behind her. "I'm sorry."

"You should be. You scared the crap out of me." Bella took a deep breath and began to calm down. "Are you okay? What happened?" She checked her watch. "I have about thirty minutes before I'm due across town, so start spilling."

Sage sat on the couch and pulled a blanket up around her. "I'm not ready to hear 'I told you so.'"

Bella joined her on the couch. "Fine. I'll save all lectures for later. Just tell me if there's anything I should presently be worried about."

"No. It's over. You were right. Wayne Easton was hiding something."

"I know. It's kind of all over the internet that he came here yesterday."

Sage made a pained face. "So you already know."

Bella leaned over and touched Sage's arm. "I don't care about him. I care about you. What happened?"

There wasn't another soul on the planet Sage would have told the truth to, but she didn't have secrets from Bella. She backtracked to their day at Stonehenge and how he'd left without an explanation. Then how she'd recognized him from a news clip. It was impossible to look her friend in the eye as she confessed how the visit the day before had gone.

"You slept with him? Oh, Sage."

Sage shrugged. "I thought—I hoped it would get him to open up to me. It did. He told me exactly what he thought of me." She blinked back tears. "Of course he thinks I'm after his money."

"He said that?"

"Not even as nicely as I'm saying it."

"What a dick."

"Yeah." Sage hugged the blanket closer. "I didn't tell you about his grandmother yet. That's the icing on this cake."

Bella's jaw dropped open as Sage told her about what Delinda had said to her the day she'd gone to apologize.

"She can't threaten you," Bella ground out. "I'll—"

"Relax, Bella, we're past that." Sage updated her on Delinda's visit yesterday. "She says she's sorry about everything."

"She should be. What a bitch."

"She was trying to protect her grandson. He was once engaged to a woman who really *was* after his money."

"According to her. You don't know if any of that is true."

Sage closed her eyes and laid her head back on the couch. "I can't live like that, Bella. I can't doubt everything everyone says."

"He lied to you."

"I tell white lies to people every day. Not all lies are equal."

"Bullshit. People are either honest or they're not."

Sage raised her head and met her friend's eyes. "Then you must have a very low opinion of me."

Bella opened her mouth, closed it, then said, "You sure know how to sway someone. You could be a barrister. You know I love you."

"I know. I'm just saying I don't know how I feel about any of this. I threw him out and told him I never wanted to see him again, and I meant it. He left and hasn't called. I should feel good about that, but I don't."

"I'm sorry, Sage. I'm sorry this guy wasn't who you thought he was."

"Me too."

Sage's phone binged with an incoming message. She checked it.

Wayne: I was an ass. I should have told her who I was.

She frowned and went to put the phone down when her phone binged again, this time from a different number.

Eric here. I was the ass. I got scared and said things she has every right to hate me for.

Bing.

Wayne: You're right. You were the bigger ass. You shouldn't have left without telling her how much she means to you.

Bing.

Eric: You could have done the same. You knew she was the one for you from the first day. Admit it, she's all you've thought about since then.

"Who is messaging you?" Bella asked.

Not yet sure what she thought of it, Sage answered, "It's Wayne and Eric. They're both sending me messages, but like they're talking to each other. Eric's arguing with himself." She held the phone up for Bella to see.

"Oh my God, that is so w—"

"Sweet? You're right," Sage said, redirecting her. Yes, she was still angry with him. Once again, she would have turned down flowers and gifts, but this self-deprecating texting was winding its way through her anger.

"Okay." Bella didn't sound convinced. "Sage, I don't know about this guy."

Wayne: It's time to tell her everything.

Eric: Do you think she would meet me for coffee?

Wayne: You? Where could you go that everyone wouldn't be snapping photos and recording your conversation?

Eric: Well, she doesn't want to see you anymore, not since she found out about the scar.

"They're right," Sage said.

Bella's eyes rounded. "You realize he's just one person, right? And that one person is fucking with you? Block him."

Sage reread the messages and shook her head. "He's apologizing."

"While revealing a possible mental disorder."

"Bella, just because you don't understand him doesn't mean he's crazy. Do you know how many times in my life my parents have questioned my sanity because I didn't fit into their definition of normal?"

"This is different."

"To you."

"Touché."

Wayne: Invite her here. She trusted you enough to show you her life. Show her yours.

Eric: Here? You mean to my haven, the one no one knows about except my electrician? She'd never come here.

Wayne: She might if you told her that it would help her understand you.

Bella took out her own phone and began to type furiously.

"What are you doing?" Sage asked.

"I'm telling my assistant to clear my calendar for today. I know what you're about to say, and there is no way in hell you're going there alone."

Sage hugged the phone to her chest. Curiosity warred with the memories of everything Eric had said to her as he left. Was having her questions answered worth risking a repeat of that feeling? "I have to know. I don't expect it to fix what's wrong between us, but I want to understand him—even if who he is isn't someone I decide to be with. Does that make sense?"

Bella grudgingly nodded. "I guess. But I'm telling my office where we're going."

"That's fair."

"With instructions to send the police if they don't hear from me once every hour."

"That's a little much, but okay."

"And I'm making sure someone knows where we are at all times."

"That might actually be a good idea." Sage wanted to assure her it wouldn't be necessary. Eric was a public figure. He wasn't dangerous. Then Sage remembered how far his grandmother had gone to protect him. She considered herself irrepressibly optimistic, but that didn't mean she was oblivious to the fact that not everyone could be trusted.

With her thumb hovering over the incoming messages, Sage wasn't sure at first which one to respond to. She finally chose Eric.

Sage: I'm still angry with you, but I'm willing to hear what you have to say.

Eric: I could come to you, but it's hard to go anywhere without some kind of disguise.

Sage met Bella's eyes, then typed, I'll come to you.

He sent her the address along with detailed instructions. Sage almost told him she was bringing Bella but decided not to. Trust was like a snowdrop; if trampled it had a difficult time recovering.

A short time later, Bella pulled her car up to the back gate of a large walled property. It opened for them, then closed as soon as they pulled past it. "This is a new suit. If I piss myself, you're paying to have it cleaned."

"There's nothing scary about an automated gate."

They drove down a long gravel driveway toward the barn Eric had described in his text. "Right there. Eric said drive toward the bushes."

"It would be nice if he met us out here. I don't like this." Bella parked several feet from the bushes. "So, what now?"

Sage texted: I'm here.

Eric: Drive into the bushes.

Sage: I'm parked right next to them.

Eric: Then just keep pulling forward.

Aloud, Sage said, "He said we should keep pulling up to the bushes."

"I'm not scratching the front of this car," Bella protested.

Sage: Where are you?

Eric: Pull into the bushes and you'll see me.

Sage: No. I don't want to scratch my car.

Eric: Trust me?

It was a loaded question and one without a simple answer. I used to.

Eric: I won't let you down again. Pull forward.

Sage read the message to Bella, who swore and pulled forward. The bushes lifted and moved to the side, revealing an entrance that led beneath the barn. Sage sat forward. It was the coolest thing she'd ever seen.

Bella turned the engine off.

Eric appeared in the opening and walked toward the car. When he saw Bella, he walked over to her side and held out his hand. "Eric Westerly."

She looked from his outstretched hand to Sage, then reluctantly accepted his grip. "I'm being polite, but know I really want to punch you in the face."

His eyebrows rose and lowered, but he smiled politely at her before heading over to Sage's side of the car. "I'm glad you came."

There was so much she wanted to say, but she held it back and merely nodded.

His eyes were dark with emotion. "I don't blame you for bringing someone with you. I haven't given you much reason to trust me."

"What did you bring me here to see?"

He motioned down the dark tunnel. "It's in there."

"No way in hell," Bella said. "Not going to happen."

Eric took her refusal in stride. "Would you feel better about coming into the main house first?"

"You call that a house? I've seen palaces that were smaller," Bella said.

"I wouldn't mind seeing the inside of your home," Sage said to Eric, and gave Bella a pleading look.

"Mind if I get in the back, then?" he asked.

Sage got out of the car, and Eric folded his large frame into the tiny back seat. Sage almost smiled at the gymnastics involved. She glanced at Bella and remembered all the reasons why she shouldn't. Eric might be charming now, but that didn't excuse how he'd behaved the day before. Would anything he said mend her trust in him? Sage climbed back in, and the three drove over to the main house without speaking.

They parked in front of a large stone staircase and got out. The sprawling, stately home was ostentatious at best. That he lived here was a negative in her book. What kind of man would own such a home? Not one she could imagine herself with. Her heart sank a little. The staff lined up at the door simply reinforced her guess that she'd have her answers by the end of her visit, but they wouldn't be ones that changed her mind.

A casually dressed, tall, thin man with dark hair appeared at the door. "Eric, the kids are home today. They're at the pool, and Axton wants to show you his new dive. Do you want to bring your friends back there? Alice wants to meet Sage, too."

Taking a guess, Sage asked, "Is that Reggie?"

"It is," Eric said with a smile. He put his hand lightly on the small of Sage's back. Desire shot through her, but she fought it. She stiffened and frowned at him. He dropped his hand. "Would you like to meet his family?"

"Who is Reggie?" Bella asked.

"My electrician," Eric said, "but lately I like to call him my butler. Mostly because it annoys him."

"Ooooo-kay," Bella said.

Sage stepped away from both of them to meet Eric's friend. Part of her was relieved that he was real. It meant not everything Eric had said had been a lie. She held out her hand to Reggie. "Sage Revere."

Reggie smiled. "Nice to finally make your acquaintance. I've heard a lot about you." He shook her hand.

Sage's cheeks warmed. "All good, I hope."

He shrugged. "Enough to know how much it means to him that you're here."

She looked around at the grounds and the frontage of the house that seemed to go on forever in either direction. It was everything she didn't value about her old life, and so much more. Eric had gilded the old English estate beyond how any royal would. If this was who he was, she truly didn't know him. "I should probably leave now. I'm not sure I need to know more than this."

Reggie leaned down and with a twinkle in his eye said, "I'll let you in on a little secret. Eric hates the house, too. I've been busting his chops for years, making it more and more tacky. If it glitters and shines, that shit is my sense of humor."

Sage did a double take. Was he serious? He was. "Why would you do that to him?"

Reggie shrugged. "I keep hoping he'll wake up and tell me to stop. One day he will."

She nodded as she absorbed that Reggie was worried about Eric. His methods of helping his friend might be unorthodox, but Sage respected that he was there trying. "Why would he live here if he hates it?"

Reggie's expression turned serious. "It was falling into disrepair, and he said he didn't want to see it get reclaimed by the wilderness. Eric cares about a lot more than he lets on. He'd sell it, but everyone inside relies on him for their livelihood. He expects people to disappoint him, but he takes his responsibilities seriously when it comes to taking care of others."

"I'm glad he has you. He speaks highly of you," Sage said.

"Really?" Reggie perked up. "Was it about me being a knight of Vandorra? Wait, I bet he told you that I saved his sister's life."

"No. No, he didn't mention any of that."

"Then he probably told you that I'm a mechanical genius."

"Sorry." Reggie's expression fell a little until Sage added, "He said he couldn't imagine his life without you in it. I was telling him that Bella is my best friend—she accepts me exactly the way I am. He said he has a friend like that—you."

A huge smile spread across Reggie's face. "You are officially now my favorite person. Outside of my family. And Eric. And some of the staff, but I've known them a long time—"

Sage laughed. "I get the idea."

"Your friend looks like she's grilling Eric."

"She's a lawyer."

"I can tell. Eh, he'll be fine. Come on, I'll introduce you to my wife and kids."

Sage hesitated. "I can't leave Bella like that."

"Eric will win her over, don't worry."

"I don't know. Bella's pretty hard to impress."

Reggie motioned for Sage to follow him. "Bella is important to you, so she's important to Eric. It might take him a moment or two to convince her, but there's a reason half the world is in love with him."

"Bella," Sage called out, "do you mind if I—"

Bella waved for her to go. Apparently, her interrogation would require more time. Sage walked away with Reggie.

◆ ◆ ◆

Eric had been chewed up and spit out by directors. He'd been hounded by the press. He'd even survived questioning by an angry prince, but Sage's friend was a pit bull.

The first part of their conversation was less about what she wanted to know and more of a rant on what she thought of him. That was followed by what she thought of his grandmother and the wrath she would bring down upon Eric as well as his family if any of them hurt Sage.

After she paused for a breath, she rained questions on him—some he answered, and some he told her were none of her business. By the time she began to lose steam, he was smiling. In a way she reminded him of Reggie—an aggressive, polished version, anyway.

"And what the hell was that tunnel you wanted us to go down when we arrived?"

"It's my secret superhero lair."

She blinked several times. "You're serious."

"I'll show it to you when I show Sage."

Bella gave him one more stern look. "Don't think that her presence here means she has forgiven you. You hurt her."

His smile faded. "I know I did."

"Don't do it again," Bella said.

"I won't." Eric remembered something Reggie had said. "Listen, I'm an odd duck. Sage is an odd duck. I know I could make her happy."

Bella didn't look convinced.

They walked up the steps and through the house to the pool area in the back. Sage was sitting on the edge of the pool, shoes off, feet in the water, laughing at the antics of Reggie's children. Alice was seated beside her, threatening the children that their lives would be shorter if they splashed Sage again.

Bella smiled for the first time since she'd arrived. "I hope you're not dangerous, because Sage would love a lair."

"Wait until you see it. Reggie doesn't do anything halfway."

Alice and Sage stood as soon as they realized Eric and Bella had joined them. Sage introduced Alice to Bella, then gave her best friend a long, pointed look.

Bella looked from Eric to Sage and shrugged. "He doesn't seem dangerous."

Eric caught Reggie's eye and pointed at his own chest, mouthing, *Not dangerous*, then wiped a hand across his forehead in mock relief.

Reggie rolled his eyes.

Looking at the relaxed scene at the pool, Eric realized the presence of Reggie's family hadn't been an accident. He mouthed, *Thank you*.

Reggie smiled and motioned toward Sage with a thumbs-up.

Eric reciprocated before turning his attention back to Sage. Yesterday she'd been throwing shoes at his head and swearing. She looked relaxed and happy at the moment, but he didn't need Bella to tell him that it didn't mean she would let him off easily.

And that was okay.

He would do whatever it took to win back her trust. As he watched her laugh at something Alice said, doubts rose within him—was he good enough for her? What would she think of him once she knew he'd put himself in rehab?

She turned and caught him watching her, and her smile fell away. She had her doubts, too.

There was a time when that would have been enough for him to delay sharing everything with her, but she deserved a full disclosure.

Everything.

And if after that she decided she didn't want to see him again, he would somehow find the strength to respect that.

Chapter Fifteen

With kids running ahead of them, Reggie and Alice with them, there was nothing intimidating about entering the tunnel entrance that led beneath the barn. Even Bella looked relaxed as she walked beside Sage.

Eric spoke as he entered. "I'd appreciate your discretion regarding the existence of what you're about to see. No one knows about it."

Bella gestured to the children. "How secret could it be?"

"Not only are my children a vault with shit like this," Reggie said with indignation, "but Axton helped me design it. People don't trust kids anymore. But I'd put my faith in any child in the kids' classes before half the adults I know."

"Amen to that," Alice said.

Sage directed her question to Reggie's oldest. "Which part did you design?"

He chattered away as they walked about the initial design, planning the electrical and plumbing, and placement of certain things. The tunnel opened up to a large area. One side was for the storage of Wayne's Ford and a collection of old things that looked like they belonged at a garage sale. The other side was flanked by large wardrobe units and a sizable mirror above a sink and table.

The children dragged Sage from one area to the next, explaining what was in each and which part they'd played in building the automated system. Sage considered herself well educated, but she didn't know half the terms the children used regarding how it all worked.

Reggie looked about as proud as any father could. "Some families play Scrabble. This is our game night."

Sage walked over to the makeup area. There, in a clear box, was the silicone scar. She ran her hand over the outside of the container. "Was it research for a part? Or some sick game?"

From close beside her, Eric answered, "Neither." He took her hand in his and turned her toward him. "To understand why I did it, you have to understand what I was seeking."

She tightened her hand around his while searching his face. "Then tell me."

In the background, she heard Alice ask Bella if she'd like to see the upper part of the barn. Bella must have agreed, because a moment later only Sage and Eric were left in the room.

Eric's eyes darkened with emotion. "I'm not proud of a lot of what I'm about to tell you, but each piece fits into the next, and without it the rest doesn't make sense. You might decide it makes no sense anyway, but at least you'll know."

Sage held her breath, waiting for him to finally let her in.

To her surprise, he started his story back in Boston. The childhood he described had been a privileged one, but only in the material sense. He spoke of his parents' divorce, which had torn his family in two, how he became someone who felt he didn't fit into either family until ultimately he left both behind. He outlined his tumultuous relationship with his grandmother and swore he would never forgive her for her latest interference.

He told her how Water Bear Man started as a favor for a friend and his fiancée before it took a dark turn. He explained how he'd never felt worthy of the money and fame that had come to him so easily and how he'd donated the proceeds of the first movie simply because it disgusted him.

He shook his head. "I feel like a thirsty man surrounded by salt water. I can't walk down the street without being mobbed. I can't take Reggie's children to the zoo or the beach. Not as Eric. Every woman I date, every person I meet, sees me in terms of what I can do for them. I could have a thousand people here if I said I was hosting a party, but not one of them would care that I love black-and-white movies. They wouldn't be able to tell you a thing about me outside of my career. I started to feel like I didn't exist anymore." He nodded toward the superhero suit. "He took over my life, and I hated him for it."

"I can understand that," Sage said.

"At first I stopped doing appearances; then I withdrew more and more. I couldn't sleep, so I took pills to help. Then I couldn't get out of bed, so I took pills for that, too. The pills stopped working, so I moved on to stronger drugs that would. I was in a bad place. Very bad. Like, I started hoping I wouldn't wake up. Had nothing changed, I probably wouldn't be here."

This was the pain she'd sensed in him; this was what he hid. "I'm so sorry."

He caressed her cheek gently. "My sister Rachelle came to London and pretty much kicked my ass into a rehab clinic. I don't know how to even begin to thank her and her husband."

"I'm sure seeing you doing better is all the thanks they need."

Eric shook his head. "No. See, that's how I used to think. Somewhere along the way, I let my focus become all about me and how I felt. I knew I could do better. I knew there was another way, but I couldn't find it as Eric or as Water Bear Man. I needed to step outside my life and discover who I am without all this. So I disguised myself with a scar, rented an apartment. I needed time as just me. Not the heir to a fortune, not a joke of an actor, not any of the versions of me I hated."

"And then you met me."

A corner of his mouth curled in a half smile. "Yes, I met you. You were not part of my plan."

My radar didn't fail me. "That's why you were upset when Bella took a photo of you. You must have been afraid we recognized you."

"I was." He combed his hand gently through her hair. "I shouldn't have lied to you about my name, but I wasn't ready to return to my life, and I didn't know you well enough to tell you any of this."

"I can understand that."

"I didn't expect to fall for you."

Sage stepped back from him as conflicting emotions swirled within her. The memory of the day before was still too vivid to simply accept what he was saying. "But you didn't fall for me. Not really. You thought I was after your money."

"Not until . . ."

His voice trailed away, as if he understood that the reason he'd doubted her was not what mattered. When his feelings for her had been tested, he'd assumed the worst of her.

Sage wrapped her arms around herself. "When we met, I thought I was meant to help you. You were different, but I felt your pain. As I got to know you, I wanted more. There were so many times when I believed we really connected. I thought you understood me in a way no one had before. Now I don't know how much of that was a lie."

"Just my name." He looked down at the scar on the table. "And what I implied about myself."

"And our connection? It couldn't have been what I thought it was. It felt real. It felt solid, but it wasn't. You didn't come in that limo because you thought I wanted that, did you? You were testing me." She swallowed hard. "How did I not see that?"

"I am so sorry, Sage. I wish I could go back and not doubt you, but I did. I messed up." He waved at the wardrobes in disgust. "Every version of me did." He slapped the side of the wardrobe with his open hand. "I am exactly as fucked-up as that sounded, but I need to know if you can love a man like me."

"I don't know." Sage's heart was breaking for him. Part of her wanted to wrap her arms around him and promise to help him make everything better, but a little voice inside her said it wouldn't be the best choice for either of them. She looked from the superhero costume to Wayne Easton's wardrobe to Eric Westerly's fancy clothes and suddenly felt overwhelmed. "I need some time to absorb all of this."

She stepped back.

He grasped both of her upper arms. "If you give me another chance, I swear on my life I will change."

"People don't change." She frowned at his hands on her arms, and he instantly released her. *But they can find their way to a better version of themselves. I have to believe it's possible, because I'm on that very journey myself.*

Is he? That would require knowing who he actually is, and how do I figure that out?

"Tell me what you want, Sage. How do I prove to you that I want you more than I've ever wanted anything? Not just in my bed. I want it all. I want to be the man I am when I'm with you."

She raised her hand in a plea for silence. She needed a moment to sort out how she was feeling. She had lost trust in herself and in him. In the past, whenever she'd felt lost, she'd told herself that she had a gift for knowing what people needed.

It takes so little for us to question ourselves, doesn't it?

It was a lot to take in—the history with drugs, the lair, his lack of faith in her. Okay, the lair was actually cool. The rest could not be dismissed. He was saying all the right things, but words meant very little in the end.

It bothered her that he had distanced himself from his family. For someone who had spent a lifetime chasing hers, she didn't know if she could be with a man who ran from his own. Wouldn't such a man one day leave her as well?

It would have been easy to walk away and say he wasn't worth the effort, but wasn't that what her parents had decided about her? *Maybe I wasn't a child who fit into my parents' lives, maybe I didn't always make it easy for them, but shouldn't love reach beyond that?*

She could almost hear Bella saying, "Don't be a doormat, Sage."

In her eyes, I should be strong enough to tell him to go fuck himself.

But that's not me, and I wouldn't like myself if it were. I want him to find happiness—with or without me. "I'll give you another chance, but on one condition."

Their eyes met and held.

"Name it," he said with conviction.

"I'd like to have dinner with your family."

"Which ones?"

"All of them. I appreciate everything you told me today, but I don't know what I believe when it comes to you. You tested me, and although I don't believe in tit for tat, I need to see you with them."

"Most of my family is in the United States."

She shrugged. "That's my condition." If he said no, she would have her answer to her other questions as well.

"When you say all of them, that doesn't include my grandmother, does it?"

Sage took another centering breath, during which she found her answer. "Yes, it does. I know you're angry with her, but families fight and make up. At least, the kind of family I want to be part of does. I know it seems like a huge request, but if you really want to prove that I matter to you—invite me to that dinner."

"And then?"

Deep breath. "Then we'll go for coffee."

With a pained expression, he said, "I have no idea if they'll all come."

"Then let me meet the ones who will."

He nodded. "Okay." He let out a slow breath. "Okay."

They stood in tense silence for several minutes. Finally, Sage said, "So, I should probably go find Bella."

"Wait," Eric said. He gave her a brief kiss so tender her toes curled. "I needed that."

Me too.

He cocked his head to one side. "Since it's a family gathering, would you like to invite yours?"

"That's not necessary." One family at a time.

Am I asking him for more than I'd be willing to do? "I don't think they would come."

A touch of wry humor entered his eyes. "They would if I told my grandmother we wanted them there."

Sage choked on a laugh. "That would get my mother there, anyway, but not for the right reasons."

"Think about it," Eric said, then offered her his hand. She accepted it. His touch filled her with warmth and desire, but also more—so much more. They walked out of the lair and into the sunshine together. Sage knew they still had a long way to go, but he wanted to work things out, and so did she.

She could worry and dissect every step they took together, or she could trust that things worked out the way they were meant to. "Eric?"

"Yes?" He bent to hear her better.

"That is one kick-ass secret lair."

He chuckled and nodded. "I hoped you'd like it."

A short time later, Eric stood beside the barn watching Sage drive off with Bella. His fantasy of her tossing her arms around his neck and begging him to carry her off to his bed because she completely forgave him hadn't quite been realized, but he didn't hate how it had turned out.

She was willing to try again, and that was the important part. *Love* was still a word he was trying to wrap his head around, but her happiness mattered more to him than any reservations he had about her request.

She could have asked him to walk over hot coals and he would have done it. She hadn't, of course, because it wasn't in her nature to cause pain to anyone else. She believed in light and hope and that there was good in everyone. It was his fault that her faith in him had been shaken, so it was up to him to do what he could to repair it.

And if that meant gathering the Westerlys—so be it.

From beside him, Reggie said, "It looks like things went well."

"Yes and no. She asked for more than an explanation and an apology."

Reggie pocketed his hands in the front of his jeans. "More what? Deodorant?"

Eric shot a glare at his friend. "Fuck you."

He snapped his fingers. "She's one of those women who wants to have twelve kids."

"We didn't discuss that, but no, I don't think so."

He brought a hand up to his heart as if experiencing real pain. "She wants you to get rid of the lair."

Eric rolled his eyes skyward. "No. She loved it. If things work out, hell, I bet she wants one of her own."

Reggie rubbed his chin. "Interesting."

"None of what she saw in there seemed to concern her."

"That's a hurdle not every woman would clear."

"Yeah. And I told her about rehab. That didn't send her running, either."

"Then what's the problem?"

"She wants to meet my family. She asked me to invite her to a dinner with all of them in attendance—at least as many as will come."

Reggie whistled. "Holy shit."

"Even Delinda. The dinner is Sage's one condition for giving us another chance."

"I'm gaining a whole new respect for your little plant psychologist. Damn. So, are you going to do it?"

"If I want to be with her, I have to."

Reggie frowned. "It sounds too easy. No woman says she wants to meet your family because she gives a shit about them."

"She said it's a test."

"Oh, that's bad. She threw down the gauntlet. All in or all out—based on one dinner. Don't take it the wrong way, Eric, but we're pulling Alice in on this one. I've met your family. They are going to need some serious prepping."

Reggie called Alice and his children over. "Okay, listen up, everyone. Eric needs our help."

Eric looked at the children and said, "Reggie, maybe we should talk about this another time."

Reggie shrugged. "If you want this to work out, we all need to be on the same page." Then he frowned. "Unless you weren't going to include us in that dinner party . . ."

Alice smoothly inserted herself into the conversation. "What dinner are you referring to?"

"We're going to a party!" Liana asked. "Will you have an ice sculpture? Can it be of a penguin? I love penguins."

Eric rubbed a hand over his face. Not a single Westerly had been invited yet, and already he'd lost control of the dinner. He looked down at smiling Liana and up at Reggie, who was still waiting for his answer. They were his family by choice. If Sage agreed to be part of his life, they would be part of hers as well. He winked at Axton. "One penguin ice sculpture—check. Do you have a special request?"

Axton considered his question seriously. "Could I install two secret doors? I could disappear and reappear as if by magic."

Eric threw back his head and laughed, then ruffled the boy's hair. "You know what? That sounds like exactly what this dinner will need. Make it so." He met Reggie's eyes over his son's head. "I hate when you're right."

Reggie hugged Alice to his side. "Then you must hate me all the time, right, Alice?"

Alice elbowed him for the smugness. "Seriously, could one of you please tell me what's going on?"

The kids lost interest halfway through Eric's explanation and ran off to play. "So, that's it. One dinner and we're back on track."

Looking less sure than Reggie had, Alice chewed her bottom lip. "Are you sure you want us there? The kids—"

Eric looked back and forth between his two best friends and said, "Might be the only saving grace to the evening. If everything goes south, at least we'll have an ice sculpture and two new hidden passages."

"You should probably invite King Tadeas. Your grandmother is on her best behavior around him," Alice added.

"Bam," Reggie said. "And that's why I married her. My woman is brilliant."

Eric nodded. "It is an undeniable fact that she's your better half."

One of the children yelled, and Alice excused herself to confirm that they were both still alive.

"What's the likelihood that this will turn out well?" Eric asked seriously as he watched Alice wagging a finger at the children, who paused, then took off again.

"I'd say 50 percent." One of the children yelled for Alice again, and Reggie cleared his throat. "Maybe 40."

Chapter Sixteen

During the ride back to her apartment, Sage was reminded why she treasured Bella's friendship. It had been a wild day full of emotional ups and downs. Bella had probably formed a strong opinion of Eric and his friends, but instead of forcing them upon Sage, she asked, "How did your talk go?"

Sage shared everything she'd learned. Despite the number of times she'd told Bella that they had different ways of seeing things, she valued Bella's opinion. She knew Bella felt the same. Without each other they might have become the extreme versions of themselves. It was why Bella shared her jaded views of the cases she worked on; Sage could sway her to a more optimistic place. Sharing gave them both the opportunity to pull each other back from the brink. "Out of everything, what bothered me the most was the way he spoke of his grandmother—how he just wrote her off."

Bella shot her a quick glance. "Because your family did that to you?"

Ouch. "Yes. I like him, Bella. I mean, when I'm with him, I feel like we were meant to be, but I don't want to set myself up for being left behind again. Maybe it's not realistic, but I always imagined marrying a man with a big family that I would become a part of."

"Oh, hon. No man, not even a great one, should be your answer to fixing what you hate about your life. You were dealt a crappy hand when it came to parents. He might have been, too. Would you want to be held accountable for yours?"

"I thought you didn't like Eric."

"I didn't, but he's different than I thought. His friends are loyal to him. His staff adores him. Those kids idolize him. You can't fake that. I'm not saying he doesn't have issues, but I'm glad I went with you today, because now I see what you like about him—he has heart."

"Yes," Sage said. "Well, now I'm afraid to tell you what I asked him to do."

"Spill it, Sage."

"I told him that the only way I'd consider giving us a second chance is if he gathered his family, even the ones in the States, for a dinner and invited me to it. I need to see him with them. Do you think that's an unfair request?"

Bella took a minute or so before answering. "I think it's genius, very intuitive. Regardless of how the dinner goes, the simple fact that he would gather his family because you asked him to will say volumes about how he feels about you. If he doesn't want to be bothered enough to do it . . . then that will say something as well."

Sage brought steepled fingers to her mouth. "He'll do it."

"That you believe he will tells me how you feel about him. I hope this works out for you, Sage. I really hope it does."

Turning somewhat in the car seat to face Bella, Sage asked, "How would you feel about attending that dinner with me?" Before Bella had a chance to answer, Sage added, "You'd have to be on your best behavior."

Bella smiled. "Aren't I always?"

"You know what I mean."

"I'll be good, I promise. I'll keep all of my opinions to myself—as long as you don't seat me next to his grandmother."

They laughed over that. A few minutes later Bella received a message from her neighbor. She played it aloud via her car's Bluetooth. "Hello, Miss Mars, I just received your invitation to the garden party, and I would love to attend, especially since it's right next door. I look forward to getting to know you better as well."

Sage's mouth dropped open. "Aha! Look who is telling fibs now."

"What was I supposed to say? 'Hello, my friend found a stranger she thinks would be perfect for you—can we bring him over'?" Bella rolled her eyes. "But I do want you to appreciate that I am opening my home to this insanity for *you*, which doesn't mean I won't have cameras set up in each room."

Sage chuckled. "Come on, you like the idea of playing matchmaker."

A telling smile spread across Bella's face. "Okay, she seems like a very nice woman. If this guy doesn't rob her blind or kill her in her sleep, it'll be heartwarming to know I helped bring them together."

Sage burst out laughing. "You're setting the bar pretty low. Imagine that as a slogan for a dating site? 'Find love through us—almost none of our couples rob and murder each other.'"

Bella shook her head and laughed along. "You make me sound horrible."

Sage held up her fingers and pinched an inch of air. "Perhaps just a teensy-weensy bit pessimistic. Hey, do you have the rest of the day off?"

"At least a couple more hours, why?"

"I could ask John Kirby if we can meet him for an early dinner. You'll be far less likely to tackle him when he reaches for any silverware if you get to know him first. He's an incredibly sweet man."

"You know, that actually sounds like a nice way to round off our day. I have a tough case to review tonight. Bring on Dog Man."

Sage sent John a text. He replied that he would love to dine with them. Yes, Bella would breathe easier if she met him before allowing him into her home, but Sage was also glad to have something else to occupy her thoughts.

Waiting for Eric to make the next move in their relationship would not be easy. She wanted to call and ask him if he was planning that dinner. And if he was—when?

Would he contact her while he decided?

Would he wait until he had everything organized?

She clasped her hands on her lap and tried to look as if her heart wasn't doing somersaults in her chest. There was a chance Bella mentioned—he might decide that what they had was not worth dealing with his family.

Or everything he'd told her could be either an outright fabrication or a creative exaggeration.

As a means of survival, she'd trained herself to reject negative possibilities. *Because I need to believe that my parents love me? Have I given them that much control over who I am?*

"They're not coming back for you, Sage," Bella had told her.

No, they're not.

And she's right—expecting a man to come with the perfect family to replace them isn't fair.

She spent the next few miles asking herself some tough questions. By the end, there was one unshakable belief still standing: she needed to see Eric with his family—not to confirm who *they* were, but to confirm who *he* was.

She wished she could believe in him—take that leap of faith. Not being able to forced her to confront her own fears and flaws.

"Bella, I have to face that Eric might never call me again."

"That's a possibility."

"And even if he does, none of this may work out."

Bella shot her a concerned look. She turned her attention back to the road and frowned. "The average number of people killed or seriously injured in car accidents each year in London is about two thousand. There are over sixty pedestrian fatalities from vehicles, and thirty more will die by being hit by some random falling or thrown object. When you start to think about that, it's scary to even leave your home. But ten or so people die each year in their own beds from some mysterious suffocation. Even before you get out of bed, there's a chance you'll start your day as a statistic."

"Is this supposed to make me feel better?" Sage joked.

"What I'm trying to say is that one of the things I admire about you is that you don't think like that. The sun shines on your face and you don't fixate on the cancer or wrinkles it's giving you. The world needs people like you."

"The oblivious?"

"The joyful. When I look at things through your eyes, I remember that not everything is a battle. You remind me to look for the good in people, to give second chances, and to put aside what I'm afraid of long enough to appreciate the wonder of the moment. Don't let any man change you. I don't know if Eric will call you or not, but I hate to see you think he won't. Have faith in him—not because he deserves it, but because you'll be happier if you do."

Sage smiled. She'd been wrong to think Eric was the first one to fully see and accept her. Bella would probably never be able to stop warning Sage to look both ways each time they stepped off a curb, but hearing the acceptance in her friend's voice brought tears to Sage's eyes. "Do you know how much I love you?" she asked.

"Right back at you. Should I tell you that I had a background check done on your John Kirby? He's clean. Not so much as an outstanding parking ticket."

"Whew," Sage said with a laugh. "And yet you are still worried about having him at your home?"

"Do you know how many felons are first-time offenders?" Bella asked in a serious tone, then winked.

Sage's mood lifted. She'd been feeling bad that she didn't have family members she wanted to introduce Eric to, but he'd already met the one who really mattered.

◆ ◆ ◆

The next day, Eric was driving across town wondering if he'd lost his mind. He could have simply called every member of his family and invited them to the dinner, but he'd kept asking himself why Sage had asked to meet them in the first place. What was she hoping to see? What would have someone like her running for the door?

He thought about what she'd told him about her own family. It hadn't sounded like a healthy situation. They'd sent her to boarding school, used her as a pawn to hurt each other, and still, for whatever reason, thought she was a disappointment. Her parents sounded an awful lot like someone he knew. Before he invited anyone to anything, he was damn well going to have a boundary-clarifying conversation with Delinda.

From Bella, Eric knew that although his grandmother had threatened Sage, she had also apologized to her. Still, she wouldn't have made the list had Sage not insisted, but he'd promised to invite her and he would. Delinda didn't have to accept, and he would also make that point clear.

He'd considered calling his grandmother, but decided to drop by her London home instead. This was a conversation best done face-to-face.

Her butler opened the door before Eric knocked. "Mr. Westerly, your grandmother will be pleased by this surprise."

"I appreciate your optimism, Michael. I wish I were as sure of the outcome."

After closing the door behind Eric, Michael said, "She had a difficult time last night. The doctor was here this morning. Nothing serious, but he suggested she rest today."

"What's wrong?"

"Her blood pressure was higher than normal. She is scheduled for some tests, but the doctor thought it might be the stress she has been under."

"The stress?" Eric asked. He was trying to absorb the idea of Delinda being anything less than an immortal force of nature.

Michael cleared his throat. "If I may be frank—she has not been herself since Rachelle was kidnapped. She believes she failed to protect her. You're aware of the circumstances around your grandfather's death?"

Eric nodded.

Michael continued, "Mrs. Westerly believes she failed him as well. She was trying to do better by you."

Eric folded his arms over his chest. "Her methods leave a lot to be desired."

"You've never acted poorly out of fear?" Michael asked after a pause. "I did not realize you were the perfect Westerly."

It would have been an uncomfortable conversation to have with anyone, but with a member of his grandmother's house staff? "I don't like your tone."

Michael stepped closer until he was nose to nose with Eric. "I don't give a fig what you do or don't like. Do you know how many times your grandmother went to your home and begged to see you? Do you feel any remorse or take any responsibility for your relationship with her? Your grandmother is eighty-two years old. If you have come here with any intention other than a friendly visit, I will personally throw you out on your ass."

Michael was several inches shorter than Eric, but something in his eyes said he was capable of carrying out that threat. Eric took a deep breath. Even though he hadn't been close to Delinda in years, the idea of losing her to the finality of death sent a mild panic through him. Perhaps it was the wrong day to discuss the dinner, but he did want to see her. "That won't be necessary."

Michael stepped back and resumed his professional stance. "Then I shall announce your arrival."

"No, I'm fine announcing myself. Where is she?"

"In her library." He pointed toward a door at the other end of the foyer.

Eric almost walked away, then stopped. "Thank you, Michael, for being there for Delinda."

Michael's lips twisted in a small smile. "She was there for me when I was in need. I am not blind to her flaws, but she does what she does out of love. Of all her grandchildren, you're the most like her. Perhaps that's why you clash as you do."

"Alike? I don't see—"

"You are both highly creative, highly sensitive people who lash out when hurt. You have difficulty trusting people. Neither of you is quick to forgive, but you're fast to judge. Oh, I'd say you have much more in common with your grandmother than you realize."

Eric walked away from Michael with those words echoing in his head. He would have loved to have dismissed Michael's assertions as nothing more than bullshit, but they rang true. He was everything his grandmother's butler accused him of and worse.

As he stood at the door of Delinda's library, he asked himself what Sage would do in the same situation. He had recent confirmation. He had hurt her, and she had not only listened to his explanation but also given him a chance to redeem himself.

Was that what she needed to see from him?

Forgiveness required allowing a person another chance to take a swipe at him, but he'd already tried the alternative. Closing people out of his life, protecting himself, had brought him to a dark and lonely place he never wanted to return to.

He opened the library door quietly and was given a moment to observe Delinda without her realizing he was there. She was seated in a chair, a blanket on her lap, looking out the window as if she were visiting a distant place or time. When not pinned down by her piercing gaze, he was able to see the frailness of her frame. In his mind she would always be a larger-than-life, overly opinionated, dominating presence—but he needed to reconcile that with the slight woman before him who would not be with him forever.

"Grandmother," he said softly. She didn't hear him, so he said it again, louder.

She turned, and when she realized it was him, such joy shone in her eyes that he was temporarily overcome with shame for the way he had treated her. She struggled to rise, but he rushed to her side and pulled up a chair beside her.

"Eric, what are you doing here?"

He wanted to ask her how she felt, but that would reveal that he knew she'd seen a doctor. Delinda was too proud to want that. Eric remembered the day Sage had brought him along as she'd looked for a new client. The answers came to her when she opened herself to hearing them. He took a breath, quieted his thoughts, then smiled as one came to him. "I need your help with something."

Delinda leaned forward, touching his hand. "Anything. You know that."

He took a leap of faith—for Sage as well as himself. "I'd like to host a dinner so everyone can meet Sage, but I'd like it to happen here in London. I'm talking about everyone: Mom, Dad, Brett, Rachelle, Spencer, Nicolette . . . spouses and children. Everyone. I'd like to do it this weekend. I know it's short notice, but could you help me make it happen?"

Tears misted Delinda's eyes, but she blinked them back and raised her chin. "I can have everyone here by tomorrow morning if you'd like."

No doubt she could.

He gripped her hand in his. If she started crying, he'd lose it right along with her, and neither of them wanted that. "By Saturday would be perfect. I'll understand if any of them are too busy to come. It's definitely short notice."

"They'll come," his grandmother said softly. "Nothing is more important than family."

After a few awkward moments, they began planning the menu as well as the guest list. Delinda said, "I'm assuming you'll want Reggie and his family in attendance?"

He was surprised that she thought their presence would be proper, but maybe there was another side to her. "I also think we should invite Michael."

Delinda cleared her throat. "Yes, I think I'll require his assistance that day."

"And your suitor is welcome as well," Eric said to lighten the mood.

"My suitor?" Delinda sniffed and her eyebrows rose. "I am too old to have a such a thing."

"Clandestine paramour?"

His grandmother shook her head, but the hint of a smile tugged at her lips. "You're incorrigible. Tadeas is a friend, that's all."

"It's not your fault, Grandmother, that even kings bow before your charm."

"My *charm*." Delinda rolled her eyes. "I'm not sure many would say that's a trait of mine."

"We all have our crosses to bear," Eric joked. "Mine is how outrageously good I look in spandex. Not everyone can pull off the look. Imagine Brett trying to."

Delinda laughed at that. "Oh, he would be too mortified to leave the dressing room."

"It sure would make his board meetings interesting."

They shared a laugh over that image, and for a moment Eric felt as close to her as he had as a child. "Grandmother . . ."

"Yes, Eric?"

Leap of faith. "I love you."

This time a tear did spill down her cheek. She wiped it away impatiently. "I am so sorry, Eric. I didn't know how much Sage meant to you. I thought you were lost and I needed to—"

He took her hand in his again and gave it a squeeze. "I was before I met Sage. She lives by her own rules. She sees the best in everyone, even those who disappoint her—and I've done my fair share of that. I understand how her career looks on paper, but when you see her in action, it's nothing less than inspirational. When I'm with her, I start to believe there might be a reason we're all here. I don't know how to explain it better than that—except that she gives me hope."

"Oliver always brought out the best in me. I miss him as much today as the day I lost him. Tadeas is the same. Maybe that's why I'm so afraid to say yes to him—I don't know if I could bear to lose another man I love."

"Sage would say he's worth the risk. I think you'd really like her, Grandmother. She's strong like you—in a much less abrasive way."

"Well, isn't that sweet," Delinda said, though she was smiling.

He wagged a finger at her. "So stop threatening to have her arrested."

Delinda sighed dramatically. "If I must. I'll even make an effort to be nice to her family."

"Nah, they sound like assholes."

Delinda let out a surprised laugh, then a thoroughly amused cackle. "You're awful."

"I learned from the best," Eric said with a grin.

The door of the library closed, bringing Eric's attention to the fact that Michael might have been listening the whole time. Rather than offending Eric, though, it was a testament to Michael's protectiveness of Delinda.

Eric decided to invite him to the dinner personally.

Chapter Seventeen

The next few days crawled by for Sage. Eric texted her each morning to say he hoped she had a good day. She responded each time that she hoped he had the same. He texted her again each evening to ask how her day had gone. She gave him a brief recap, then asked him about his day. The strained texts highlighted how much both of them were holding back. She desperately wanted to ask him if he was organizing a dinner with his family, but she didn't. He claimed to miss her, but he didn't ask to see her again. It was a test of Sage's ability to remain positive, but she did. Not for him, but, as Bella had said, because Sage wasn't happy when she expected to be disappointed.

Midafternoon, Sage was retrieving her mail from the first floor of her apartment building when her phone rang. Her heart fluttered with excitement until she saw the number was her mother's. "Hi, Mom."

"How are you, Sage?"

"I'm good."

"I wanted to thank you for finally doing something right. I received a call from Delinda Westerly. She said she met you and was so impressed that she needed to meet me as well. *Needed*, can you believe it? We're having tea tomorrow."

"And you'd like me to join you?"

"Oh my goodness, no. I'm calling to see if there is any lie I need to maintain regarding what you do for a living or anything else you might have told her." *Of course. Delinda couldn't like me unless I lied about myself.*

Sage tapped the mail on her forehead and said, "Mom, I love you. I will always love you. That doesn't mean I like you. Every time you call, I think this time will be the one when you want to see me because you miss me, because you finally realize that I'm more important than everyone you try so hard to impress. You might never make that call. You might always remain self-centered and narcissistic, but I'm not giving up hope on you. I am a good person, and I will keep my heart open so that if you do wake up and want a real relationship, it'll be possible. But I'm also a busy person who doesn't have time for you when you're like this. Good luck tomorrow, Mom. I have a feeling you'll need it." Her mother was sputtering in annoyance as Sage hung up on her.

And that was okay.

Sage looked at the mail in her hand and saw that one piece hadn't come through the post but had been delivered directly to her mailbox—a large, rectangular ivory envelope with gold-embossed print. She tore it open.

Careful script on expensive card stock held an invitation.

Sage,

The entire Westerly family invites you to join us at my home tomorrow evening, Saturday, at 5:00 p.m. for a meal and whatever mayhem might ensue as a result of our gathering. Please feel free to invite anyone you would like to accompany you.

RSVP as soon as you receive this, because I'll be holding my breath until you do,

Eric

After hugging it to her chest, Sage reread the invitation again and again. He had done what she'd asked. She texted Bella with the news, then read the invitation a few more times.

She stuffed the rest of her mail back into her box and headed out into the afternoon sun. She took out her phone while she walked and texted, I would love to.

He replied almost instantly. They're all here except my youngest sister, Nicolette. She's flying in tomorrow morning.

At the corner of her street, she let her feet guide her and smiled when she realized the direction she'd taken. I'm hungry. I think I'll get a sandwich at the place next to our coffee shop.

Eric: I'm always hungry.

Sage: Maybe I'll see you there.

He didn't respond immediately. I'll have to come as Wayne, unless you're okay with having absolutely no privacy.

She understood now that the scar was not a lie—it was a tool that freed him. I like Wayne. The only problem I ever had with him was his aggression toward clowns.

Eric: ??? Oh. Yeah. That's Reggie's sense of humor.

Sage: I figured.

Eric: It'll take me about thirty minutes to get to you.

Sage: I'll get us a table.

If Sage's feet touched the pavement after that, she didn't feel it. She kept smiling at strangers along the way as she texted Bella where she was going. Not only had he arranged the dinner she'd requested, but like her, he didn't want to wait until then to get together.

She accidentally bumped into someone going in the other direction. Sage apologized and was about to keep walking when the young woman asked, "Were you in the Eric Westerly video? The one with the flowers and the limo?"

"Uh, no. No, I wasn't."

"Sorry, you look just like her. Can I take a selfie with you anyway?"

Sage was shaking her head to refuse, but the woman had already lined up her shot and had taken it. She obediently smiled when the woman told her to, mostly because the entire exchange had caught Sage off balance. She was used to being invisible.

"Thanks, my followers will love this. I'll just say you might have been her. That'll be good enough. Cool." With that, the young woman disappeared into the crowd.

It was Sage's first taste of being in the public eye, and it gave her a new appreciation for what it must be like for Eric. It also made her worry that someone might see them together and see through Eric's disguise. He was hiding in plain sight. The only reason the scar worked was because no one had a reason to doubt it. She didn't want to be the reason they did.

Since he was probably already en route, she called rather than texted. "Hey."

"Hey, yourself. I'm halfway there."

"I'm not sure we should meet in public."

"Why?"

She told him what had just happened. "It was only once. It might be nothing, but I thought you should know. I'd hate for people to draw a connection between you and Wayne."

After a pause, he said, "I have an idea. It'll mean I won't be there for another hour, though. Is there somewhere else you need to be?"

There wasn't, but she couldn't imagine an appointment she wouldn't cancel to see him that day. "Don't worry about me. I love this area. I can definitely find something to do for an hour."

"Why don't we meet at the bathrooms of the fast-food place at the corner instead?"

"The bathrooms? That sounds deliciously clandestine," she joked.

He laughed. "Sage, if that sounds exciting, you'll love what I have planned for the rest of the day."

"Do we have plans for later?" Sage asked with coyness.

"We do now," he purred.

Bella would have needed to know why he wanted to meet by the bathrooms. She would have asked for an itinerary for the rest of the day. Sage preferred to trust in the magic of what was budding between them. "Then I'll see you in an hour."

"Sage?"

"Yes?"

He seemed to want to say more but finished with, "See you soon."

Eric rushed from store to store until he found the perfect gifts for Sage. Seated in his Ford, he put them all into a gift bag and sped to meet her. Barring any unforeseen traffic snafus, he'd be right on time.

A short while later, he scored an amazing parking spot, grabbed his gift bag, and sprinted into the fast-food place. He didn't trust easily, but he knew she would be there . . . based solely on the fact that she'd said she would be.

And there she was—standing near the bathroom doors. He had the luxury of watching her expression light up when she saw him. Never, no matter how long he lived, would he forget how her smiled rocked through him. She was his as surely as he was hers. He could picture everything in that moment—waking up beside her, holding their first child, growing old with her. It was all right there in her smile.

He kissed her lips lightly in greeting, not wanting to call attention to either of them yet. Then he slid the gift back into her hand. "Open it in the bathroom. I'll grab two sodas and meet you at a table."

She had a wonderfully dazed look after their kiss, but nodded and disappeared into the ladies' room. He was just about to sit at a table nearby when she emerged.

Her brown eyes were now green, hidden partially by nerdy black-rimmed glasses. Her beautiful chestnut curls were covered by shoulder-length straight blonde hair. She was still attractive, but just different enough so that anyone who had seen her on social media wouldn't recognize her.

The huge grin on her face said everything he needed to know. He waved her to the table, and they sat across from each other, sipping their sodas as if it were the most normal day for both of them.

"Hello," he said. "My name is Wayne Easton."

She bit her bottom lip. "Hi. I'm—I'm—Lorna St. Cloud."

"Perfect!" he said, reaching across the table to take her hand in his. "Depending on how much you enjoy this date, we could make it official and get you identification." Her eyes rounded and he quickly added, "For your new name. Reggie can arrange credit cards, driver's license, an online presence, everything."

"Oh, of course." She smiled in relief, but there was a funny look in her eyes as if for a second she'd thought he was asking a much larger question. "I'd like that. Although I'll write my own bio."

Eric laughed. "That's probably for the best." Part of him wanted to announce that although he wasn't prepared to propose that day, he could see it happening soon. He'd already attempted to say it, though, and had expressed himself poorly. He decided to take it slower with her. He would have loved to drag her out of there and into the nearest hotel room, but there would be time for that later. When dealing with forever, there was no need to rush. "You'll be meeting my whole family tomorrow. Tell me more about yours."

She described being brought up by nannies as a young child before being sent off to boarding school full-time when her parents divorced. Although she was kind in her descriptions of both of her parents, he already knew how deeply they had disappointed her. What he hadn't known until that conversation, though, was how she had taken that pain and grown it into a philosophy of finding happiness through helping others. He fell a little more in love with her with each new thing he learned about her.

They broke down and ordered fast food, then decided to walk it off. Time flew when he was with her. They talked about her life, his life, everything they had in common, and everything they didn't. She had endless questions about the people she'd meet the next day, and as he described his family, he realized there was something he admired about each of them. With her, he could finally admit that the rift between them had been his fault as much as theirs. He hadn't known how to fit into either family.

"Delinda, my father, and Brett were nearly identical in beliefs and work ethic. None of them understood my desire to be an actor. My mother and younger siblings had gone off and created an entirely new family. She didn't want my father's money or anything to do with his lifestyle. I would visit and see Rachelle, Spencer, and Nicolette doing chores to earn a minuscule allowance. It didn't matter as much when we were young, but things got tense when I drove up in an expensive car while they were working part-time jobs. Their animosity toward my father spilled over into what they thought of me. I have never been good when it comes to talking about how I feel—but I want to be. I see the change in Brett, and I know there's a better way." He hugged her to his side as they walked. "I didn't know how my family would respond when I invited them to London. I was half-afraid they wouldn't care enough to come. They're here, though. Staying at my house, and it's so much better than I had ever dared think it could be. I have you to thank for that."

Her eyes shone with happy tears. "It's what I do."

"It really is." He stopped then and gave her a long, tender kiss. "I want to show you something and get your thoughts on it."

"Lead on," she said, hugging him tightly before stepping back but maintaining her hold on his hand.

They walked all the way to his apartment building. He described it on the way and also told her his plans for it. As they approached the front steps, a woman on the first floor called out to Eric, speaking to him in a West Indian creole. He smiled and waved.

Sage answered the woman in slow French the woman seemed to understand.

"What did she say?" Eric asked.

"She said it was nice to finally see you with a woman, but that I had better be good to you because she has a lot of single nieces. I promised her I would take good care of you."

"Tell her I am so impressed by how she is raising her son."

The woman answered, "Thank you," in English, then added more in her language.

Eric looked to Sage for translation.

Sage said, "She says that's all she knows in English. She also said her cousin has a laundromat with a job opening if you need one."

"Do you see why I love this place?"

"I do."

"Tell her thank you and how grateful I am. And that I'll keep it in mind if my present job falls through."

The woman nodded, then closed her window.

"Are you really going to buy the building just to help these people?"

"That's the plan. Brett lent me one of his people to get everything up and going. The purchase will happen soon. After that, I want to help without being obvious. I'd love your input."

"You really mean that?"

He pulled her into his arms. "You know I do. There's no one I know who is better at sensing what people need."

The smile returned—the one that made him wonder how he'd lived a single day without it. "Thank you, Eric. Thank you so much."

All that gratitude and squirming sent his immediate concerns spiraling in a different direction. "I want to take you inside, but—"

"But?" she said breathlessly.

"I want our next time to be perfect. Not here in my shabby one-bedroom. I went to you for all the wrong reasons last time, and I want our next time—"

She wrapped her arms around his neck and silenced his words with a kiss. It was a kiss like nothing he'd experienced. She didn't have to say the words—the love was there. He swung her around, kissed her deeply, and thanked whoever or whatever had sent her his way.

She followed her heart without inhibition or reserve. He vowed to follow his own. He ended the kiss and framed her face. "We should wait."

She cocked her head to one side in question.

He took a deep, calming breath and said, "I want you—you have no idea how much, but I want more than that with you. Could you wait for our wedding night?"

She blinked several times. "Are you saying—"

He tucked her against his chest and hugged her tightly. "I'm saying you matter, this matters. I want to fall asleep at your side every night. I want to wake up to you. But not as Wayne and Lorna. Not as two people who are still figuring each other out."

She closed her eyes and rested her head on his chest. "I'm sorry. You're right."

"Don't you dare be sorry." He cupped her chin and raised her face so their eyes met. He was torn between wanting to be the best version of himself before they were intimate again and wanting her to understand how much he wanted to be with her. "This isn't about me. It's about us. If you want, I'll toss you over my shoulder right now and carry you inside." He winked. "Or fuck you in those bushes. Or—"

She blushed clear down to her toes, but smiled. "Or?"

"Introduce you to my family. Show you my life. Become your best friend, your husband—and then your lover. I've done so many things wrong in my life, I want to do this right. With you, I want—forever."

A tear spilled down her cheek. He removed her glasses, pocketed them, and wiped it away gently. "Am I saying everything wrong?"

She threw her arms around his neck again, this time just hugging him with all her might. "No. No you're not." She hugged him again. A voice called out from the building. Sage laughed into his chest. "She wants us to break this up before her son comes home, because he's a good boy and she doesn't want him getting any ideas about how to behave in public."

Eric stepped back and waved to the woman.

She shook her head and closed the window, but she didn't look upset.

As he and Sage walked away, Sage said, "You could arrange for her son to win a full scholarship somewhere. First find out his grades. He may need a step before that, like a tutor. Maybe make something available through his school. He can't be the only one you help, and it can't be easy for him. He needs to earn it. She wouldn't want her son to be given money."

"And her?"

"The boy you described will take care of his mother. I don't think you'll have to worry much about that. Maybe just fix up the building a little. We'd need to know more about her to really know. This is going to be so much fun." Sage squeezed his hand in excitement. "You don't mind if I spend all your money, do you?"

"You're welcome to try."

As they started back down the street that would lead to where he had parked his car, he felt lighter and—happy. Truly happy for the first time in a long, long time. He told her about his conversation with Delinda and why he'd asked her to help him. "Are you okay with seeing her again?"

"She apologized. We're good." She paused and pulled him to a stop. "She invited my mother to tea. Why do you think she'd do that?"

Eric groaned. "I told Delinda a little about your mother. She feels that your mother would benefit from speaking with her. Since she knows I care about you, and that I intend to make you part of my family, it might be to tell your mother how to behave."

"Part of your family," Sage said in a dreamy voice.

"Don't get too excited. You haven't met them yet," Eric joked, then turned serious with his next point. "Do you want me to call Delinda off?"

Sage didn't take long to ponder that. "No. No. My mother could benefit from that talk." She shot him a guilty smile. "That's not wrong, is it?"

"Not at all." He shook his head and chuckled. "And you're going to fit in just fine."

Chapter Eighteen

The next evening, in a simple knee-length blue linen dress, Sage pulled up to Eric's long front driveway in Bella's car. "I hope they like me."

Bella parked behind a Bentley. "They will love you. And since when do you worry about what anyone else thinks?"

Sage clasped her small purse on her lap. "He saw forever, too, Bella. This is big. If they ask me about what I do—should I tell them? Or should I let them get to know me first?"

"Want my opinion?"

"Uh, yeah."

"I think that house is full of people who are more worried what you'll think of them than what they'll think of you. From what you've told me, this is a big night for them as well. They want to be part of his life, and they're the ones on trial, not you. Even if a riot breaks out in there, something tells me you and Eric will be in a coffee shop tomorrow laughing over who threw the first punch. You want his family to love you? Do what you do best. And don't be embarrassed about it—Eric needs you. His family needs you. Go in there and just be yourself—because you're pretty fucking wonderful."

Sage hugged Bella. "I am."

"You are," Bella said with laugh.

Sage threw open her door and made Bella's words into an affirmation. "I am *fucking wonderful.*"

Reggie surprised her by being right there. "Maybe tone that shit down a little. It's your choice, of course. Just offering a bit of advice."

"Reggie, stop teasing her," Alice said, at his side. "Hi, Sage. You look beautiful." Bella came around the car to join them. "You, too, Bella. Love that pantsuit."

Sage looked up at the house. "Is everyone here?"

Reggie shook his head. "Nicolette canceled at the last minute. Something about a photo shoot she couldn't reschedule."

Alice leaned closer and lowered her voice. "Eric was disappointed, but he doesn't want to talk about it. So . . ."

"I won't ask," Sage assured her. "How has it been having everyone staying here?"

"Busy," Alice said, "but good. They're different than I imagined. More down-to-earth. And they seem to really want to reconnect with Eric. It's kind of sad and beautiful at the same time. I hope we see more of them after this weekend."

Bella shot Sage a "told you so" look.

Eric appeared at the door, wearing a dress shirt and dark trousers. The scene belonged on the big screen. Did he have any idea how truly handsome he was? "You came," he said as if he hadn't been sure she would show. He rushed down the steps and greeted Sage and Bella each with a kiss on the cheek.

"I told you I would."

"I know. I just—" He shook his head, held out his hand to her, and laced his fingers through hers.

He really does need me.

She went up on her tiptoes and kissed his lips impulsively, tugging him down so she could say something softly into his ear. "It'll be fine."

"Stay tonight." He kissed her then—a deep, soul-searching kiss full of promises and hunger. "What was I thinking leaving you at your door last night? I spent all night kicking myself for saying we should wait. You're all I think about."

"We can all hear you." Reggie cleared his throat. "Let's tone that down as well. I've got kids in there."

Alice linked one arm through Reggie's and her other through Bella's. "Come on. They need a moment. We'll see you inside."

Once they were alone, Sage searched Eric's face. He was so serious, so earnest, she wanted to bring a smile back to his face. "I don't think I'm strong enough to carry you off, though I could definitely pull you into those bushes." She winked. "But I like your plan better."

He laughed, then sobered again. "Sex never meant much to me. It felt good, but I didn't care who it was with. I never asked myself if I was good enough to be with them, because I didn't look that far outside of myself. You met me while I was working on figuring myself out. There are still parts of my life that are under renovation. You'll see what I'm talking about as soon as you step inside."

He's worried. Sage's heart swelled. She didn't need to ask herself how a man who had so much could be so unsure. He understood what it was like to be left behind and how it made a person wonder if it had been their own fault. His recovery encompassed more than just his drug use. Another man might have tried to hide that from her. His honesty was a humbling gift.

"I was scared about tonight, but Bella said that even if a riot breaks out in there, she knows you and I will share a laugh about it over coffee tomorrow."

He hugged her to his chest. "Bella rocks."

"Yes," Sage murmured against his chest. "So does this."

Chapter Nineteen

The wave of introductions began as soon as Sage and Eric entered an enormous sitting room that could easily have been used to entertain fifty people. It wasn't nearly as overwhelming as it would have been had Eric not already told her about each of them. Eric's older brother, Brett, had the aura of a hard-core businessman, but his wife and child softened him. No special gift was required to see how much he loved them.

Rachelle gushed over Sage and Eric, a little too eager, but she obviously wanted the evening to go smoothly. Prince Magnus stayed beside his very pregnant wife like a guardian angel. He was polished and polite, but his approval would need to be earned.

I don't mind that.

Spencer had an easy sense of humor. His wife, Hailey, and her daughter, Skye, gave Sage a warm, friendly greeting. After talking to them for a while, Sage agreed with Alice that Eric's family was more grounded than many would have been at their level of wealth.

Eric introduced Michael as if he were another brother but left off the tag of how he fit into his family. Sage remembered meeting Michael at Delinda's house. That Delinda had included him and that he was being treated as one of the family did a lot to improve Sage's opinion of Delinda.

Reggie and his wife fit into the group with more ease than Eric. Their precocious children appeared and disappeared from the room, just as they said they would.

At Sage's prompting, Axton and Liana invited Skye to join them and—whoosh—she was off and laughing. Eric assured Spencer that she'd be fine. "Probably. She's not afraid of heights, dark places, or snakes, is she?"

Spencer excused himself to check on where the children had gone.

After he'd gone, Eric leaned toward Hailey and said, "I shouldn't tease him, but he's so easy."

Hailey laughed and wagged a finger at him. "Careful. Payback's a bitch. Spencer has become surprisingly protective of Skye. It's kind of adorable."

"Adorable?" Eric scoffed as he watched his brother emerge from one of the secret passages, looking worried. "It looks painful."

"Parenthood is," Hailey assured him. "At least it was at first. I did a lot of panicking. It's easier now. We take turns freaking out. Look at me, cool as a cucumber because I know Spencer's on this one."

Eric gazed warmly down at Sage. "Everything is different when you have someone to share it with."

A small commotion in the corner caught Sage's attention. Young Skye had her hands on her hips and was laying down the law to Spencer. He headed back over toward Hailey.

"Oh no!" Hailey exclaimed. "He can't let her win." By way of explanation, she said, "Skye spends a lot of time with Delinda. It's been good for her, but . . ." As she walked away, she could be heard saying to Spencer, "No, *I* can't do it. You have to go over there and tell her you meant what you said."

Sage exchanged a look with Eric and said, "A mini Delinda?"

With equal mock horror, Eric said, "Can the world handle two?" They shared a laugh.

"Where is your grandmother?" Sage had just realized she wasn't in the room. *Oh no. Please. Please. Please. Don't let them be together.* "Where's Bella?" She started to walk around, hoping to spot one of them.

"Reggie," Eric called out as he kept in step with Sage, "have you seen Bella?"

Reggie pointed toward the French doors that led outside.

Sage quickened her pace. She had no doubt Bella could hold her own, but the Westerlys were from a power tier far above her friend's. Not even for Eric would Sage allow Bella to be mistreated or threatened. Nope, not going to happen.

Eric halted Sage gently. "What are you worried about?"

Sage searched his expression. Her usual unwavering optimism shook beneath the weight of recent experiences. "I'm sorry. It's just that they are both strong personalities, and I've seen the other side of Delinda."

"You never will again," he said with a confidence that calmed Sage. The loyalty in his eyes said he would go to battle for her, even if it was against his own family. "I won't let anything happen to you or your friend. My grandmother and I have discussed—healthy boundaries."

"Okay." She believed him. Even Delinda deserved a second chance.

Alice came through the French doors and walked over to join them. "Oh my God, Eric, your grandmother is a hoot."

"Is Bella out there as well?" Sage asked.

Alice nodded. "And King Tadeas."

"How is it going?" Eric's hand on Sage's back tightened even though he asked the question calmly enough.

"They're fine," Alice said with a laugh. "I have a king's promise that they will all behave. Don't worry, Eric, we've got your back."

Sage hugged Alice right then. Eric often thought of himself in terms of what he'd done wrong, but friends like Alice were evidence that somewhere along the way he had done just as much right. Alice returned her hug just as warmly.

"Dinner is about to be served. Please make your way to the grand dining room," a member of Eric's staff announced.

When he opened the door to the outside, Bella's voice carried inside.

Her tone was excitedly amused. "You did not say that."

"I did," Delinda said in a more restrained but equally amused voice.

"I wish I had been there to see her face. I don't think it'll change her, but good for you for giving it to her."

"Hopefully, after the sting abates, she will see how much she is missing by acting the way she is. We have to allow our children to choose their own paths."

Sage exchanged another look with Eric. "Do you think they're talking about my mother—"

At the same time, Eric asked, "If that's about your mother, are you okay—"

They both answered, "Yes," in unison. Then paused. Exchanged another look.

Eric said, "Just wanted to make sure."

Sage spoke in perfect unison with him again.

They stopped, realized what they'd done, and both started to laugh.

Bella, Delinda, and King Tadeas entered the home smiling. Bella pointed toward Delinda, then framed her hands into a heart.

"We may have to worry about those two for an entirely different reason," Eric joked. "My grandmother took her wedding band off. I believe things are about to get serious."

"Queen Delinda?" Sage lowered her voice. "They're coming this way. I've never met royalty. What do I do? Curtsy? Bow? What do I call him?"

"In private you can call him Tadeas, in public Your Majesty. But why the sudden nerves? You weren't worried when you met Magnus."

Sage's hand flew up to her mouth. "I totally forgot Magnus was a prince."

Eric chuckled, pulled Sage to his side, and kissed her forehead. "And that is why you're the woman for me."

Sage flushed with pleasure. With Eric, even when she was wrong, it was somehow right. She laid her head on his chest. After a lifetime of yearning, she had found where she belonged.

The moment was cut short by Delinda saying. "Eric, might I steal Sage away for a moment? We'll meet you at the table."

Eric looked from his grandmother to Sage's upturned face. "That's entirely up to Sage."

Second chances are what I do, Sage reminded herself as she stepped out of Eric's arms. "I'll be right in."

Before they departed, Sage was introduced to King Tadeas. He was an older, gentler version of Magnus. Just as Eric had said, in private he preferred to go without his title. He looked somewhat reluctant to head into dinner without his escort.

Delinda waved him away.

Bella offered the king her arm.

Sage shook her head at both. Only Delinda would dismiss a king, and only Bella would think she could manage him as well.

King Tadeas took Bella's arm, and the two walked off chatting. Eric lingered a moment more, but when Reggie called to him, he reluctantly headed into the dining room as well.

Delinda stepped closer to Sage. The tense moment crackled with uncertainty. Sage wanted to believe the best of the older woman. She told herself to keep her heart open to her. As one moment dragged to two and Delinda said nothing, Sage began to squirm. "Was there something you wanted to say?" She was old, after all. There was a chance she might have forgotten.

Delinda held out her hand.

Sage took it cautiously.

"You are not a weed," Delinda said. "I'm sorry it took me so long to recognize that."

"I'm not sure I understand, but thank you."

Squeezing her hand, Delinda said, "You have no idea how much it means to me to have my family in one home like this. Almost all of them. I wish Nicolette—" Delinda stopped herself. "What I'm trying to say is: thank you. I gave you reason enough to want nothing to do with me or my family. But here you are, and so are they. It says a lot about your character as well as how much you care for my grandson. I see the way Eric is with you, and I wish I could go back—"

"Delinda—"

"Sage, let me say this. Promise me something . . ."

"Delinda—" *Please don't say something to ruin how much I want to hug you right now. You can do this. Be nice.*

"Call me Grandmother."

Sage blinked back tears and nodded again. "Of course."

Delinda pursed her lips and gave Sage's hand another squeeze. "And tell me when you see me crossing a line with Eric, because I don't want to lose him again."

I just might be able to love this woman as well. "I will. He loves you and doesn't want to lose you, either. He told me about how close the two of you used to be. I hope you find your way back to that." Sage released Delinda's hand with a smile. "And I understand everything you did now. All you were doing was trying to protect him. You're someone I would be proud to call Grandmother."

Delinda sniffed. "Oh, you're a little heart tugger, aren't you? Or I'm getting soft in my old age."

"No, *soft* isn't the word I would choose to describe you," Sage said with a straight face.

Delinda laughed. Her expression turned almost tender. "I spoke to your mother. I understand you better now as well. I wish there were something I could do to—"

"She'll come around one day. I'll keep my heart open, and it'll happen."

"I may have been a little harsh with her."

"Me too," Sage said, meeting Delinda's gaze. "It was time."

Delinda's eyebrows rose in surprise. "Welcome to the family, Sage. You're going to fit in just fine."

"Hey, Eric said the same thing to me. Is it a compliment?"

Delinda's expression remained carefully blank. "Why don't we head into the dining room?"

"I'm taking it as one," Sage announced as she and Delinda made their way in.

Delinda chuckled.

◆ ◆ ◆

Never had Eric imagined he would see his grandmother enter a room laughing with Sage as if they were old friends. He rose from his seat to hold out Sage's chair and noted Tadeas did the same for Delinda.

"It looks like the two of you found common ground."

She smiled up at him and said, "We did. We both love you."

Eric swayed on his feet as her casual declaration washed over him. *Sage loves me.* He took a seat beside her, feeling dazed and jubilant all at once. *I'll have a second chance with her, and this time I'll get it right.*

Across the table, his mother and father did not sound as happy with one another. His father said, "What exactly was it that Nicolette thought was more important than being here?"

"She said there was a photo shoot she couldn't postpone. The invitation *was* last minute," his mother said in defense.

"You make too many excuses for her, Stephanie. The rest of us were able to drop everything to be here."

A tension filled the room.

"I'm not excusing her absence, Dereck. All I'm saying is that this is a new career for her, and she might not have felt that she could leave—"

"She doesn't need a career, Stephanie. If you let her, she'd have enough money to do as she pleased."

Spencer took his wife's hand. "Here we go."

Stephanie threw her napkin down beside her plate. "It's always about money with you. Always. Can't you see that Nicolette needs—"

"She needs to be here. But you wouldn't tell her she should be. You're still punishing me and using the children to do it."

"Oh my God, *this is not about you.*" Stephanie threw her hands up in the air. "Just once could you let it be about someone else?" She looked around as if only now realizing how unprivate their conversation had been.

A painful silence fell over the room, broken only by Reggie telling his son, "It's okay, they're divorced. We probably shouldn't have sat them together."

"What does divorced mean?" Skye asked Delinda.

Without missing a beat, Delinda said, "It means I shouldn't have been the one to ask Nicolette to come."

Skye turned to Hailey. "I don't understand."

Hailey looked down at her daughter with a sad expression. "Sometimes even when people love each other, they can't get along. They separate. That's divorce."

Skye frowned and addressed Delinda. "What does that have to do with Nicolette?"

Spencer answered before Delinda could. "Grandmother Delinda was trying to say that she also feels bad that Nicolette isn't here."

Skye's face crumpled. "Auntie Hailey, you love Spencer. I love Spencer, too. I don't want you to separate."

"Oh, honey. That's not going to happen."

"But that's what divorce is." Skye pushed her chair back and ran from the room.

Both Hailey and Spencer took off after her.

"Well, that's just perfect," Dereck said.

Brett leaned across the table. "Dad, don't—"

"Don't what? Ask about my daughter? She is my daughter as well." Dereck turned to glare at his ex-wife. "No matter how much doubt you've filled her with. Unless she's not mine, and then why don't you finally admit it? Because I can't live like this anymore—not knowing. Is she Mark's or is she mine?"

Stephanie gasped. "Do you really think now is the time or the place to discuss this? All you've done was upset Spencer."

"Spencer will get over it. Tonight was about Eric," Dereck said.

The dinner suddenly crystallized why Eric had put an ocean between himself and his family. He understood but could not condone his father's behavior. His mother had cheated and then married the man who had fathered at least one of the children she'd claimed were Dereck's. His mother was jumping to the defense of the children she'd taken with her when she'd left her husband—the same three she'd built her new life around—a life that hadn't included Eric.

Eric closed his eyes briefly, then turned to check how Sage was handling the scene. She took his hand in hers, and there was more love in her eyes than he felt he would ever deserve.

Spencer stood near the door of the dining room. "Is it safe to bring Skye back in? Tell me now, because I'm not doing this to my family."

Rachelle said, "Spencer, we are all your family."

"I'm not saying you're not," Spencer countered. "But my first priority is my wife and child."

"As it should be," Magnus said.

Sage stood up. "Eric, do you have Nicolette's phone number?"

Eric also rose to his feet. "I do." He brought it up and handed his phone to her.

All eyes were on Sage as it rang on FaceTime. Nicolette's face appeared on the screen. "Eric? Wait, who are you?"

Sage said, "I'm Sage, but Eric is with me." Sage turned the phone to scan the table. "Everyone is. We're having dinner at Eric's, and everyone was just saying how much they missed you."

"They were?" Nicolette asked slowly.

"See for yourself. I'll pass the phone around, and you can say hi to everyone."

"Hold on," Nicolette said. "Could I please speak to Eric?"

"Of course." Sage handed the phone back to Eric.

Nicolette looked uncertain. "Is everyone else really there?"

"They are," Eric said.

"I . . . My shoot was . . . I'm sorry."

Eric glanced up and met Sage's gaze before answering. "Make it up to me by visiting soon." He smiled at her. "I'm proud to see you following your dream."

"You are?" Nicolette asked as if she was waiting for the conversation to take a sour turn. "Thank you."

On impulse, he pulled Sage closer so she was in the shot with him. "Nicolette, this is Sage, the woman I intend to marry. I haven't officially asked her yet, but I'm pretty confident about what her answer will be."

Sage laughed, and Nicolette joined in.

He lowered his voice. "If our family doesn't scare her off."

"No chance in hell," Sage chimed in.

Taking a chance and following his gut, Eric said, "Dad was just asking about you. He misses you, too. Want to talk to him?"

"Sure," Nicolette said with caution.

Dereck did indeed look happy to talk to his daughter. He asked her about the shoot and even added that he would love to fly out and see her on location.

Stephanie's eyes filled with tears as she listened. Eric almost told his father what to do, but Dereck's next action showed that he understood what Sage was trying to do for them. He said, "Nicolette, Mom is missing you as well. I'm handing you off, but I'll call you tomorrow."

"I'd like that, Dad."

Stephanie took the phone, spoke to Nicolette for a few minutes, then handed the phone to Brett. Peace returned to the room, and a moment later so did Skye and Hailey.

When Eric saw Delinda accept the phone from Spencer with a smile, he couldn't hold in how he felt. He whispered, "I love you. I don't know what you see in me, but I'm not buying you glasses."

He kissed her then, oblivious to the young and old around him, lost in the woman who had returned light to his life.

Reggie's voice broke into his bliss. "It's okay, they're getting married. We probably shouldn't have sat them together, either. Easy on the PDA, guys."

Eric raised his head and smiled. "Will you marry me, Sage Revere?"

Without hesitation, Sage answered, "Yes. Yes, a thousand times, yes."

They kissed again, briefly this time, since a round of applause kept them very aware of their audience. Eric hugged Sage to him and looked around the room. Bella held up the phone to show that even Nicolette was cheering, "Congratulations!"

Reggie's daughter asked loudly, "Are they going to make a baby?"

He answered, "Hopefully not until after dinner."

Alice rolled her eyes skyward.

Still laughing, Eric bent and whispered to Sage, "Want a houseguest tonight?"

She swatted at him, but she didn't say no.

Delinda loudly clapped her hands together twice and informed the staff to hurry dinner along. Eric turned his attention her way. He expected to see irritation, but she was smiling from ear to ear.

Eric held out Sage's chair again, and they retook their seats. One family dinner survived. One proposal delivered and accepted. Looking around the table, Eric saw his family through Sage's eyes. They were simply people, as flawed as he was, but trying to do better. They'd let each other down, hurt each other along the way, but they were all there—and it was his choice to decide if that was a good or bad thing. When he saw them through that lens, he found his place in both families. He'd be the bridge. He took Sage's hand in his again. *They'd* be the bridge.

Chapter Twenty

Sage was still smiling later that evening when she unlocked the door to her apartment and held it open for Eric to follow her inside. The night had held a series of highs and lows, but she and Eric had weathered them together.

His family had issues, but none that were insurmountable. What they had on their side was that they wanted things to work out. That was the first step to fixing any relationship. She hoped her own mother one day reached that place.

Sage met Eric's eyes, and the drama of the evening fell away. All that mattered was the man before her and the look of love on his face. Sexual tension filled the air. Reluctant to be the initiator again, Sage said, "Wasn't it funny to see Bella drive off with Delinda and Tadeas? They got along much better than I imagined."

Eric stepped closer while unbuttoning his shirt. "The only one I care about right now is you." He dropped his shirt to the floor.

"Well, if you're going to be that way." Sage unzipped her dress and stepped out of it.

He lifted her up in his arms and easily carried her to her bed, then laid her gently down on it. "What way? This way?" He ran his hands over her in worshipful caresses. His lips followed the tender trail, kissing her breasts through the lace of her bra before working their way lower. His hot breath warmed her sex through the thin material of her panties.

He straightened and stripped naked, then removed the last of her clothing. Even though his cock stood in testament to his hunger for her, he didn't rush. When he kissed her, it was an invitation more than a claiming—and one that she eagerly leaned in to meet.

Slowly, gently, he brought her pleasure. It was an entirely different experience than their first time, although that had been good as well. This was a slow burn, a whispered proclamation of love. She cried when she came. Just when she thought she could not love him more, she saw a tear slip down his cheek.

They fell asleep tangled in each other's arms.

The next morning, Sage woke to a smiling Eric raining kisses on her face. She pushed him onto his back and confidently straddled him. Tender. Rough. Slow. Frenzied. She wanted it all with him. "Do you know how much I love you, Eric Westerly?"

With a lusty grin, he ran his hands up her legs to cup her breasts. "Why don't you show me?"

She spent the next hour doing just that. She loved him with her mouth, her hands, her sex, until they collapsed into each other's arms, sweaty and sated.

"What about now?" she asked cheekily.

He raised one eyebrow playfully. "I think so. Maybe we should go over all that again, just to make sure. But after I recover."

She chuckled.

He rolled closer and tucked her into his side. "I love you, Sage."

"I love you, too."

"I told everyone we'd have lunch with them tomorrow before they go home. Are you up to that?"

Sage went up on one elbow and framed a side of his face with her hand. "I love your family because they're part of you. Plus, I've always wanted a big family."

"Even a batshit-crazy one?"

She kissed his chin. "It'll keep things interesting." She ran her hand over his chest. "They're not as bad as you think, Eric. They love each other. It'll all work out."

He kissed her warmly, then said, "I do believe it will."

The next few weeks flew by for Eric. During the day, as Wayne and Lorna, he and Sage organized the changes to his building and the families living there. They also went ring shopping. A disappointing number of people were rude to them when they asked to see larger diamonds. Apparently neither Wayne nor Lorna looked as if they could afford them. However, when they finally met a woman who went out of her way to make them feel comfortable and worked with them to get just what they wanted, Eric and Sage asked Brett's assistant to see what she needed. Since her home was in foreclosure, they paid it off for her.

Making people happy had never been so much fun.

Sage wrote up Lorna's background to support a career as a plant psychologist—a.k.a. botanist extraordinaire. As Wayne, Eric strolled the streets of London with Lorna, looking for people in need. He would never tire of watching her introduce herself to someone and work her way into their life.

As Eric and Sage, they introduced John to Bella's neighbor. If John cared that Eric's scar had mysteriously disappeared or that he was a big screen actor, he didn't give any indication. From the moment John met Bella's dog-crazy neighbor, not much else mattered. The man was instantly smitten.

Helping others became its own addiction. Eric funded shelters for the homeless, purchased land for neighborhood garden projects, and worked with schools to fund needed programs. He and Sage made sure it all stayed anonymous, and Eric had never felt better about himself.

The day came when the acting CEO of Eric's film company asked him to make another *Water Bear Man* movie. Eric was half-inclined to refuse to produce another, but after talking it out with Sage, he decided the good outweighed the bad. More money meant he and Sage could continue to have resources to bring joy and financial relief to countless *clients*. Water Bear Man was no longer a fraud—he had a noble purpose as well.

Eric was happier than he could ever remember being. It was for that reason that a mild panic filled him the day Sage left his house early and texted him to meet her because she wanted to talk to him about something important.

Was that code for things not going as well for her as they were for him? She told him to come as Eric and gave him an address in the theater district.

Was she taking him to a play? Why the secrecy? He told himself it was probably something good, but raced to her side anyway.

As instructed, Eric parked in a small lot behind the theater and knocked on the rear door. A man opened the door and beckoned him inside. He led him to the back of a stage and told him to wait there.

Sage appeared, and she was smiling. Eric started to breathe more easily. "What's this about?" he asked.

She handed him a script. "Mr. Kirby's friend owns this theater and supports new playwrights. I told him you might be interested in auditioning for a role in their next production."

Eric scanned the first page. It was a drama, not slapstick action. "I just agreed to produce another Water Bear Man movie."

"They'll work around your schedule."

Eric read the second page of the play. His heart started beating wildly in his chest. Could he do this? Could he return to the stage as a serious actor? "The theater really wants me? Not Water Bear Man?"

"He's willing to take a chance on you." She winked.

Hating himself for not instantly jumping at the chance, Eric scanned another page of the script. "I've tried to take serious roles before. The audience wasn't receptive."

"Then show them what they're missing," Sage said emphatically.

Eric devoured the next page of the play. The dialogue was contemporary and moving. He flipped another page. "I'll do it."

"Easy, tiger," Sage said. "First you must audition."

"You're serious," Eric said, pointing toward the stage. He caught a look in her eyes that told him he was missing something. "*Why* am I auditioning?"

The smile she'd been holding back spread across her face, easily making her the most beautiful woman he'd ever seen. "Because Nicolette is out there waiting to see her brother take his first step toward following his dream."

Eric peered around the curtains and saw that his sister was indeed out there. As were the rest of his brothers and sisters, his parents, his grandmother, and her royal boyfriend. With the script still in one hand, he picked Sage up and spun her around. "How did you get them all here?"

In unison, they both said, "Delinda."

"Marry me while they're all there. This weekend," Eric said. Never had anything felt more right.

Still laughing and clinging to him, she asked, "Can we do it that fast?"

"We can," he said, "because we play by our own rules."

They kissed deeply, then Sage gave him a push and said, "Now get out there and break a leg."

As Eric read the page of dialogue the director handed him, he found the character's voice. For a moment, he was more than Eric Westerly—more than Water Bear Man—he was who he was meant to be. Acting, this kind of acting, filled him with a joy he'd thought couldn't return. When he finished, there was a pause, then everyone rose to their feet to give him a standing ovation.

He motioned for Sage to join him on the stage. Holding her hand, he took a bow. She chuckled and bowed as well. The Westerlys kept clapping.

In a voice just loud enough for him to hear, she said, "I feel silly up here. I didn't actually do anything."

He turned and framed her face with his hands. "They're clapping because, like me, they know that a successful performance is just as much about what happens backstage as onstage. You gave me back a piece of myself I thought I'd lost."

She placed one of her hands on his. "I didn't give you anything, Eric. It was always there, you just didn't see it."

He turned and looked at his family, who were all now quietly watching them. They might be an unconventional family, but they were his and they loved him—he no longer doubted that. "I am going to spend the rest of my life finding ways to make you as happy as you've made me."

Her face lit up with a smile. "That's funny. That's exactly what I intend to do for you."

They shared a laugh and took one final deep bow before leaving the stage to meet with his family and a very pleased-looking theater director.

Epilogue

Still glowing after their honeymoon, Eric and Sage returned to their English estate. Excited, Reggie immediately led them to Eric's lair and unveiled a new section . . . one just for Sage. As grand as Eric's, it had three labeled wardrobes. One for Sage, one for Lorna, and one for Water Bear Woman. *Water Bear Woman?*

Sage's mouth dropped open when she saw a gray spandex superhero costume similar to Eric's, but smaller. *Oh no.*

"I took the liberty of working with your writers to create a new character." Reggie dramatically lowered his voice. "There's been another accident. This time in the waters off Antarctica. A chemical spill that only one woman knew how to clean up. Sadly, she slipped into the sludge—sludge filled with water bears—and was bitten by thousands of tardigrades . . . becoming . . ."

"Water Bear Woman?" Sage asked with a nervous laugh. He had to be joking. He didn't look like he was. She turned to Eric.

"Come here, Mrs. Water Bear Man," Eric joked, puffing his chest out with mock pride.

Sage shook her head and stood her ground. "I am not wearing that thing." Spandex was unflattering on the best of bodies. Even as she refused, though, she had to admit there was something endearing about being invited into this corner of Eric's life. They would be truly partners—in the real world as well as on the big screen.

"Not even for the children?" Eric asked with puppy-dog eyes. "Come on, imagine the team we'd make visiting children's hospitals together. Try it on."

There was no refusing him when he looked at her that way. Smiling, Sage pointed at his suit. "I'll wear mine if you wear yours."

"Deal," Eric said.

In an unspoken race, they each flew to their own areas and changed. Reggie politely left the room just as the clothing began to fly. A few minutes later, Sage and Eric stood facing each other. Feet apart, Eric had his hands on his hips, his chest pushed out, and his chin arrogantly in the air. Sage mirrored his stance.

A serious expression darkened his eyes. "Before you, I didn't know who I was, and I didn't think I liked any of my options. Now, I see that it doesn't matter what people call me or even what I call myself—I'm me. And with you at my side, I feel like that's good enough."

A wave of love for him washed over Sage, and she blinked back tears. "It's better than good enough. Before you, I pushed people away. Sure, I helped them, but then I cut them from my life. I was so afraid that if I opened my heart to someone, really let them in, they would leave me, like my parents did. You showed me that love is worth that risk. My family is crazy. Your family is nuts. But somehow we'll make it work. Together."

Eric wrapped his arms around Sage and kissed her deeply. It was a kiss full of gratitude, love, and promises.

Reggie returned and snapped a photo of them. "Now look this way," he instructed, and took another. "For the first time, I officially present to you, Mr. and Mrs. Water Bear Man."

They struck a pose worthy of any superhero movie poster. Reggie snapped more photos.

He shared them with their friends and family via social media: **#HollywoodHeir #HappyEnding**

Acknowledgments

Thank you to:

Montlake Romance, for letting me explore my superhero side. Special thanks to Lauren Plude for rolling with the schedule when I broke my leg. My very patient beta readers. You know who you are. Thank you for kicking my butt when I need it.

My editors: Karen Lawson, Janet Hitchcock, Marion Archer, Krista Stroever, and Marlene Engel.

About the Author

Ruth Cardello is a *New York Times* bestselling author who loves writing about rich alpha men and the strong women who tame them. She was born the youngest of eleven children in a small city in northern Rhode Island. She's lived in Boston, Paris, Orlando, New York, and Rhode Island (again) before moving to Massachusetts, where she now lives with her husband and three children. Before turning her attention to writing, Ruth was an educator for two decades, including eleven years as a kindergarten teacher. *Hollywood Heir* is the fourth book in her Westerly Billionaire series. Learn about Ruth's new releases by signing up for her newsletter at www.RuthCardello.com.